"*Bristol Bay Summer* made m
written story includes the joys
Frontier."

—Jewel, singer-songwriter, author, and proud native of Homer, Alaska

"Having spent twenty-three delightful summers in Bristol Bay myself, I'm thrilled that Annie Boochever has written a book that so perfectly captures both the coming of age of a young adult in this uniquely Alaskan setting, but more importantly, provides insights into the profound rich cultural heritage of this fishery. *Bristol Bay Summer* is a must-read for anyone—young and old alike—wishing to better understand the critical importance of the Bristol Bay salmon fishery to both feeding the world AND feeding the soul!"

—Sue Aspelund

"Books about the real Alaska are few and far between. *Bristol Bay Summer*, the newest addition to the canon, is the real thing. Through the eyes of Alaskan newcomer Zoey Morley, we fall in love with the power and beauty of Bristol Bay and its people. Annie Boochever's prose is as fierce and elemental as the land itself; her story takes readers to the edge of the cliff and back again."

—Debby Dahl Edwardson, National Book Award Finalist and author of *Blessing's Bead* and *My Name is Not Easy*

"When Zoey's parents divorce, her dad disappears, and her mom uproots her—twice. She feels angry and alone. Through the hard work of living in a wild part of Alaska, she comes to rely on strengths she never knew she had. She learns compassion for those around her, coming to understand that their lives are at least as difficult as her own. This is a powerful story of a girl becoming a woman, a story of land and sea and artistry."

—Peggy Shumaker, Alaska State Writer Laureate 2010–2012

Bristol Bay Summer

Annie Boochever

ALASKA NORTHWEST BOOKS®

Library of Congress Cataloging-in-Publication Data
Boochever, Annie.
Bristol Bay summer / by Annie Boochever.
pages cm
Summary: "Against the backdrop of the great Bristol Bay salmon fishery, thirteen-year-old Zoey Morley struggles with her parents' divorce, her mom's bush-pilot boyfriend, and the pangs of growing up during her summer in the 'real' Alaska"— Provided by publisher.
ISBN 978-0-88240-994-8 (paperback)
ISBN 978-1-941821-27-5 (hardbound)
ISBN 978-1-941821-25-1 (e-book)
[1. Bristol Bay (Alaska)—Fiction. 2. Divorce—Fiction. 3. Self-reliance—Fiction.] I. Title.
PZ7.B64483Br 2014
[Fic]—dc23

Edited by Michelle McCann
Design by Vicki Knapton
Maps by Ani Rucki

Front cover photos: salmon © iStock.photo.com/andyKRAKOVSKI; airplane © Ruedi Homberger; chapter opening photo: © iStock.photo.com/eAlisa; back cover photo: © iStock.photo.com/xposedpixel.

Published by Alaska Northwest Books®
An imprint of

P.O. Box 56118
Portland, Oregon 97238-6118
503-254-5591
www.graphicartsbooks.com

To my children
Liorah, Zachary, Megan, and Spencer,
who steady the boat when the wind kicks up.

Contents

Maps ... *10*

1. Departure ... 15
2. Last Stop ... 21
3. Latrine Business ... 27
4. Chez Jensen-Morley ... 33
5. Night Visitors ... 39
6. A New Boy ... 46
7. Darth Vader ... 56
8. Colorado Honey ... 60
9. Thomas to the Rescue ... 64
10. Naknek ... 72
11. Knives and Fur Hats for Sale ... 79
12. Captain ... 86
13. A Gift ... 92
14. Patrick ... 98
15. Fishing Begins ... 106
16. Rulers of the World ... 112
17. Bag Balm ... 119
18. A Cake in the Coleman? ... 124
19. Blue Skies and Brown Bears ... 128
20. Swallowed a Lead Line ... 133

21. Dancing with Mosquitoes.....139
22. A Not So Happy Birthday.....148
23. Payday.....155
24. Dillingham.....158
25. So Many Fish.....166
26. Midnight.....173
27. Japanese Typhoon.....179
28. Refuge.....184
29. After the Storm.....192
30. An Uncertain Good-bye.....196
31. Dad.....204
32. Crash Position.....213
33. MayDay! MayDay!.....222
34. It'll Work Out.....230
35. Ghosts in the Water.....235
36. Home Again.....243

Glossary.....*247*
Acknowledgments.....*253*
Discussion Questions.....*255*

"Clouds come floating into my life,
no longer to carry rain or usher storm,
but to add color to my sunset sky."

—Rabindranath Tagore, *Stray Birds*

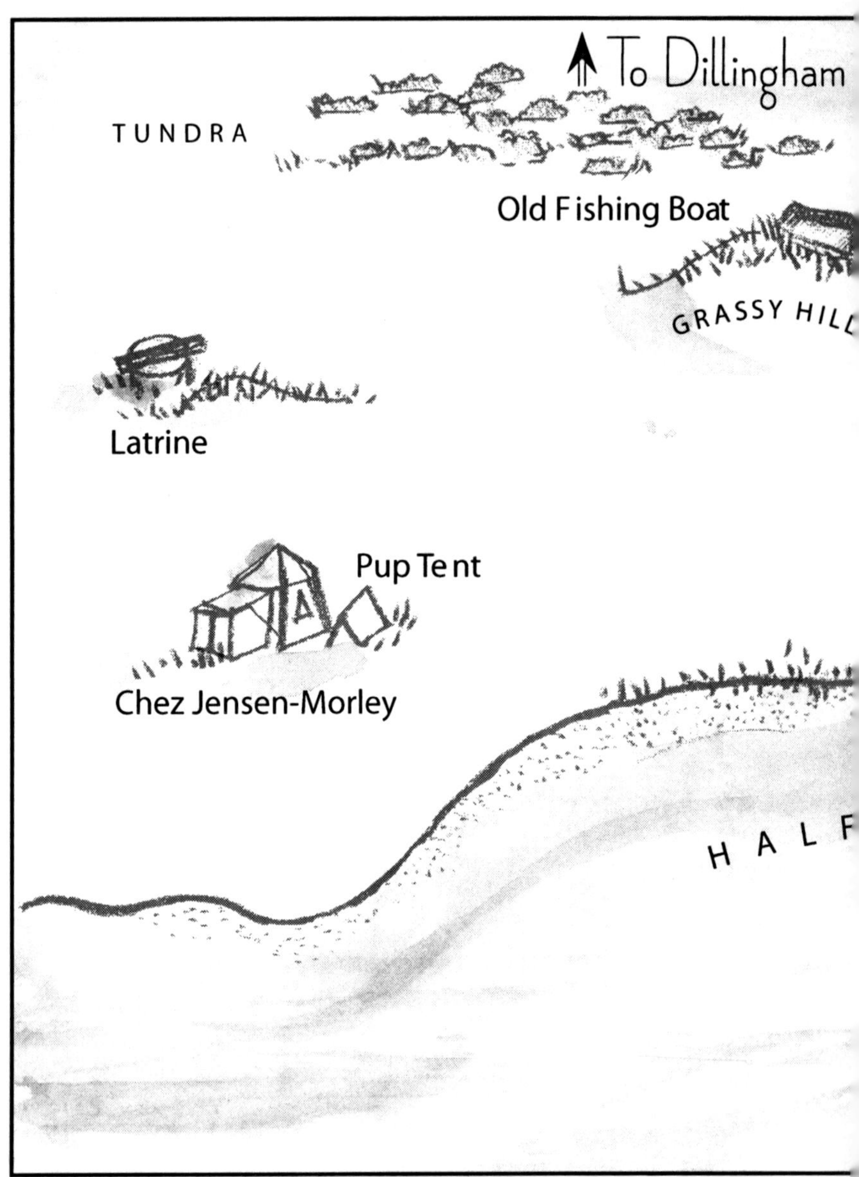
To Dillingham
TUNDRA
Old Fishing Boat
GRASSY HILL
Latrine
Pup Tent
Chez Jensen-Morley
HALF

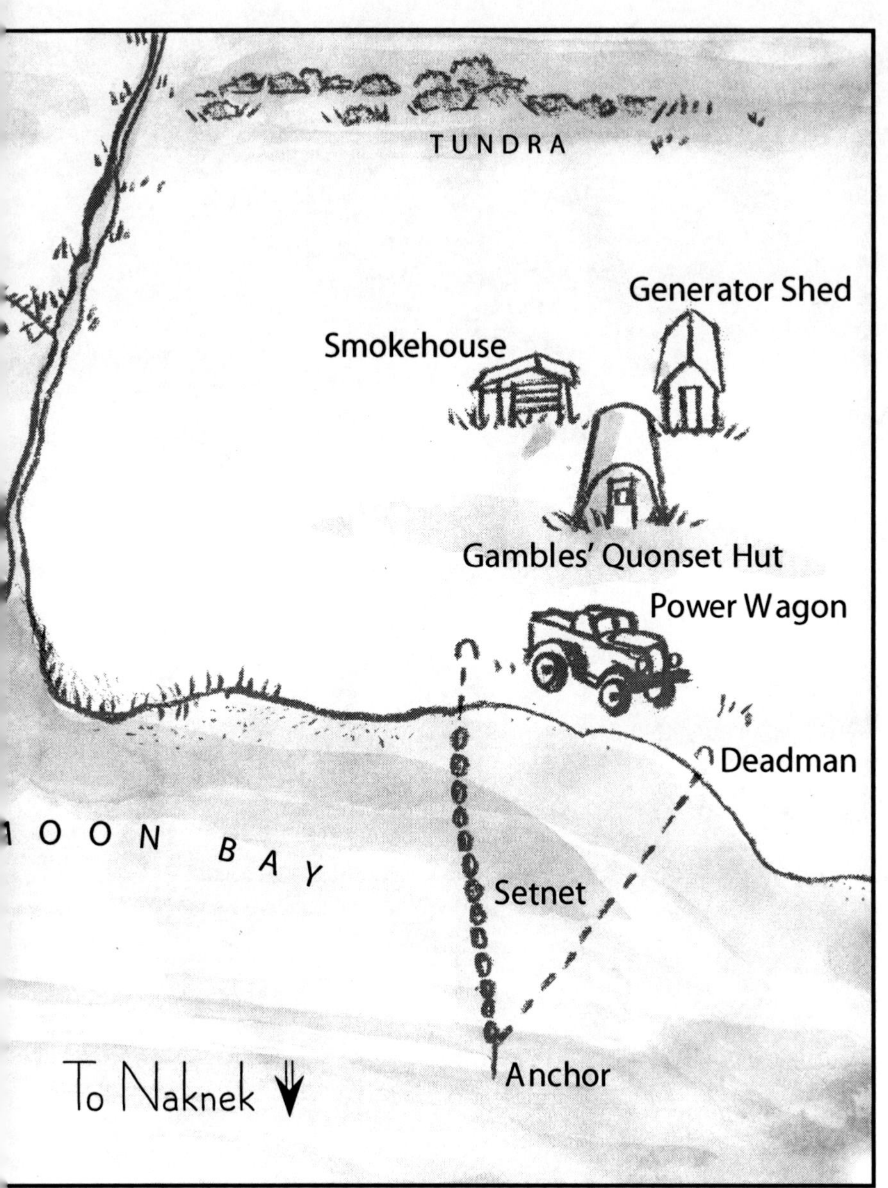
TUNDRA
Generator Shed
Smokehouse
Gambles' Quonset Hut
Power Wagon
Deadman
OON BAY
Setnet
Anchor
To Naknek

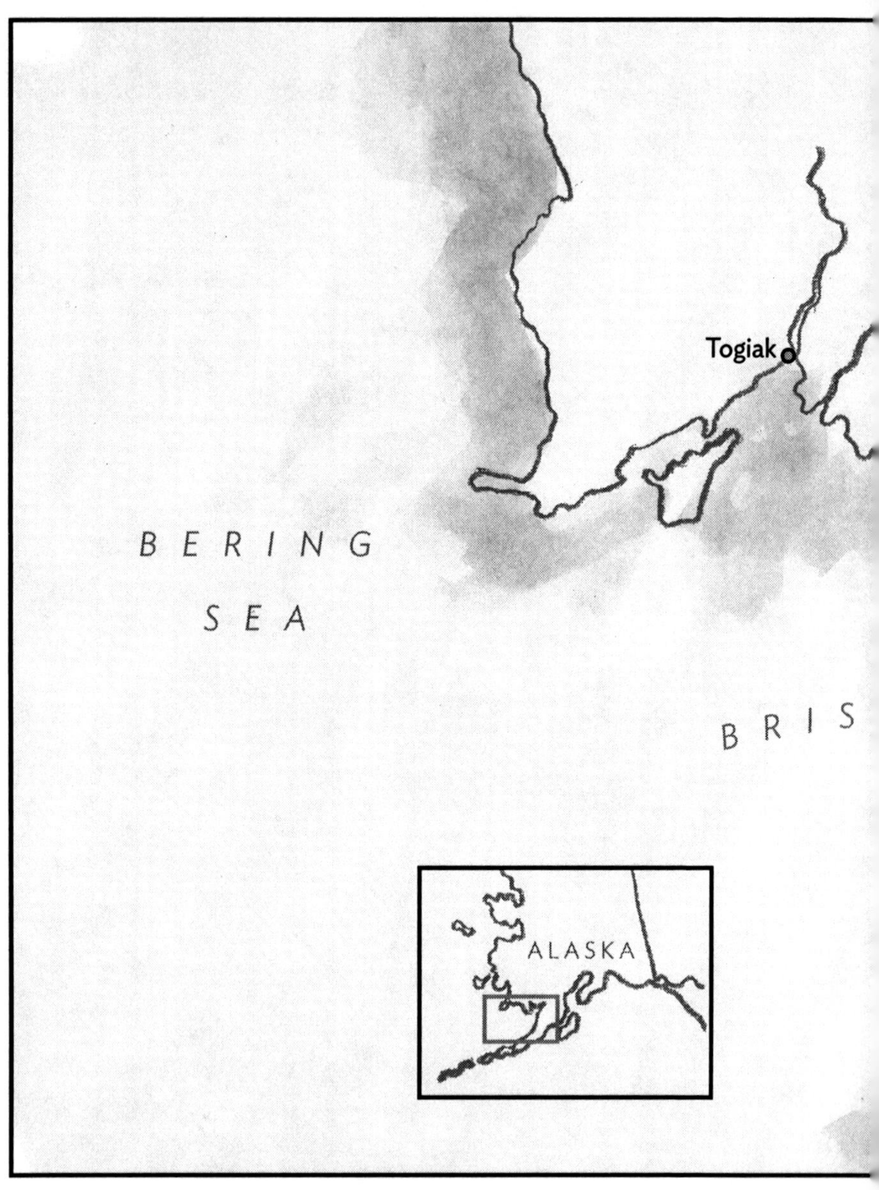
Togiak
BERING
SEA
BRIS
ALASKA

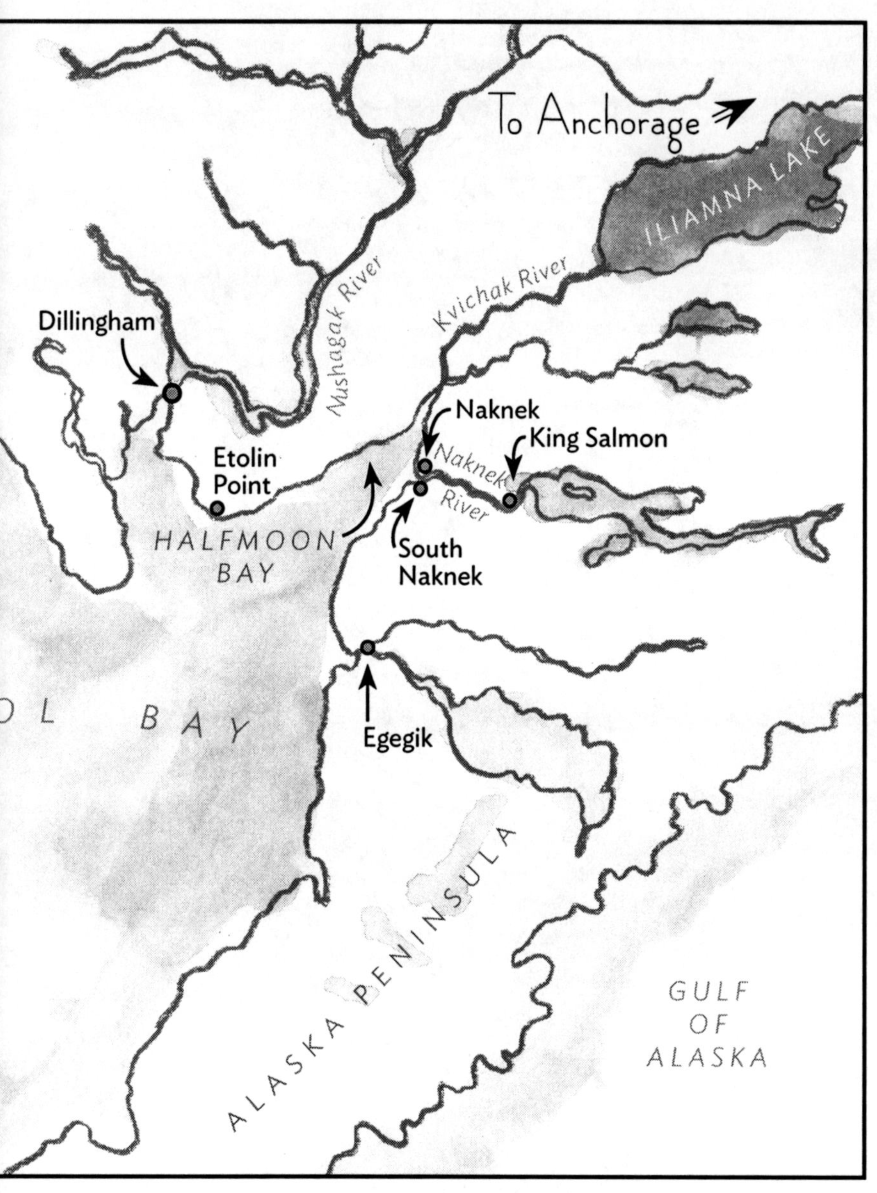

To Anchorage
ILIAMNA LAKE
Nushagak River
Kvichak River
Dillingham
Naknek
King Salmon
Etolin Point
Naknek River
HALFMOON BAY
South Naknek
L BAY
Egegik
ALASKA PENINSULA
GULF OF ALASKA

1
Departure

Alaskans like to call their state "The Last Frontier." It even says that on the license plates. Like a big adventure is around every corner, and every one of those cars is revved up and ready to go exploring. And the families inside are excited to take on the wilderness, with a song in their hearts and stacks of sourdough pancakes in their tummies.

Maybe that's what Alaskans are like, but Zoey Morley was definitely not there yet.

"That's your airplane? You couldn't afford one with three real tires?" Zoey frowned at Patrick and shook her head. "You can't be serious."

"Taildragger," her mother, Alice, had called it, and now Zoey understood. The plane had one small wheel under the tail and two bigger wheels in the front.

"All of us in that little thing with all our stuff? It doesn't. . . ."

Zoey's voice trailed off. It was no use. Every time the Bristol Bay idea had come up, she was very clear: "I'm not going!" But here she was, standing on the dusty pavement at Merrill Field in front of the most rickety, pathetic-looking plane in the whole airport.

Even with its yellow and white paint job, the little airplane seemed sad and tired. That's how Zoey felt too. Sad every time she thought of her mom and dad before the breakup. And tired from the packing, the days of driving, the unpacking, the new neighborhood, the new school. Most of all, she was tired of being sad.

Zoey tugged at a blonde braid and thought again of Colorado last summer, the car jammed with stuff and her dad in the driveway looking so clueless. He got smaller and smaller in the rear-view mirror as they drove away. Then he was gone. So was the life she had always known.

When they arrived at her Aunt Linda's house in Anchorage, the days were already getting dark and cold. Now after a longer winter than she had thought possible, the sun finally felt warm, the snow had melted, and here they were leaving again.

In that!

"Zoey, if you can't say anything nice." Her mom, again. "Now make a line and help pass boxes."

Zoey glared at her mother and pushed a box containing packages of cereal and spaghetti at her six-year-old brother, Eliot. He croaked out a raspy "Kraak, kraak," and passed it on to their mom.

He's being a raven again. What a weirdo. She looked at his mismatched socks, the old jacket with the duct-tape patch on the sleeve, and the straight blonde hair that hung in his eyes. He was more like a lost puppy than the mysterious Raven, the famous star of so many Alaska Native stories.

Eliot brushed his bangs aside with one hand. The box finally reached the tall, rugged man in the doorway of the plane. Their mom's boyfriend, Patrick. He was a bush pilot, and this mess was his big idea.

"We need to earn some money, Zoey," her mom had said.

Zoey agreed with her there. Ever since her parents had split up, all she heard was, "Too expensive, Zoey. Not now. I need to pay the rent." *Your dad's not paying any child support.* Her mom didn't say that, but Zoey knew she was thinking it.

Most people who need money find a real job. Zoey's mom taught piano lessons in their living room. This Bristol Bay thing wasn't a job either. It was, well . . . Zoey didn't know what it was, except crazy.

"Wanna check out inside?" Patrick patted the wing above the door.

Zoey paused.

"Can I see?" Eliot rushed past bumping Zoey on the way.

Zoey rolled her eyes. "Whatever."

Eliot climbed up and peered inside. "Cool! Come on, Zoey. You gotta see." He stepped down to make way for his sister.

Zoey sighed. She grabbed the wing strut and levered herself up on the metal footrest below the door. Inside the plane, pieces of stuffing spilled from split fabric on the seats, and a shredded lining hung from the ceiling like cobwebs. The area behind the seats was stuffed with boxes.

"What's wrong with it? Why is it all raggedy?"

Patrick set a box in the doorway. It was labeled "Food Supplements" in her mom's swirly writing. "It's an old plane. But the price was right."

"Mom! You said. . . ."

"Zoey, that's enough."

"Hang on a minute, so I can make enough room for you guys to sit."

Zoey lowered herself back to the tarmac. Patrick tucked his frame through the door, pushing boxes of canned vegetables ahead of him.

Zoey's mom shook her head. "Zoey, we've been over and over this. Most kids would love to fly in a small plane. And Bristol Bay? It's the most famous sockeye fishing area in Alaska, maybe in the world. Just wait till you see it."

"I don't ever want to see it! How many times do I have to say this? We just got here, and now we're moving again! It's not fair!"

Her mom sighed and shook her head. Patrick backed out the door.

"Zoey, it's pretty clear your mom can't teach enough lessons to pay the rent, and I can't help out unless we get this plane out west where I can haul fish. There's a lot of money to be made out there, but it's a short season. There's no time to waste. Now, let's get this baby in the air."

He gently picked up their old black lab, Lhasa, and eased her onto the floor behind the passenger seat. If Lhasa was concerned about the plane, she didn't show it. Eliot was next.

"Don't worry, guys; the engine's real solid," said Patrick.

"Raven Boy ready to fly!" Eliot shouted.

Patrick reached his hand down to help Zoey. She ignored him, pulled herself up, climbed over Eliot, and sandwiched herself against a window. Zoey didn't know much about Patrick. But she knew she didn't like him.

She made sure her duffel was wedged under the seat. In it was an art kit she had won in the poster contest last year. She had carefully packed the markers, brushes, and big tubes of paint. She was not going anywhere without those.

Zoey craned her head around to look behind her. The cabin was so crammed with boxes and gear she couldn't even see the back windows. She looked at Eliot. He wore a bulky sweater and a dark bandanna Patrick had tied around his head, and he was sitting on a box so he could see out the window. It made him tall enough that his head brushed the shredded material from the ceiling, causing him to cock his head first one way then the other. Maybe he did look like a raven after all.

Zoey's mom climbed in and Patrick followed. His seat rose directly in front of Zoey. His curly black hair blocked most of her view forward, but she could see her mom shut the passenger-side door, latch it, then sit strangely still for a moment, staring out through the front windshield. Her mom's mouth made tiny movements at the corners just like it used to when their dad didn't come home when he said he would.

Zoey wiped her sweaty hands on her pants and hunched her shoulders up to her chin. She felt like throwing up. This was really happening. All her summer plans with her new best friend, Bethany—swimming at Jewel Lake, staying up late at the Fourth of July concert on the Park Strip, and celebrating Zoey's thirteenth birthday at the new dance club—all those plans were gone.

She and Bethany had planned it all out. They were going to take turns babysitting, and Zoey was going to use the money to fly to Colorado to find her dad. Only Bethany knew about that part. But Zoey was sure she could convince her mom when the time came. Instead, now she would be stuck in a tent in the middle of nowhere.

Her mom had been firm, almost angry. "Zoey, we are a family and we are going out there *together*."

And the letter she sent to her dad to see if she could stay with him? Returned to her stamped "Address Unknown." How could that be? They had lived in that house her whole life until this last year. Where was he? Nearly a year had gone by without a single word from him, not even one letter. She was determined to find out why. But now this Bristol Bay–summer plan was like a freight train that just kept coming no matter how many things she tried to throw in front of it.

"Are you guys all right back there?" Zoey's mom turned to look at them and burst out laughing. "You look like real pioneers, all squeezed in there with everything you could possibly want for the next few months. Off to a new world where, who knows? Anything can happen! Where's the camera?" She plunged an arm into her bag.

"Ready? Smile!"

Zoey didn't. Lhasa panted, so Zoey reached down and rubbed her head.

"Clear prop!" Patrick yelled. He turned a key, and the engine sputtered to life. Its roar overwhelmed even her thoughts. Then they were moving. Patrick wore a headset and spoke into a microphone, but with the noise Zoey had no idea what he was saying. They taxied to the end of the runway. Patrick swung the plane into the wind and revved the engine. They rolled slowly, then faster.

Zoey held her breath. The cabin was shaking so hard she worried the engine would fly right off the plane. All around her things rattled and buzzed. Why hadn't they taken off yet? She dug her toes under the seat in front of her as if to lift it off the ground and watched the back of Patrick's head for any sign he might be in trouble. Faster and faster.

Then the plane felt smooth and light. No more rattling, although the wings wobbled just a little. They were flying, but to where? Into some mysterious place Patrick called "the real Alaska." A place she couldn't even imagine. A place her dad would never find.

2

Last Stop

It was still too noisy to talk. Zoey watched shadows dance across the Anchorage skyline. Patrick banked the plane, and they headed toward the open water of Cook Inlet.

"Kraak, kraak!" Eliot yelled, his eyes fixed on the horizon. He tried to flap his arms in the confined space.

Zoey had never flown in a small plane. She thought of the big Alaska Airlines jet they took to Juneau to visit Nana and Papa. This felt more like riding a lawn mower hung from an old kite.

Trees, roads, and cars fell away as they climbed higher and higher.

The streets, houses, and tall buildings of downtown Anchorage seemed small in front of the towering Chugach mountain range behind them. Then, all too soon, they disappeared altogether, replaced by the seething waters of Cook Inlet. Zoey felt her connection to her old life shrink too. Her new one was a big question mark. Patrick had shown them Bristol Bay on a map, but it wasn't a real place to Zoey. Not yet.

I'm going to tell my dad all about this someday, she decided. But it didn't make her feel any better.

Her mom turned and gave them a thumbs-up. Zoey could see Patrick's hand on her knee. Why was her mom suddenly so attached to this poor, dumb pilot? Not that they had been rich, or all that happy in Colorado, but did she really think he was an improvement?

Trying to understand her mom was like trying to figure out why the wind changed direction. You never seemed to have enough information. This whole divorce thing just swooped in one day like a harsh wind trying to blow their family apart. Lots of families live their whole lives in the same place. Why not hers?

But Zoey knew lots of families didn't. Bethany's mom was divorced too, and her boyfriend was creepy. Zoey and Bethany both thought so. All they knew for sure was that it just wasn't fair.

The sound of the airplane engine smoothed out. Sun broke through the clouds, and a waterfall of dazzling light spilled over the Sleeping Lady, a mountain across Cook Inlet that was easy to see from Anchorage.

Zoey had heard the old Indian story. A beautiful maiden was sleeping before she was to be married. The man she loved was away from the village, fighting off a warring tribe. When he was killed, no one had the heart to awaken the sleeping lady, so she slept on and on and finally turned into the famous mountain.

Just as well, because they would have gotten divorced anyway, Zoey sulked.

This was the first time Zoey had seen the mountain from the air. It really did look like a woman asleep, with her arms folded and her long hair cascading into the sea. Directly below them, the tide and wind churned the water green and white with brown streaks and extravagant swirls. So wild and scary and beautiful all at the same time.

They left the Sleeping Lady behind, and soon Zoey spotted even bigger mountains. White smoke puffed from one snowy peak then another. Her mom pointed and yelled above the din of the engine.

"Mounts Iliamna and Redoubt. They're volcanoes."

"Wow! Are they going to erupt?"

Her mom shook her head and laughed. "Not today, I hope!"

Zoey slid her duffel out from under Lhasa, and pulled out her sketchpad and a pencil. With one hand on the paper and her brown eyes darting between the view and the pad, she swiftly made lines to capture the lights and shadows of the landscape. Stuck in this plane she couldn't fly, on the way to a place she didn't want to be, Zoey felt herself grow calm. Drawing was something she could control. No one could make her put a line where she didn't want one.

Lhasa stopped panting and nudged her head against Zoey's arm. After a few minutes, Zoey yawned, closed the pad, and squeezed it between her seat and the door. She stroked the dog's silky ears with her fingertips.

Eliot was already sound asleep. The cabin felt warm. The leaky volcanoes were long gone. Zoey closed her eyes.

When she woke an hour later, the scene had changed dramatically. On both sides of the plane, rocky cliffs rose sharply from a jagged white river. The mountaintops were wrapped in snow. Sheets of blue glacier-ice spilled into valleys. Milky waterfalls launched themselves hundreds of feet onto hungry-looking rocks.

"Lake Clark Pass," shouted Zoey's mom.

It was so narrow. What if they met a plane coming the other way?

Did Patrick really know how to fly this rattletrap? As if to answer, he pointed out the window. Below them, on a ledge in the side of a cliff, lay the fuselage and wing of a small airplane that looked a lot like theirs.

Oh, great. She didn't need to worry about finding her dad, because they were all going to die this afternoon!

Eventually, though, the pass opened to a wide river valley. They followed the drainage another half hour to a point where the shoreline turned sharply away on both sides. Before them a flat sea stretched so far it curved to meet the sky. Their mom turned and pointed excitedly.

"Zoey, Eliot. That's Bristol Bay!"

When the water was directly below them, Patrick let the plane drop to just a few hundred feet above it, then turned to the right and followed the shoreline for several minutes until they flew over a small point of land followed by a gentle curve in the beach. The engine slowed. Zoey's mom turned again, this time with a big smile, and pointed downward.

"And that's Halfmoon Bay down there!" More smiles. Zoey wished her mom would get a grip on herself, but she said nothing and looked out the window. Below she could see a shallow dent in the edge of what seemed like an endless shore. Apparently, this was it.

"Halfmoon Bay is this tiny little section of Bristol Bay, which is so big you can't even see the edges of it," Patrick yelled back at them.

"Over that way," he pointed above the water in the direction of the left wing, "is a place called Naknek. That's our closest town, but you can't see it from here."

As the plane dropped still lower, Zoey thought she glimpsed the roof of a small building on the beach, but whatever it was quickly disappeared behind them.

"Home to the largest sockeye salmon runs in the world," Patrick crowed.

Zoey wished he would concentrate on being a pilot instead of a tour guide.

Eliot woke up just as the earth rose to meet them. Zoey's stomach seemed to lodge somewhere between her pounding heart and the roof of the plane. This maniac was going to land on the beach. She squeezed her eyes shut and glued her fingers to the bottom of the seat.

Good-bye, world.

I love you, Dad.

The tires bounced a couple of times then miraculously rolled smoothly. As if he were simply parking the family car, Patrick turned the plane into the wind and stopped the engine. In less than three hours, they had gone from the parking lots and paved streets of Anchorage to nothing but water, beach, and a broad brown-green plain Patrick called the "tundra."

"Last stop. Everybody out." Patrick climbed down first, then opened the passenger door for Zoey's mom with a little bow. Lhasa bolted over Eliot and jumped to the ground, sniffing wildly at this new world.

Patrick lifted Eliot down and extended a hand to Zoey, who found the footrest and climbed to the ground on her own. She stumbled on a smooth, round rock and glared at Patrick when he grabbed her arm to steady her.

She shrugged him off and looked around. The plane had landed on a level stretch of sand and gravel. An expanse of pebbles sloped gradually from where she stood down to the choppy, foam-streaked sea. A couple of distant fishing boats broke the monotony of the watery view, and far behind them a ghostly line of mountains lay along the horizon. Somewhere out there was the town Patrick had said was nearest to them.

She turned her head in the direction they had come, but saw nothing of a building, or any other sign of people. Higher up the beach, the stretch of "landing strip" ended at a line of tall grass and behind that, as far as she could see, spread a carpet of low-growing mosses and scrubby plants. The tundra: a wide wetland without a single large tree. At a spot perhaps a football field back along the beach, the grassy border of the tundra swelled into a low, rounded hill covered by more grass. Other than that, the world was flat as far as Zoey could see.

Looking up the beach in the opposite direction made the wind-whipped sand sting her face. Nothing there, either, except that she could make out a place not too far away where the beach curved out toward the water and just seemed to stop. That must be where Halfmoon Bay ended and the shoreline blended into the larger outline of Bristol Bay.

All she could hear were waves, wind, and seagulls.

The ocean air was thick and sharp in her throat.

This was their summer home.

3

Latrine Business

Patrick gave orders as he handed down bags from the plane. "First thing is to get our tents up so we have a place to sleep."

Zoey's mom tossed two nylon duffels toward Zoey. "You and Eliot are in charge of the tents. This one's yours." One duffel dropped at Zoey's feet. The wind sent the other tumbling down the beach. Lhasa barked and took off after it.

Zoey's mom yelled, "That's the rain fly, Zoey. Get it!"

"Why should I?"

Her mom did that squinty thing that made her look like she was lining up a gun barrel.

"Okay." Zoey walked slowly after the bundle. She trudged back with the small stuff sack that held a thin nylon sheet that would stretch over their tent to keep out the rain. Sand jumped from the beach and pricked her face like needles.

"Hey, Eliot, give me a hand," said Patrick, and the two of them disappeared into the high grass that lined the beach. They returned dragging an assortment of boards.

"Where did those come from?" asked Zoey.

"I dropped these out here on my last trip. There's some plywood, too. We need it to build platforms for the tents. Maybe you guys can find some flat driftwood for shelves."

Zoey sighed. She was about to say "find your own driftwood" when Eliot grabbed her arm.

"Zoey, Zoey, we can explore while we look for wood."

"Now hold on everyone," Zoey's mom said. "Don't forget where we are. We need a rule so we all stay safe. How about . . . never go walking alone, and always stay within sight of the camp. Got that?"

"That's two rules," Zoey grumbled.

"Your mom's right," Patrick said. "I didn't see any bears when we flew in, and they usually stay clear of the camps, but you never know. See that grassy mound up the beach near the tundra? You can go as far as that, but stick together."

It wasn't that Zoey didn't agree with the rules. Even in Colorado they had learned that bears were no joke. She just couldn't stand it when Patrick tried to be the family boss. She didn't need that at all.

Eliot and Zoey walked in the direction Patrick had indicated, squishing their feet through a line of seaweed left by the tide. Nose to the ground, Lhasa soon veered off, a scent leading her into the high grass. Eliot and Zoey followed the dog to the upper edge of the beach where the tundra began.

Away from the water's edge, the sharp ocean air mixed with an earthier smell. Seagulls soared above and scolded as though mocking her family for trying to set up housekeeping where they didn't belong. Zoey stared at the strange landscape and thought of the moon-landing video they had watched at school. "One giant leap" . . . in the wrong direction.

Eliot tugged Zoey toward the grassy hill Patrick had pointed to.

"I bet we see bears this summer," he said. "I bet we see lots of stuff."

"I bet we don't get to see any movies. I don't see any theaters on this beach." Zoey and Bethany had planned to go to the latest movie with that cute *Star Wars* guy, Harrison Ford, *Raiders of the Lost Ark*. Guess that wouldn't be happening.

Eliot pulled on Zoey's jacket, and she put her hand on his shoulder to slow him down. They had walked only about five minutes, but the airplane was out of sight behind the hill, and the wind was quieter here.

"What's that?" Eliot pointed ahead.

"It looks like an old shack."

"No, it's a boat!" He shook off her hand and charged down into a hollow that lay just in front of them.

"Don't forget what Mom said. Stay with me or I'll. . . . Eliot! Wait!"

"A boat! A boat!"

She caught up with him.

In front of Eliot, the remains of an old wooden fishing boat, about twice as long as a pickup truck, nestled in the sandy gravel. Years of wind, tides, snow, and ice had pummeled the stern section nearly flat. But the cabin stood up like a lookout post, and the bow remained intact.

They quickly climbed up the slanting deck. Eliot pushed through the cabin door and headed straight for the steering wheel.

"Captain Raven of Bristol Bay!" He tried spinning the wheel, but it wouldn't budge.

Sand and a couple of soggy magazines littered the floor along with a few shards of pottery probably from an old coffee cup. Zoey noticed an open hatch near her feet. A slanted ladder descended into the hold. Next to the ladder an old rain hat, barely recognizable, hung on a rusty nail.

Who had worn that hat? What had happened to the people who used to fish in this boat? Was it a family? A storm must have washed it all the way up here to the tundra. Was anyone on board when that happened, or had they already abandoned ship? She peeked down the stairway. *Was there a skeleton down there?*

A motion through the cracked window in front of the steering wheel caught Zoey's eye. A shadow slid along the ground under the bow.

"Lhasa?" she called, but the dog was busy digging on the grassy mound. It was eerily quiet, except for her own heart beating. She peered outside. A bear maybe, or some crazy old fisherman? Nothing. She breathed out, a little disappointed.

A gust of wind vibrated a pole on the roof, sending a weird moaning sound deep into the wooden hull. Eliot raised his eyebrows, grinned, and shrugged. He crawled up into a cramped bunk in the bow and started to paw through debris.

"Kraak, kraak!" he cried, holding up an old leather boot. "Pirates!"

"Hey, I thought you guys were gathering driftwood," their mother's voice interrupted from outside. "You're supposed to be out on the beach."

"Raven Boy find pirate treasure," said Eliot, carrying the boot out on deck.

"Wow! You two hit the jackpot!" Zoey's mom surveyed the old boat. "Patrick," she hollered.

No response.

"Come on, Eliot, let's go tell Patrick to bring a crowbar. Maybe he can get some good planks from this wreckage. Zoey, you stay put."

Zoey watched Eliot trot off down the beach with her mom, the old boot bouncing in his arms.

A few minutes later, Zoey could hear Patrick's steps approaching. "You can't take our wood," Zoey called out. "We found this boat, and we like it in one piece."

"I'll just grab a couple of boards from the stern, here. They'll make good supports for the platforms. Don't worry, I won't hurt the cabin." He started ripping out a loose plank. "Come on, give me a hand."

Zoey picked the smallest piece of wood and limply dragged it back to camp. She remembered the moving shadow and turned to examine the beach around the wreck again. Empty.

The wind died down, and a lukewarm sun poked through the clouds. Zoey watched her mom. Dressed in a shapeless blue raincoat and oversized pants stuffed into big rubber boots, she struggled to haul boxes of supplies from the plane to the tent site. Clumps of her wavy brown hair fluttered from the edges of a gray wool cap.

She can't really like being out here in the middle of nowhere, can she?

Zoey remembered when her mom had taken them to chamber music concerts all dressed up. Her dad never wanted to go.

Dad!

She had been so busy since they landed, she hadn't even thought about him. She would write him a letter tonight.

In spite of herself, Zoey helped her mom organize the rest of the gear at the campsite. It was hard work, but something caught her, like being a pioneer putting down roots in a new country. Zoey could understand that kind of pioneer. The kind that wanted to build a home and stay put.

"Let's stop for lunch," said Patrick. "The platforms are almost done. After we eat, we can erect Chez Jensen-Morley."

"Shay what?" said Eliot.

"He means it will be our very own castle," said their mom on her way back to the plane to find the sandwiches.

Eliot announced he had to pee.

Their mom turned, "Go ahead, Patrick. Tell them."

"If all you have to do is pee, go up on the edge of the beach grass, but no farther. It's good for us to claim our territory, let the animals know this is our spot."

"Cool!" yelled Eliot as he romped up the beach and dropped his pants.

Zoey turned away. "Yuck!"

Patrick and their mom laughed. When Eliot bounded back to them, Patrick continued, "Later I'll show you where to go if you have to do more than pee." He was still chuckling as he led them back to the campsite. Zoey grimaced. Just great—no people, no houses, no beds. And no toilet!

4

Chez Jensen-Morley

Chez Jensen-Morley turned out to be an old, army-green pup tent for Zoey and Eliot, and a big, tan, Eureka wall-tent for Patrick and their mom, and for family meals and activities. With a little complaining, they finally got both shelters up. Patrick attached ropes to the platforms and drove long wooden stakes deep into the sand. Then he pounded together some driftwood benches while the others began to organize the food. Finally, he hung a kerosene lantern high up on the pole in the middle of the tent.

"For our late-night poker games," he laughed.

The sun played hide-and-seek as they worked, shining long enough to make them loosen their jackets, then slipping away again until the chill breeze made them zip back up. Every so often the clouds spat out pellets of cold rain.

Patrick grabbed a bucket and two plastic jugs and took Zoey and Eliot along the beach past the low hill that hid the old fishing boat. Not far beyond, a small creek spilled from the tundra through a broad V in the sand and ran across the beach and straight into the water of Halfmoon Bay. Patrick led them to a pool of water where they filled the containers.

Then they lugged the water back to the tent platform, stopping several times so Zoey and Eliot could rest their arms and shoulders. When they arrived at the tent platform, their mom clapped her hands to celebrate their hard work and immediately dropped a small tablet into each jug.

"Iodine."

"Why can't we just drink it? There's nothing around to get it dirty," said Eliot.

"Even though there are no people, you can still get parasites from the stream," said their mom.

"Little bugs," said Patrick. "They live in your intestines and grow up into huge aliens that burst out through your chest and begin eating. . ." He slurped menacingly.

"Patrick!" Their mother fired a squinty look at him. "Eliot, they do not grow into aliens. They're just tiny critters that can make you feel sick. So, just to be safe, we use the iodine tabs. Don't worry. You won't even know they're in there."

Zoey hid her smile. She didn't want Patrick to know that sometimes she thought he was funny. Bethany thought he was cute. Cute, schmute is all Zoey had to say about that. She watched him finish building a stand for the Coleman cookstove.

"Want to come check it out?" Patrick picked up the wooden frame and gestured for Zoey to follow him into the tent. "It's starting to look pretty homey in there."

"Yeah, if your home came from the Goodwill," she said.

But when they got inside, even Zoey was impressed. They had set the tent up in Anchorage a couple of weeks ago, but she had forgotten how big it was. The ceiling stood taller than Patrick in the middle, and she and Eliot could stretch toe to toe on the floor of the sleeping area and not touch the walls with their fingers.

The entry flap was now enclosed by an extra awning their mom had sewn to make a space for cooking and eating. With the awning area full of food on driftwood shelves, the camp was nearly like a tiny two-room house.

Their mom tested the new cooking stand with the big soup pot. Patrick dragged in a piece of driftwood for another chair. Somehow, it *was* starting to look like a home after all.

Finally, it was time to cook their first Halfmoon Bay dinner. Zoey's mom lit the primus burner to boil water for spaghetti. Zoey looked at her watch. Eight o'clock at night, and the sun was still shining. Her mouth watered as she watched the steam rise from the pot. Maybe all those cans of tomatoes weren't such a bad idea.

Later, they all sopped up spaghetti sauce with pieces of French bread bought fresh that morning in Anchorage. Zoey did not remember liking spaghetti so much. Soon she was full and felt too tired to move. Her mom opened a tin of cookies. Bethany's cookies.

After they had all packed into Patrick's old Chevy to go to the airport, Bethany had waved from her yard.

"Don't leave yet!" Bethany and her mom had hurried up to the truck.

Bethany had held out the blue tin with a picture of a Christmas tree on the lid.

Zoey promised to send letters. "I've got your address somewhere. Patrick said there's a post office in Dillingham. We'll be at 'general delivery' or something. I'll write and explain."

Zoey remembered trying to get her arm free in the crowded seat for a final wave. Then the truck turned the corner and her friend disappeared.

"Earth to Zoey. You gotta at least have one." Her mom stood in front of her, cookie tin in hand.

Maybe she wasn't *that* full.

When nearly half the cookies were gone, Patrick grabbed the

kids' packs. "Come on, guys. Let's get your sleeping bags laid out. You've got your very own bedroom next door."

Their mom filled the teapot from the jug of iodine-treated water and put it on the stove. "I'll clean up here. You go ahead."

Once outside, Patrick finished their toilet lesson. Zoey, Eliot, and Lhasa followed him along the beach in the opposite direction from where they had found the boat. Up over the high grass and down onto the tundra. There, sheltered from most of the wind, was a hole in the ground about three feet deep with a couple of logs laid over it for a seat.

"This is our latrine. I dug it on my first flight out to scout the beach."

"You can't be serious. No way!" Zoey crossed her arms and turned away.

"Well, you have two choices," explained Patrick. "You can either go here, or you can squat down on the beach near the water. If you go down there, put your toilet paper under a rock, so it doesn't blow around before the tide comes in."

Zoey and Eliot stared at Patrick. The seagulls cried along the shore.

Finally Patrick said, "I suppose I could rig up a lean-to over it. You know, give you a little privacy and maybe keep the rain out. I'll see if we have enough lumber. But don't worry, no one can see you behind all this grass anyway."

Zoey fumed. This was way worse than she had imagined. There was nothing to give her any privacy from Eliot. And what if a plane flew over? *How embarrassing!*

"Eliot, I'm going to make a sign that says 'KEEP OUT!' Any time you see that sign sticking out of the sand over there, you will

NOT, NOT, NOT come any closer, or you will die a horrible, painful death. Got it?"

Eliot was silent a moment. Then he smiled his sweetest puppy smile. "Got it, Zo."

Or was that Raven, the trickster, talking? Zoey was not reassured.

They hiked back to the campsite without a word. Patrick helped them blow up air mattresses and spread out their sleeping bags.

"Goodnight, guys. I think you're going to like it here. I hope you will. Your mom and I are right next door if you need anything." He disappeared through the tent flap.

Zoey slid the duffel with her art kit between her sleeping bag and the wall of the tent. The pack with her clothes and books she pushed down to the far end. Then she crawled inside her sleeping bag. It was still light out, but the green nylon of the tent shaded them. Eliot snuggled up to Lhasa and was soon asleep.

So this was their new life. Zoey wondered what Bethany was doing. Maybe watching the *Kate and Allie* show, or listening to Cindy Lauper sing "Girls Just Want to Have Fun" on the radio. Zoey softly hummed it until she felt tears in her eyes. Some fun she was having. Anchorage seemed like a million miles away. And where was her dad? What would he think of her now? She wanted to write to him right then but she was too tired. It would have to wait.

Eliot's mouth hung slightly open. The sound of his breathing mixed with the whisper of the waves, as though the ocean were breathing too. She tried to match her own breaths with her brother's and then with the water as it whooshed in . . . and out. . . . Finally, they were all breathing together, like one big family, Eliot, Zoey, and Bristol Bay.

That was the last thing she remembered until Lhasa barked. The dog sounded frantic.

What was wrong?

5

Night Visitors

Zoey glanced at her watch, eleven o'clock. She fumbled for the zipper, opened the tent flap, and peered out. The sun was gone, but the sky was still light! Eliot stirred inside his sleeping bag. Patrick emerged from the big tent, a rifle in his hand. "I hope she hasn't found our first bear."

As the seriousness of the situation hit them, Zoey and Eliot squirmed from their sleeping bags and yanked their clothes on. Seconds later, they raced out of the tent and ran to catch up. Patrick was jogging toward the stream where they had filled their water jugs. They heard Lhasa bark somewhere ahead of him.

Where the sun had set, a deep red glow bloomed from behind the distant mountain peaks like the coals of a dying fire. Thin clouds overhead were shot with pink and gold, and the sand seemed to glow. Zoey and Eliot caught up with Patrick before he reached the creek.

"Stop right there," Patrick whispered.

Ahead, on their side of the creek, Lhasa crouched and barked furiously. Across the narrow stream, a fierce looking creature, something like a giant weasel, and almost as big as the dog, bared its teeth and growled.

Zoey's mom shouted in a firm voice, "Lhasa, come!" The dog turned toward her, but continued to bark.

In a half whisper, Patrick said, "It's a river otter, and the dog's got it all riled up."

A shadowy movement near an old log a short distance up the beach from the big otter caught Zoey's eye. More of them! Babies! Zoey pointed her index finger and shook it with excitement.

Four tiny animals stumbled from behind the log and one at a time paraded along the creek bank toward the ocean. The big otter, which Zoey decided must have been the mother, carefully stayed between the babies and Lhasa and looked scarier than ever. But the babies were another matter, so cute with their smooshed up faces and long snaky tails. When they walked, they scrunched up in the middle and then oozed out the way an inchworm does, only faster. Zoey was half thinking of picking one up to pet when Patrick hissed at them.

"Don't get too close."

Lhasa wasn't listening. She inched toward the biggest otter. It backed away in a fit of toothy snarls and growls. The babies scurried back toward the log, bumping into one another as they backpedaled. Lhasa bared her teeth, too, and growled ferociously.

Suddenly, the mother otter crossed the stream and lunged at Lhasa. They merged into a rolling ball of fur, sand, and ear-splitting screeches. Lhasa, bigger and heavier, was able to keep the otter off balance, but the mother showed she was determined not to let the dog get any closer to her pups. After a few seconds the two animals once again faced off, this time with their muzzles only inches apart.

"Lhasa!" Zoey screamed and leaped toward the animals.

"Get back here, Zoey!" Her mother grabbed Zoey by the arm, but Zoey broke loose and charged forward.

"LHASA!" Zoey's scream was immediately lost amid a new explosion of squeals, yelps, and hisses as the two animals clashed again.

Zoey knew it was foolish to get too close. She instinctively covered her ears with her hands. Sand churned around the animals making it impossible to see exactly what was happening. Zoey's heart pounded. What if Lhasa was killed? She grabbed a handful of sand in each hand, darted forward, and threw it in the midst of the fight with another shout, "STOP IT!"

Lhasa's bark choked into a yelp, and at the same moment the otter broke free and retreated across the stream to the log. Lhasa whimpered and slunk to Zoey's side. Zoey grabbed the dog by the collar and pulled her back toward Patrick and the others.

Meanwhile, the frightened babies rushed from behind the log once again, and their mother herded the whimpering brood down the creek to the ocean, turning often toward Lhasa as if to say, "Don't even think about it!"

When the little ones reached the deeper saltwater, they dove, then surfaced several yards from shore. The mother was the last to enter the water. When she was fully submerged, Zoey loosened her grip on Lhasa and the dog trotted over to Zoey's mom, wagged her tail, and panted.

"Zoey what did you think you were going to do to that mother otter?" Patrick scowled. "She could take your hand off in one bite."

Zoey put her hands on her hips. "Somebody had to help Lhasa. She's part of our family. You can't just watch like it's some Disney show."

Patrick grabbed her by the shoulders. "You *never* chase after a wild animal, Zoey. NEVER. You have no idea what even a small one like an otter could do to you. We can't afford to make mistakes out here. It's sixty miles to Dillingham, and the only way there is by plane. If you screw up, and no one's around to help, you could die. Got it?"

He released her, and Zoey turned away. Her lower lip trembled. She tried hard to stay strong, but a few tears escaped and snuck down her cheeks.

"Who does he think he is?" she demanded.

Her mother put an arm around her, but Zoey shook her shoulders violently. "Leave me alone!" She stomped toward the tent, shoving each foot hard into the gravel.

"Look!" It was Eliot.

Zoey turned to see one more baby otter slink from behind the log. Zoey's mom grabbed Lhasa's collar and the dog's ears snapped forward. The little otter squealed as it hurried after the rest.

"Awwwwww," said Eliot.

Zoey kept her distance from Patrick and her mom, but stood and watched too. She was furious at Patrick for being so tough on her. Her dad would never have done that. She thought of the time her mom had yelled at her because Zoey had taken most of Eliot's Halloween candy away.

But Zoey was just trying to keep him from getting sick. Her dad seemed to understand. He said he and Zoey were going for a moonlight walk. And that's what they did, just the two of them. Her dad had pointed out Orion and the Big Dipper. Standing there on the beach two thousand miles from their old home, Zoey thought of trying to find those constellations in the sky, but it wasn't even dark yet.

Zoey called Lhasa over to her. Other than a cut on her nose and a slimy coating of sand and otter slobber, the dog didn't seem hurt. The otter family soon disappeared in the dark, shimmering water.

Back in the tent, Zoey waited until Eliot was asleep. It was bad enough being all jammed up in a dinky tent with her Raven

Boy brother, on the edge of nowhere. She was not going to take orders from her mom's stupid boyfriend.

Outside the wind picked up. The tent quivered. The nylon sides sucked in then snapped back out. It began to rain. Little drops at first, but soon it sounded like a corn popper had gone crazy. Zoey could no longer hear Eliot's breathing over the din.

She reached for her duffel bag and shuffled through it until she found the photo. Eliot on a rope swing behind their old house in Colorado. Near the edge of the photo, watching the action with his crooked old grin and shaggy hair, was her dad.

Sure, her parents had fought sometimes. *They all do that, right?* But her mom said it wasn't "normal." The fights had gotten worse. Something had to change, she said. In school, teachers separate kids when they can't get along. So, that's kind of what happened, only no one told her parents to separate. They just did it one day, without asking Zoey about it at all. Later, her dad said he didn't want the divorce, but her mom wouldn't budge.

"My favorite girl," he used to say. Then he just fell out of her life.

"It's for the best," Zoey's mom had told her. "You don't know everything that was going on. We will all be happier this way, I promise." Easy for her to say, but now Zoey was just one more kid in a "single-parent household." So maybe her mom and dad didn't like each other anymore. Why did they have to go and mess up *her* life?

A few weeks later, they had packed up and moved to Alaska, where all her mom's family was from. They stayed a while with Zoey's grandparents, Nana and Papa, in Juneau, a place Zoey had visited a couple of times before. It rained the whole time they were there.

Then it was on the ferry and back in the car for three more days of driving to Anchorage, where her mom's sister, Aunt Linda, lived. And finally to the little house up the street from Bethany where Zoey and Eliot shared a basement bedroom. A room that felt as far from Zoey's old life as a hotel on the moon.

"Someday you'll understand," her mom had told her.

Oh yeah? When would that be?

She placed the photo back in the duffel and grabbed her stationery. Her dad would want to know what was happening to her, to all of them. She was sure he would write soon, and then she'd have his address.

June 20

Dear Dad,

You won't believe where I am. Bristol Bay, Alaska! It's all Patrick's idea (that's Mom's new boyfriend). Maybe you already heard, but he dragged us all out here in his ratty airplane so he could haul fish.

Don't worry, Dad, I show Mom what a dork he really is every day.

Guess what we saw tonight? Otters! A whole family of them! I couldn't believe the babies. They were so cute. I thought Lhasa and the mother otter were going to kill each other, but thanks to me, they didn't.

Anyway, how are you? I really miss you. I was hoping to earn babysitting money this summer so I could come visit you, but now I can't do that. Don't worry, I'll figure something out. I'm going to buy a plane ticket . . . somehow.

But where are you now? How come you haven't called?

I guess this is it for a while. Oh, I didn't tell you about our "bathroom." Disgusting! An open pit on the beach! What is Mom thinking?

I hope you get this letter. I'll have to keep it here until you write so I'll know where to send it. I'm so tired. I'll write more later. I really love you, Dad.

Your Faraway Daughter,

Zoey

6

A New Boy

Zoey woke to a shrill call. An eagle? That wild sound. It reminded her of Juneau. There were lots of eagles there. The complaint sounded again somewhere overhead: "Eeeeeeeee." A seagull joined in, and soon bird cries filled the sky. No rain, but the wind still rustled the sides of the tent. Underneath all that, she heard the steady roll of waves hitting the shore.

She stretched as far as she could in the little pup tent and looked over at Eliot. He was propped up on one elbow studying her. Lhasa was sandwiched between them, which didn't leave a lot of extra room to move around.

"How long have you been watching me?"

"You were twitching. Were you having a dream?"

"I don't know. I can't remember." She listened to the ocean, and something else—an odd raspy sound.

It was Eliot. When he breathed out, he hissed like a leaky tire.

"What's wrong with you? You sound like Darth Vader."

"I don't know. I just woke up this way."

"That's how you were after we played in Bethany's attic, and Mom had to take you to the doctor, remember?"

"I'm okay, Zoey."

Lhasa sat up and pointed her ears toward the door flap.

Zoey sat up too. "What was that?"

Over the sound of the wind and waves came a soft tapping. Zoey rolled onto her stomach, and Eliot did the same. Zoey lifted the tent flap so they could see outside, but whatever had tapped was out of view. Lhasa inched forward between them. Eliot put his arm around her and sat absolutely still.

Tap, tap, tap. It was coming from the side of the tent.

Eliot looked at Zoey and tightened his hold on the dog. Zoey slowly unzipped the mosquito netting.

"Lhasa, stay." She half crawled out of the tent and peered around the corner. A large black raven was pecking at the shiny metal spikes Patrick had hammered into the wooden platform to hold down the tent.

Slowly, the raven hopped its way toward the front of the tent as Zoey tucked herself back in. There. They could both see the raven only a few feet away. Fine, black feathers covered its head. Bigger ones cloaked its throat and chest like the dark armor of King Arthur's knights. One thick feather in the bird's tail stood out. It was dusty gray. The bird saw them and cocked its head. As if on command, Lhasa, Zoey, and Eliot cocked their heads too and stared back.

"Eeeeeeeeee," shrieked the eagle from high over their heads, and the raven skittered away from the tent. It flew low down the beach and landed on the sand, still within view.

"Let's follow him!" Eliot was already pulling jeans and a sweatshirt from the bottom of his sleeping bag. He crawled out on the tent platform to put them on.

"Wait for me. Do you think Mom's still asleep?" said Zoey, nodding toward the big tent and pulling her sweater over the long-john top she liked to wear for pajamas.

They listened but didn't hear anything. The front flap on the big tent was closed.

Zoey found her own jeans and they each slipped on a pair of thick rubber boots and finally their rain jackets. Eliot pressed his ear against the door flap of the big tent.

"Mom and Patrick are still in there," he whispered.

Zoey nodded and they moved silently past the tent.

"How's your Darth Vader thing?"

Eliot still sounded funny, but he said, "It's okay. Come on."

The sky was a cold gray. Zoey took a deep breath of sea air and clutched Lhasa's collar. Every time they got close to the raven, it would fly off a little farther down the beach. When the raven was nearly to the stream where they had seen the otters, it turned and flew up along the streambed toward the tundra and disappeared behind the grassy hill. They followed behind. When they rounded the edge of the hill, close to the old boat, they stopped short.

The raven was perched on the roof of the wheelhouse. Below it, a boy worked with a knife, carving something into the side of the boat.

"What's your name?" called Eliot when they were still some distance away.

The boy looked up, startled. His hooded sweatshirt hid much of his face, but Zoey could see straight dark hair framing a pair of equally dark eyes. She thought he looked Alaska Native, related to the people whose ancestors had lived in Alaska thousands of years before white people showed up.

Lhasa pulled so hard that Zoey let her go. She wagged her tail and bounded up to the boy, who took a step back, then kneeled to pet her. Zoey and Eliot moved closer.

The boy put his knife in a sheath on his belt and pulled back the sweatshirt hood. His straight nose and angular face gave him a proud look, and Zoey's first thought was that those brown eyes were somehow laughing at her. When the boy pulled Lhasa's face right up to his and gave her a big grin, Zoey knew she wanted to find out more about him.

"I'm Thomas." He scratched both of Lhasa's ears at once. "Who are you?" He said this to the dog, as if he were more interested in her than in Zoey or Eliot.

"That's Lhasa. Do you live around here?" asked Eliot.

"Were you here yesterday?" asked Zoey, remembering the shadow she had seen. Thomas looked up. "I saw you come in. Our fish camp is down the beach." He pointed with his head toward the area of Halfmoon Bay they had first flown over, on the far side of the stream.

He was about a head taller than Zoey, and he looked maybe two years older. It had never occurred to Zoey she might find someone close to her age on the beach at Halfmoon Bay. She tried to think of something else to ask, but she couldn't find the words. He seemed so different. Zoey felt her face flush and hoped he couldn't see it from where he stood.

"Zoooooeeey! Ellllllllliot!"

Mom.

The boy pulled his hood up and started walking away.

"Wait, don't leave yet." Zoey blurted.

He stopped but still faced away.

"Are you the only other kid around here?"

He turned partway toward Zoey. "Not sure who is coming out this year. Depends. You're the only city kids."

Zoey bristled. "What's that supposed to mean?"

"You're from Anchorage. I've been there before. Gotta get

back to camp." He turned and jogged down the beach. The raven hopped twice on the cabin roof and flew off in the same direction.

"Wait!" Zoey called, but Thomas was gone.

The only other kid out here, and he's either stuck up or weird.

Zoey walked over to the boat to see what the boy had been carving. Dug into the peeling black paint were the letters SOC. Below them, she could see the start of some kind of carved design, but she couldn't make out what it was supposed to be. And what did SOC mean?

Zoey's gaze followed the boy. She tugged at her pigtails. It was time to get rid of these. He probably thought she was about ten.

As Thomas disappeared down the beach, Zoey noticed the raven again. Sunshine pierced the fog and made the back of the bird glisten as it flew. Zoey sighed.

Eliot joined her. "This could be our secret fort."

"Yeah, but it's not very secret anymore. He could come back."

Their mom shouted again from down the beach: "Zooooey! Elllllllliot! Where are you?"

"Coming."

When they got back to the tent, they found their mom searching through boxes, mumbling about whole grain pancake mix. Patrick sat in a corner of the kitchen with a calculator and a notebook.

"Mom, Mom," shouted Eliot as he burst through the door flap. "We just met a boy." Their mom set a box down hard.

"His name was. . . ."

"Listen, you two, in case you haven't noticed, we are *not* in Anchorage anymore. You can't just take off without telling us. And when I call you, I want to hear an answer."

Zoey didn't get it. "But we said we were coming."

"Not until I called twice," her mother shot back. "I want you to have a good time, but this can be a dangerous place. And you left your tent flap open. Don't come crying to me when you have mosquitoes and sand fleas and who knows what else in your beds."

"And lions and tigers and bears," said Patrick without looking up. "Especially bears."

Their mom frowned.

"Go wash up for breakfast in the big bucket outside. Tomorrow, I'll heat some water so you can bathe."

Zoey hated it when her mom scolded her like a little kid. She didn't seem to realize her daughter was growing up.

"Mom, give me a break. First you just about kidnap us from Colorado, then when I finally start to get used to Anchorage and find someone to hang out with, you haul us out to this pit. Is there some kind of plan here? Because, if there is, somebody forgot to tell me. Where's it going to be tomorrow? We're practically to Japan as it is. But I get it. Don't leave the tent flap open. That's what's important to you now."

Zoey stomped out of the tent. Eliot followed her, reached a hand out, and touched her shoulder.

"Quit patting me! I'm not a dog!" She stared at the bucket of water. "Why can't this be a *normal* family?" She plunged her hands into the icy water. "Hasn't anyone out here heard of plumbing?"

Eliot turned to look at the spot where the raven had pecked earlier. He bent down and traced his fingers over little indentations in the wood around the tent spikes.

"That raven has a strong beak. Hey, Zoey! Look," whispered Eliot.

Not six yards away the raven had reappeared. From the back of its throat came a sound like someone drumming on a wood block. The bird looked at them as if waiting for something.

Zoey returned to the awning and slipped inside the big tent. "I know you don't care, but our raven is back. What can we feed it?"

Patrick shook his head. "It's never a good idea to feed wild animals, even a bird. They get dependent on handouts."

"Oh, come on!" Zoey rolled her eyes and wiped her wet hands on her pants.

"Patrick, it's only one raven." Zoey's mom spooned the batter onto the griddle.

"Dad would have let me feed him, and you know it, Mom."

Eliot burst into the tent. "He just flew away, but he'll be back. His name is . . . Blackie! Blackie the Raven!"

"Blackie? How about 'Midnight?'" said Zoey. "It's more mysterious."

"Yeah, Midnight!" said Eliot.

The batter bubbled sweet smells that filled the tent. "If your new bird friend is out there when you're done eating, I'll make him a pancake, okay?" Zoey's mom said.

"Don't pay any attention to me. Bird's perfectly capable of taking care of itself. But I give up." Patrick shook his head, poured himself a cup of coffee, and went back to his notebook.

Zoey and Eliot sat down around the old cable spool that was their dinner table.

Patrick closed the notebook. "I gotta get going. I'm supposed to pick up a guy in Dillingham today who's working on the setnet. Plus, I need to find out when they're going to open the season." He patted the notebook. "Better be soon so I can start paying some bills. If we're going to make this thing work, Fish and Game better give the green light."

"We need some groceries, too. Milk, eggs, maybe some apples," Zoey's mom said without turning away from the stove. "Oh, and you said something about getting a radio for us so we could call you if you weren't here?" She lifted the edge of the pancakes with the spatula. "Do you really have to go all the way to Dillingham? Without us?"

"You'll be fine. Besides, you can feed that raven to your heart's content. Feed him 'til he bursts if you want."

"Get over it, Patrick." She flipped both pancakes and smacked them with the spatula as they landed back on the griddle.

Patrick pulled his backpack from a shelf as Zoey's mom plopped a pancake onto each plate.

"Now, what about this boy, Zoey? Where did you see him?" her mom asked.

"Was it Thomas?" asked Patrick.

"Yeah," Eliot said. "How'd you know his name?"

"That's Carolyn Gamble's son. He can tell you a thing or two about fishing."

"He wasn't very friendly," Zoey said.

"They're our next-door neighbors, from down past the creek where we get water. Give him a chance. You might be surprised."

"What are they doing here? Are they fishermen?"

"That's who I'm hauling fish for. And Thomas's uncle Harold is who I'm picking up today in Dillingham." He stuffed his note-book, wool jacket, and hat into the knapsack and slung it onto his back. He grabbed an old handheld radio off the shelf. "I'll see if I can get parts for this—too expensive to buy a new one. Besides, it won't do much good. The range is terrible. Only works if the plane is just about right overhead."

He grabbed a couple of pancakes off the top of the stack. "For the road. Be back before bedtime." He gave Eliot and Zoey each a pat on the head, and kissed their mom on his way out.

Zoey finished her pancake and sopped up the syrup with the last bite. She wanted to lick her plate but thought better of it.

"Let's get this kitchen cleaned up, and we'll go say 'Hi' to Carolyn. We'll take her some of the wildflower honey I saved from Colorado. They have blueberries, blackberries, huckleberries, cranberries, and salmonberries out here, but I don't think they have many honeybees. You two go to the bathroom first."

Go to the bathroom? Did Mom think they were two years old?

Zoey waited till Eliot came back before she went to the latrine. When it was her turn, she thought how foolish she must look balanced on a log with her jeans on the sand. Still, if she pushed her head up, she could see miles of Bristol Bay right there in front of her. Eagles. Seagulls. Even salmon jumping in the water. Like a magazine picture, but with sound effects.

Back by the tent, Zoey heard the airplane start far down the beach where Patrick had parked it. Her mom's hand appeared through the flap holding two pairs of rain pants.

"Put these on."

"It's not even raining."

"They'll block the wind and keep you warm." Her hand disappeared back inside.

I can pick out my own pants.

Zoey heard Patrick's plane taxi down the beach away from them. When the engine revved, she and Eliot looked up, hoping to see him fly by.

Once in the air, the plane doubled back and flew directly over them, dipping its wings to wave "good-bye."

"Show off," said Zoey.

They watched the plane disappear over the horizon, then Eliot grabbed Zoey's hand.

She was surprised to see how pale he looked. "What's wrong, Eliot?"

"Zo, I don't feel so good."

7

Darth Vader

"Let me hear you breathe."

Eliot took a deep breath and let out a raspy wheeze.

"Oh, Eliot. I thought it was gone. You've been breathing fine all morning." Zoey pulled the flap open on the big tent and stuck her head in. "Mom! You better look at Eliot. He's not breathing very well."

"What do you mean?"

Eliot went to his mother and let her feel his forehead. He breathed out hard so she could hear the funny sound.

"You feel a little warm. How long has this been going on?"

"Since I woke up."

"Why didn't you say something before Patrick left? Without a radio, I have no way to reach him."

Her voice went up several notches. "What am I supposed to do now. I don't know if I even brought that inhaler. You had asthma *once* in your life, and that was months and months ago!"

Lhasa, curled in a corner, stretched her legs and yawned.

"It's okay, Mom." Eliot moved next to the dog. "I'll just lie down here with Lhasa for a little while, and maybe it will go away."

"Go rest on my sleeping bag." Their mom turned a box upside down onto the floor. Hand lotion, bug spray, rubbing alcohol, and a stream of other tubes and jars spilled out. "I can't believe neither of you said anything! Asthma . . . I never thought. . . ." She shook a corkscrew curl of hair out of her eyes. "I can't even find my hair ties. Where would that inhaler be?"

Eliot stood up and crossed the tent to the sleeping area.

Their mom got to her feet but looked sort of deflated. She kneeled and tore into another box. "Maybe our new neighbors can help."

Zoey squirmed. Watching her mom get all frantic was worse than when she was overprotective.

"I'm going to my tent to read."

Eliot pulled the puffy sleeping bag up to his chin. "Which books did you bring, Zo?"

"*Bridge to Terabithia*, two Nancy Drews, and *The Mixed-Up Files of Mrs. Basil E. Frankweiler.* Remember that one? The one I read you where Claudia and her little brother Jamie are just like you and me. Except *they* didn't get dragged away for a stupid fishing trip. They ran away and solved a mystery at the New York Metropolitan Museum of Art."

Zoey's mom looked at her sideways. "Right, just like you and Eliot." She shook her head and held up the jar of honey as though it were a prize. "Well, at least I found this. But where's the inhaler?"

"Could you read it again to me, Zo?"

Even though she wanted to get away, Zoey couldn't resist. She often read Eliot to sleep. It relaxed her too.

"I guess so."

Zoey went to her tent and came back with the book. She lay down next to Eliot, propped her head on a pillow, and began reading. Almost at once her brother was asleep. Zoey read silently for nearly an hour, then closed the book and stretched. In the story,

Claudia had run away. Maybe Zoey could too, even from Bristol Bay. But how?

She needed a plan. As of today, she would start thinking of one.

Zoey noticed Eliot's breathing again. It didn't sound any better. It was rough, like a rattley old engine, or like something was stuck in his throat.

"Any luck with the inhaler?" Zoey asked her mom in a soft voice.

Her mom came and put her hand on Eliot's forehead. "No, I can't find it anywhere. He feels really warm. Must be a fever."

"He sounds terrible, Mom. What can we do?"

"We have to do something, and soon. If it gets worse, his throat could swell up and stop him from breathing. He could die." Zoey's mom paced the tent.

"Zoey, I need you to go down the beach and find that boy's mom, Mrs. Gamble. Tell her your little brother isn't breathing well and might need a doctor. Ask if she knows where we can get some help. Or an inhaler."

Zoey's mom grabbed the jar of honey. "Here, take this with you."

"Are you kidding?"

"We've never even met them. It wouldn't be polite to go empty-handed. Don't argue with me!"

Zoey zipped her jacket and stuffed the jar in a pocket.

"Come on, girl," she called to Lhasa and hurried down the beach, walking stiffly in the rain gear.

"These plastic pants make me feel like a sausage," she muttered to no one.

Lhasa bounded ahead. Soon Zoey arrived at the little creek and waded across, careful to not let the water go over the tops of her rubber boots. As she climbed the bank on the far side, she realized she had never been this far from their camp before. She remembered the roof she had seen from the airplane while they were landing. Is that where she was going? If so, she figured she had about another ten minutes to walk. She looked several times for the raven with the gray feather, but it did not appear.

Zoey smelled the Gambles' camp before she could see it. Smoked salmon. You couldn't miss that. Then, not too far off, she saw a building. Definitely not a tent. As she got closer, a big husky ran toward them. Lhasa barked and the husky growled and bared its teeth. Zoey froze.

8

Colorado Honey

She didn't dare go any closer. She knew about huskies. They could be unpredictable. Lhasa stood her ground, and Zoey held her breath.

"Kenai! Get over here." The voice came from up near the building.

Several gulls near the edge of the grass took flight, crying angrily. Just beyond, past a line of seaweed left by the high tide, Zoey saw the boy from the day before. The husky gave a deep bark, turned, and trotted toward him.

When she got closer, Zoey recognized the building as a Quonset hut. There were lots of them near the military base in Anchorage. It was about the size of a stretched-out, one-car garage. The curved metal roof looked like half of one of those big drain pipes that run under highways. The wall facing her had one window and a door. Smoke trickled from a rickety-looking chimney, and off to the side of the hut more smoke came from a tall, skinny shed. A smokehouse.

The muffled sound of a gas engine, like a lawn mower, came from another shed behind the larger building. A generator. *They must have electricity!*

Thomas had moved near the doorway, still holding Kenai by his collar.

"Don't worry. He's just telling your dog who's boss." Thomas looked hard at the dog, let go, and opened the door. "Kenai. Go lie down."

The husky went inside.

"Where's the little guy? Your brother?"

"That's why I'm here. He's sick."

"Come on in." Thomas started into the cabin.

Zoey looked at her dog. "Stay here, Lhasa. I'll be right back."

Inside, a small woman with dark hair washed dishes in a real sink. Zoey's eyes widened as she looked around the room. It was a mansion compared to their tent. Another window and door let light in at the far end.

Thomas's mother nodded to Zoey. "You flew in yesterday with Patrick?"

"Yeah, that was us. I'm Zoey."

"Carolyn Gamble. Nice to meet you." She gestured to a small kitchen table. "Sit right here, dear. You want some tea? You've met Thomas."

The boy nodded and quickly cleared the last two dishes off the table.

Zoey looked around. Almost a real house. With furniture and even curtains on the windows.

"Thank you, Mrs. Gamble, but I can't stay. My little brother, Eliot, is having trouble breathing. He has asthma and Mom can't find his inhaler. My mom sent me to ask if you know where we can get him to a doctor."

Thomas's mother wiped her hands on a dishtowel and crossed the room to where Zoey stood. "There's sometimes a doctor at the clinic across the Bay in Naknek. Anyway, they'll have medicine there. When is Patrick coming back? I heard his plane leave."

"Not until late tonight or tomorrow morning, but Eliot can't wait that long. He's coughing this raspy cough and Mom says he has a fever. She's worried he'll get worse."

"It would be good to have someone take a look at him. Thomas can take you all in the skiff."

Zoey looked from Thomas to his mother. *Was he really old enough to take them all to this Naknek place by himself?*

Carolyn smiled. As if she'd read Zoey's mind. "Don't you worry about a thing, dear. Thomas is fifteen and he's made that trip a hundred times. He knows how to drive a skiff just fine."

"Okay, Mom." Thomas got up and grabbed a piece of scratch paper and pencil. "Anything else we need from town?"

"Potatoes and. . . ." Carolyn took the paper from him. "You go get ready, I'll make a list."

"How soon do you want to go?" Thomas pulled a small booklet from his pocket and flipped through it.

"How far is it?" Zoey felt like they should leave right now.

"Not far. Only an hour or so if the water's flat, but that's not often," said Carolyn. "Thomas, what's the tide doing?"

Thomas ran his finger down a page in the booklet.

He seemed older to her now. So in control. His eyes weren't just dark. More like the color of the coffee beans her dad used to grind in the morning. Today they looked kinder. He didn't seem stuck up anymore. At least he hadn't called her "city girl" again.

"High tide is twelve forty-seven."

Zoey checked her watch. Eleven o'clock.

"We should go soon," Thomas said. "We have to dodge the sandbars going across, and we need to get into the Naknek River while the tide is still up."

Sandbars? Papa had talked about those in Juneau. He said

they were like little underwater islands made of sand. When the tide was low, people could get their boats stuck on them and have to wait for hours for the water to come back in again. Zoey had never seen one.

Mrs. Gamble rinsed her cup in the sink using water from a big jug that hung on the wall. "How about if Thomas picks you up at your camp in half an hour?"

"Okay." Zoey headed for the door. "Oh, I almost forgot." She reached in her pocket and pulled out the honey. "From my mom. She brought it from Colorado, where we used to live."

Carolyn held the golden syrup up to the light of the window. "Thank you, Zoey. This will be a real treat."

Zoey turned the doorknob and over her shoulder said, "It was nice meeting you, Mrs. Gamble."

Carolyn laughed. "Just 'Carolyn', dear. Long as the weather holds, you'll be fine. Tell your mom to try not to worry."

As the door closed behind Zoey, the wind hit her hard in the face. She and Lhasa hurried down the beach. What if Eliot had gotten worse? What if the weather didn't hold? Could Thomas really get them to a doctor safely?

9

Thomas to the Rescue

When Zoey got back to the tent, Eliot had a thermometer in his mouth.

"I take it you didn't find the inhaler."

"I've turned every box upside down. Nothing."

Zoey told her mother of the plan for Thomas to take them to the clinic.

"Carolyn thinks we need to go right away."

"She's right. I don't want Eliot to spend the whole night like this. If his throat closes up he'll be in big trouble." She read the thermometer. "A hundred and two degrees!"

Just then they heard the skiff in the distance. Thomas was coming already.

"Go get a change of clothes for you and Eliot. Hurry!"

Zoey rushed out to the sound of her mom muttering about Tylenol, vitamin C, and rain gear. A minute later she was back with her duffel. She helped get Eliot dressed. Her mom grabbed an armful of rain pants from the hooks, herded them outside, and closed the tent flap.

"What if Patrick comes back while we're gone?" asked Zoey.

"I'll leave him a note. Help Eliot down to the boat. I'll be right there."

When they got to the shore, Thomas guided the skiff toward the beach. At the last second he tilted up the outboard engine. The boat drifted in to the beach, but the waves washed it sideways. Thomas leaped out wearing rubber boots and dragged the bow farther up on the sand. Then he pulled three bright orange life jackets from the skiff and threw them on the beach.

"My mom said to wear these. They'll keep you warm."

Zoey buckled Eliot's life jacket. She found herself wanting him to caw like a raven, but he was silent as a rag doll. She put her life jacket on, and soon her mom was beside them doing the same.

Thomas steadied the boat while Zoey's mom climbed in. He passed Eliot to her and pointed to a small seat in the very front.

"Face back toward the engine. That'll give you a little protection from the wind and spray."

Lhasa ran along the edge of the water barking and whining. When no one paid attention to her, she dug furiously in the sand and barked some more.

"Take the middle seat," Thomas said to Zoey. "When you get there, grab that oar and help push us off."

She kicked her leg up high to get it over the side of the boat. Holding on and bending low, she made her way toward the back. The words "Johnson 40" were printed on the battered little motor in faded letters. Zoey wondered for a moment if the "40" was its age, then realized it must be the horsepower.

At Thomas's direction, Zoey put one end of the oar into the water and shoved it against the sandy bottom.

Thomas pushed hard until the boat was completely off the beach, then he jumped in and climbed past everyone, putting his hand on Zoey's shoulder for an instant when the boat lurched. Zoey pushed again with the oar as Thomas pulled the cord on the engine. After a couple of tries the rusty machinery whirred and caught. Zoey pulled the oar in and took her seat, just a few feet from Thomas.

He backed the boat into deeper water and turned it around. "Not bad, City Girl."

There it was again.

Lhasa barked and swam toward them.

"Lhasa, go home!" yelled Zoey, but the dog kept coming.

Thomas looked at the dog then back at Zoey. He shook his head, stood, and guided the boat through two-foot choppy waves out into the Bay, gradually turning the throttle up as they moved away from shore. Finally, Lhasa turned and swam back toward the beach.

The skiff seemed to climb up the side of one wave only to be met by another. Zoey's stomach grew queasy. She didn't feel like a city girl. More like a rubber duck in a washing machine. They'd just started and already she couldn't wait to get back to dry land.

Then the engine picked up speed and the skiff leveled off. Pretty soon they were flying along with the wind hard on their faces. Zoey cinched her hood down, held on tight to her seat, and tried to look ahead.

Eliot closed his eyes, and Zoey turned her head back toward Thomas.

He kneeled and pulled out a pair of ski goggles, eased them on over his wool cap, and pulled gray wool gloves out of his pocket. He slid them on and faced into the wind, his green jacket flapping.

They were on their way to Naknek, a strange boy was in charge, and Zoey was scared to death.

"Keep an eye out for sandbars," Thomas shouted at Zoey over the engine noise.

The sky darkened. Zoey tried to be alert, but pelting rain stung her eyes. She shouted to Thomas. "What do I look for?"

Thomas smiled. "Extra ripples. That means shallow water is breaking over rocks or sandbars."

Zoey nodded trying to hide the shivers that were creeping up her arms. She reached under her raincoat hood and rolled her wool hat down almost to her eyes, all the time scanning the line where the gray soggy air met the water for anything that might snag the little skiff.

Thomas had to slow the engine so the boat wouldn't bounce so hard, but Zoey still gripped the underside of the bench seat with one hand. Periodically, she caught sight of a fishing boat through the rain, but the boats didn't pay any attention to them. She felt tiny and out of place surrounded by the angry, churning water.

"Where's Naknek?" Zoey shouted over the noise of the engine.

"Straight across this part of the Bay from where our camps are. When we get closer, you'll see the mouth of the Naknek River."

All Zoey could see ahead of them was water and the distant mountains. If there was a town in that direction, she had no idea how to find it. What if a big wave capsized them? She knew it happened a lot in Alaskan waters. The Coast Guard visited her school last year, and the officer said more people drown in Alaska than in any other state, mostly because the water is so cold. After just a few minutes in it, your muscles cramp up and you're gone! Stay with the boat, they said. Don't try to swim for shore. Stay with the boat. They said that over and over.

But how could she hold on to the boat and Eliot at the same time? And who would ever find them?

A plume of spray appeared in the distance through the rain, as if someone were pointing a garden hose at the sky. Thomas saw it too and pointed.

"Whale," he mouthed. As they got closer, big black fins cut through the choppy water.

"They're not belugas!" she yelled. She had heard about the many belugas in Bristol Bay and couldn't wait to see them.

"Orcas," shouted Thomas. "Sometimes they drive the belugas into the mouth of the river and try to trap them there against the shore. That's why they're called 'killer whales.' Good hunters."

Zoey had seen whales while visiting her grandparents in Juneau. But those were humpbacks. They rolled through the water sucking big mouthfuls of tiny shrimp. These killer whales swam like torpedoes.

Six or seven huge dorsal fins barreled straight for the little skiff. They looked like they could cut right through it without even noticing. Zoey held her breath.

In a flash of spray, the dorsal fins veered just behind the skiff, slicing through the wake of the outboard and vanishing into the gray mist. Zoey shuddered at the cold emptiness in their wake. Suddenly, she remembered her lookout assignment and jerked her head back around. No extra ripples. Everything looked okay.

Zoey finally found a rhythm in the waves, and although she still held on, she relaxed her grip on the seat. She looked at Thomas. He concentrated intensely on the water ahead. Still, he seemed comfortable, as if . . . what? As if he belonged here. In this tiny metal shell on the surface of a huge nothingness, at the edge of a wet, wet nowhere. He actually looked happy.

Thomas was at least as tall as her dad, and there was something no-nonsense about him. None of the fancy outdoor gear you saw on the streets of Anchorage. Just jeans and an old army jacket stained with who-knows-what and half soaked with rain and spray.

Her dad had done all the rowing when they fished in Colorado. What would he think of her now? She tried hard to remember what her dad looked like but realized the only images she could recall were from photos. One with her mom in front of the old house. Another of him holding a big trout. His eyes, she was sure, were sky blue, but the face that held them had become a blur.

She had to get back to Colorado.

"He's getting worse," Zoey's mom shouted. Zoey looked back at her brother. His eyes were barely open and his head bobbed heavily.

Just then, the boat slowed and swerved sharply to the right. Eliot's eyes opened. That same sky blue.

"What's happening?" Eliot could hardly talk.

Zoey didn't know. A wave slapped the bow and spray shot back at her. When she looked over the edge of the boat she could see the bottom.

Thomas yanked the engine up. The prop whirred in the air. Metal scraped against gravel as they ground to a halt.

Zoey felt sick inside. This was her fault. She was supposed to keep watch, but all she did was daydream.

Thomas looked right into her eyes. *How could she feel a look?* And in the pit of her stomach.

"Don't worry," he said. "You couldn't have seen that coming. It happens a lot." He turned and killed the motor. They were stuck. Immediately, waves sloshed into the boat.

"I'm really sorry. I don't know what happened."

"We'll be okay." Thomas grabbed an oar and pushed off the bottom. They inched along.

"Mom," Eliot whimpered. "I feel like I'm going to throw up."

He gagged and heaved the breakfast pancakes all over himself and his mom.

He tried to cry, but what came out were strangled whines and croaky gurgles.

"Hush, Eliot. You have to stay calm." Their mom tried to mop up the mess with her handkerchief.

Meanwhile, the boat twisted back and forth in the rough water. A big wave pushed them several feet sideways and Zoey realized they were floating free again.

Quickly, Thomas put the engine back down into the water and worked to get it started.

"Don't let us float back onto the bar. We don't have an extra shear pin."

"A what?" said Zoey.

"If the prop hits a rock or something else hard while the engine is running, this little metal pin breaks off, and you have to put on another one. Otherwise the prop won't turn. But we don't have an extra one, so if it breaks, we're stuck."

"So then what?"

"Then we row."

Zoey realized he was completely serious, but at the same time, he didn't seem concerned. As if he would just do whatever it was he needed to do to get them all to Naknek.

Finally, the engine caught. Thomas put it in gear, and the boat slipped quickly into deeper water.

"Don't worry, it's pretty clear from here, until we get to the river."

It seemed to Zoey that the number of ways you could get into trouble in Bristol Bay was too big to even count, let alone prepare for. People who live here all their lives still get surprised. Zoey didn't like surprises.

A few minutes later, they were running smoothly. The rain dried up, the clouds cracked, and a slit of sunshine spiked the water ahead of them. Soon, a bright path glinted, all the way to the approaching shore.

Thomas sat down but kept his eyes straight ahead.

"See that cliff where the sun's hitting, way up there?" he said. "That's where the Naknek River comes out. It'll get a little bouncy from the current, but things'll calm down when we get around the point."

Zoey nodded and took a deep breath. Eliot and her mom were sort of cleaned up and Eliot's head rested against her side. He looked like he was asleep.

After what seemed like hours of waves and splashing, the water finally calmed. They were almost there. At last, Zoey let go of her seat bottom.

10

Naknek

"We're heading into the river current. We might get pushed around a little," Thomas announced.

Zoey could see where the Naknek River poured into the Bay in a broad, brown streak. Huge muddy swirls tentacled out on each shore. Clumps of fishing boats clung to anchor lines along the riverbanks. The skiff rocked in the surging flows.

After a minute or two, Thomas maneuvered them across the river flow and they were moving smoothly close to shore. Bluffs on both sides of the river cut the wind. At their base, looking like they drifted in on a high tide, stood a scattering of rough shacks, some with hand-painted names: "The Mansion," "Pete's Retreat," "The Willsons." Zoey wondered if people actually lived in them.

"We're headed up there." Zoey followed Thomas's finger to a high spot on the beach where a saggy pier stuck out from the bank.

Zoey pointed and called to Eliot, but he didn't even open his eyes.

They approached the shore. A few children played by the nearest shack, while two adults nearby handled a long fishing net. All up and down the beach people in rubber pants and jackets chatted in groups, bent over boats, or worked on fishing nets. Eliot sat up and looked around half-heartedly, then closed his eyes and leaned back into his mother.

Thomas pulled the engine up like before and the skiff drifted the last few feet to the beach. This time there were no big waves to push them around. Thomas leaped out, and Zoey's mom lowered Eliot to him. He took the boy's weight easily in his arms. With one hand, Thomas held the bow steady, with the other, he reached out first to Zoey's mom, who climbed out, then to Zoey. She put her hand on his arm near the elbow and was surprised at how solid it felt. She jumped to the ground and immediately sank to her ankles in mud.

Then they all squished up the beach toward the cabins. It wasn't until the mud under her boots gave way to sandy gravel that Zoey felt she was really back on land. Thomas set Eliot down while he tied the boat's rope around a big rock.

Zoey looked at Eliot leaning against their mom. "How do you feel?"

Eliot did that barking cough again and shook his head. Their mom picked him up this time. The mud from his boots made thick black lines on her pants.

As they approached the cabin, the children Zoey had seen earlier looked up. They were about Eliot's age. Behind them a woman wearing a blue jacket and a scarf tied around her black hair stepped forward. She was joined by a man in rubber overalls, boots, and a wool hat.

"Is that you, Thomas?" said the woman.

"Hi, Clara. Lee Roy."

Zoey's mom interrupted them. "Do you know where we can find a doctor? Eliot here is having trouble breathing. He needs medicine."

As if on cue, Eliot coughed.

"Lee Roy," the woman said, "go get the rig. I'll stay here and work on the net while you take them to the clinic."

Lee Roy turned and walked quickly up the beach.

"These guys are staying at Halfmoon with the pilot who hauls our fish," said Thomas.

"Sorry, I'm Alice Morley. This is my daughter, Zoey, and son, Eliot."

"Welcome to our fish camp," Clara said pointing up the beach.

The building she waved at wasn't much bigger than a gardening shed. Various pieces of rain gear hung on hooks by the door, and a rusty stovepipe poked through the roof. The only window Zoey could see was covered with plastic sheeting.

Could they really be living in that?

Zoey went over to Eliot and put her arm around his shoulder. "How are you feeling?"

Eliot shrugged her hand away with a big wheeze.

She took a second look at him.

"Mom, what's wrong with his face?"

Zoey's mom pushed Eliot's bangs aside. "Oh, my God."

Eliot's once smooth white cheeks were covered with weird red splotches. He held up his hands and turned them so the backs were facing his mom. More of the same.

"They itch, and I'm really hot," Eliot croaked.

A pickup truck that might have been blue many years ago bounced down the beach toward them on oversized tires. A big winch squatted on the front bumper, and a rusty spotlight jiggled on a pole above the roof like the eye of a Cyclops. The cargo bed was built from rough planks. Zoey had never seen such a tough-looking truck.

Lee Roy hoisted Eliot into the passenger's seat and his mom climbed in after him. Thomas vaulted neatly into the cargo bed and once again held his arm out to Zoey. She didn't look up, but grabbed his hand and braced her foot on the bumper. Two seconds later, she was standing next to him still feeling the warmth and roughness of his fingers. They stepped over a pile of old rope and sat with their backs against the cab. Zoey looked at Thomas's hands, brown and streaked with mud from the beach. A moment later Lee Roy revved the engine, and they lurched forward.

The truck trundled along the beach past shacks lined up like tired old lookouts staring out to sea through dark window-eyes. *Were they watching for fish?* Patrick had said the salmon were already pressing up the Naknek River. Various people along the way waved as the truck lumbered along.

At the wheel, Lee Roy picked his way through ruts and boulders, careful to avoid the occasional metal post that poked out of the sand.

"Deadman," Thomas said pointing to a bright blue post. "That's where a fisherman died." Zoey's face froze in horror and Thomas's smile slipped into a grin. "No. We attach our net lines to those metal posts. Not sure why they call them deadmen, but they go way down in the sand. You'll see."

What a strange place!

Zoey held tight to the side of the truck. She had never been allowed to ride in the back of a pickup truck. Here it seemed perfectly normal. Ahead was the pier she had seen from the skiff. It blocked their path and extended a long way out over the water. They followed a track up the hill behind it. A sharp curve and a huge pothole later, and they were on a real road.

"Alaska Peninsula Highway," said Thomas.

Zoey nodded then turned to peek through the truck's back window at Eliot. She could only see him from the side, but he didn't look any better. The wrinkles around her mom's eyes told Zoey his condition was still serious.

She turned back in time to see "Fisherman's Bar" painted on a wall above a big window. Several men huddled near the doorway. Nearby another hand-painted sign on a long blue building said, "Hilton."

Thomas leaned over to Zoey. "That's where the cannery workers sleep. There are bunkhouses like that all over town."

Zoey thought of the fancy Hilton Hotel in Anchorage and got the joke. But she didn't feel like laughing.

"King Salmon is up that way."

"Is that a fish or a person?" asked Zoey.

"It's a town," said Thomas with another grin.

Zoey wondered what a place called "King Salmon" might look like.

"It's a little bigger than Naknek. The jet lands there."

Zoey sat up straight. "You mean a jet that can take you out of here, like down south?"

"I guess so, but mostly people just take it to Anchorage."

Zoey's mind raced. She would have to find out how much it would cost to fly from King Salmon to Denver.

"I suppose if Eliot was sick enough they might fly him to Dillingham or Anchorage," said Thomas, interrupting her thoughts.

Zoey felt terrible. Her little brother was really sick and all she could think of was leaving. She wondered how much it would cost if Eliot had to be flown out. In fact, she wondered how her mom planned to pay for the doctor visit. Weren't they stuck in Halfmoon Bay because they were broke?

The truck picked up speed and the chilly wind made Zoey wrap herself tighter in her jacket. A few similar looking trucks rolled by them going the opposite direction toward the beach. She could smell Thomas next to her. Gasoline, fish, and some kind of soap. She didn't look at him, but instead stared out over the tailgate.

Clouds of dust swirled behind the truck. Through it Zoey saw boxy houses surrounded by scrubby bushes and open lots dotted with all sorts of mechanical gear. Naknek only had a couple of streets. Still, it felt a lot more like civilization than Halfmoon Bay.

Every yard they passed was piled with stuff. Most held at least one four-wheeler and a couple of boats. Snowmachines and gear she didn't recognize were draped in bright-blue plastic tarps. Fishing nets and floats of all sizes. Here and there an old bicycle. Then right alongside of their truck, on the dirt that paralleled the highway, a kid about Thomas's age sped past them on one of those four-wheelers. He had on a wool watch cap and a raincoat that flapped in the wind. He waved at Lee Roy.

What was she doing here? How had her life gotten so, so . . . lost. She felt stuck in a bad dream. But she was awake.

She realized she felt better sitting next to Thomas. This boy they didn't even know was taking care of them. Then she remembered, "city girl." He probably just thought of her as a big pain. But he had smiled a few times.

"That's the restaurant," said Thomas pointing to a homey-looking, barn-like structure. *The* restaurant? The only one? Zoey was hungry. Everything had happened so fast, they hadn't eaten in hours. If her mom had brought food with her, she had forgotten to give it to anyone, so Zoey would have to wait until they got to the clinic.

At a sign that said "School Road," Lee Roy made a sharp left. The school was big and new-looking. Across the road was a building with "Camai Community Health Center" hand-painted in black letters over the front door. As they pulled into the parking lot Thomas pointed farther up the road.

"I live down that way." *So Thomas didn't live at Halfmoon Bay. This was his hometown.*

Inside the clinic, the receptionist, a thin woman in white pants and a Seattle Seahawks sweatshirt, greeted them.

Zoey's mom stepped forward. "My son is really sick. He needs to see a doctor."

"I'm afraid the doctor only comes through here once a month, dear. We're too small to have our own. But our health aide is here and she's seen just about everything, including some things you don't even want to know about. If she has any questions, she'll call one of the docs in Dillingham." With that, she led Zoey's mom and Eliot down a hallway.

"I'll be back soon," her mom called over her shoulder. "Don't worry." And then they were gone.

11

Knives and Fur Hats for Sale

Zoey sat in the waiting room absently flipping the pages of a magazine with a moose on the cover.

"Vroom, vroom." A little girl pushed a plastic truck past a table that held crayons and paper. A woman nearby balanced a sleeping baby sprawled on her lap. Lee Roy and Thomas stared out the window to the parking lot and talked in low voices. Soon they came over to Zoey.

"How you doin'?" asked Lee Roy.

"I'm okay."

"High tide tomorrow is around noon," Lee Roy went on, "so that's the soonest you could float the skiff and get back to camp. You think your brother will be better by then?"

"I don't know. If he's not, we'll probably have to take him to Anchorage."

"I'm gonna leave you two here a while and run up to my sister Rose's house. You could maybe stay there tonight."

Thomas added, "Everybody around here knows Rose and her husband the Captain. I would take you to our place, but a bunch of cannery workers are staying there for the season. Mom's idea to save some money."

Lee Roy turned to the door. "Be back shortly. Good luck with the little guy."

Zoey thanked Lee Roy and watched him leave.

"So, how do you like Naknek?" Thomas asked.

Zoey didn't know how to answer. Naknek was a little like the old mining towns in Colorado, with their bleached-out wood buildings, falling-down wire fences, and old pickup trucks. But those places were dry and dead-feeling. Naknek felt alive. The salmon were coming. The fishermen were getting ready.

"I'm not sure yet. It's a lot different from Anchorage." She put her magazine down. "How long have you lived here?"

"Grew up here."

"Do you have brothers and sisters?"

"No. Just me. And my mom." He turned toward the window. Zoey waited, but Thomas was quiet.

"Do you want to draw while we wait?" She grabbed a few sheets of paper and a handful of crayons, and sat on the floor.

"I think I'll just watch."

Zoey skillfully worked a crayon to re-create what she had seen earlier that day.

After watching a few minutes, Thomas said, "That looks just like the fish camps down by the river. How'd you learn to do that?"

"I don't know. No one taught me. I just like doing it."

The little girl with the truck stopped playing and moved closer.

"Can I color too?"

"Sure. You can help me draw Naknek. We're going to make the whole town." She grinned at Thomas and gave the little girl the sheet she had been working on and a couple of crayons.

"Can you fill in the building there?"

The girl studied the drawing for a moment, then bent down, her nose almost to the paper.

Zoey moved away and Thomas followed.

"What about your dad? What does he do?"

Thomas stared at the floor and didn't answer. Behind him, Zoey saw her mom coming down the hall. Where was Eliot?

"Well, it's a good thing we came," said her mom. "Thank you so much, Thomas, for bringing us. Eliot probably has a virus. The health aide thinks he should be better in a couple of days. He's breathing better. That rash though—they don't know what that is. They're waiting for a call back from the doctor in Dillingham. Come on, you can see him now."

They followed Zoey's mom back to another room.

Eliot lay on a small bed. A boxy machine hummed on the tray next to him. It was connected to Eliot by a tube that wound up to his mouth. White smoke snaked inside the tube whenever he inhaled.

Zoey felt dizzy. Was Eliot on some kind of life support? She forced herself to act normal and was about to ask if he needed to go to a hospital when the receptionist entered the room.

She smiled at Eliot. "You've just about got it all." She took the tube from his mouth and turned off the machine.

Eliot looked tired, and his face was still puffy and red. He managed a smile.

"Hi, Zo." He pointed to the machine. "I've been neverlized." He took a deep breath. "No more Darth Vader!"

"What was that white smoky stuff?" Zoey felt a little better.

The woman put the machine in a cupboard. "It's a mist of the same medicine in his inhaler. It's called a nebulizer."

The phone rang and the Seahawks lady answered. She described Eliot's condition, then turned to them.

"What did Eliot have for dinner last night?"

"Spaghetti. We have it all the time."

"Did you give him any medication before you came here?"

"I did give him a couple of Tylenol." She paused in thought. "Oh, and a couple of vitamin C."

After relaying that information the receptionist talked some more, then hung up.

"The rash might be an allergic reaction to a medication or food, but the doc thinks it's part of the virus. Should be better in a couple of days. If not, bring him back in."

Zoey felt like jumping up and down. Her little brother wasn't going to die.

"Zo! See what I got." Eliot opened his hand and revealed a little red Chevy tow truck. "A matches truck!"

"Matchbox truck," Zoey corrected. "Guess what? Thomas says we can't leave until tomorrow. Something about the tide."

But Zoey's mom didn't seem to be listening. She looked tired. "Sure. That sounds good. I don't think Eliot's ready for another boat ride yet."

"But, Mom, have you thought about where we're going to stay tonight?" It surprised Zoey to hear the edge in her own voice.

"No, Zoey," her mom shook her head. "I haven't gotten that far."

"Lee Roy says maybe we can stay with his sister. He went to ask her." Zoey threw the information out like a punch.

Zoey's eyes met her mom's, and Zoey turned away. Why was she always so mad at her? It's true, her mom was an airhead sometimes, but today had been a hard day for everyone.

"Fine. I don't want to argue about it," her mom said. "Let's let Eliot rest. Come on, back to the front room." She gave Eliot a kiss and walked out, leaving Zoey to follow her down the hall.

In the waiting room, the little girl was gone, and the drawing lay on the floor. Zoey's mom was chatting with the receptionist, and Thomas sat on the floor, back propped against the wall and hat low over his eyes. He was sound asleep. Zoey picked up the drawing and took it back to Eliot.

"Since you were out of it most of the way here, this is what Naknek looks like."

Eliot smiled, but he was too tired to keep his eyes open. Zoey rolled the picture up, tucked it in his jacket, and tiptoed out.

As she sat waiting for Lee Roy to return, Zoey wondered what the mystery was about Thomas's father. Maybe his parents were divorced too. His dad must have moved away somewhere. Soon she saw Lee Roy's pickup roll into the parking lot. Zoey's mom must have seen it too, because shortly after, she walked Eliot into the waiting room. Soon Lee Roy was driving them all to the home of someone named Rose.

They had gone less than a mile when Zoey noticed a small sign on the side of the road that said "Knives and Fur Hats for Sale." Lee Roy turned right onto a small dirt road that led to a house with a huge TV dish on a pole in the yard.

The pickup stopped a few yards short of a rickety-looking garage. The front door opened and a large, gray-haired woman wearing a bright yellow apron greeted them. Turquoise glasses hung from a beaded necklace.

"Oh my, the sick child. Come in, sweetheart, come in."

She hugged Thomas. "You've grown a foot since school let out. Or maybe it's just your hair." She pulled his bangs down below his eyes. "I've got some good scissors. Be happy to help."

Thomas smiled broadly. The biggest smile Zoey'd seen on him yet. "Hi, Rose."

Rose led them into what must have been the living room. In the middle of the room was a table made from an old door and two sawhorses. On it sat an ancient-looking sewing machine. Animal skins covered the walls. Rose must have noticed Zoey's wide-eyed expression because she pulled one down and passed it to them.

"These are for my hats. This one's a muskrat. Funny little rodent but real nice fur. Go ahead, it won't bite. Not anymore." Her laugh made Zoey think of tropical birds she'd seen on the nature shows.

Zoey's fingers tingled as they brushed the pelt. "It's very soft." She put it to her cheek. Eliot mashed his face into the fur until their mom gently pulled him back. "Time we got you to bed."

She turned to Rose. "If that's okay. He's pretty wiped out."

"You should eat first," Rose said in a voice that said the matter was already decided. "Then the little one can rest in the spare room. Later, you and Zoey can share the foldout couch. I'm sure Thomas is okay with a sleeping bag on the floor." She peered at him over her glasses.

"No problem," said Thomas.

Half an hour later, they were sitting around the kitchen table slurping chicken noodle soup and munching peanut butter sandwiches. Zoey scarfed down a sandwich and started on another. Eliot didn't show much enthusiasm. When he had managed most of a bowl of soup, Zoey's mom took him to the bedroom.

"Where's Captain?" Thomas asked as he picked at the last crumbs from his plate.

Rose turned to Zoey's mom. "That's my husband. He used to be a guide up in Lake Iliamna, then he came out here to do driftnetting. He liked giving orders so much that everyone calls him 'Captain'." More birdcall laughter. "Except me!"

"Driftnetting?" Zoey asked.

Rose smiled. "The nets attached to the shore, like the ones Thomas's family has, those are setnets." Zoey nodded. "The fishing boats around here are called driftnetters. They have bigger nets and they catch more fish. Sometimes the setnetters and the driftnetters have, you know, disagreements, over whose fish are whose." She looked at Thomas and laughed again.

Thomas rose and took his plate to the sink. "Driftnetters think they own the Bay, but they have to let us catch our fish. That's the law." He didn't sound angry, but his eyes flashed. "Is Captain in the workshop?"

"Been holed up all afternoon. I don't think he even knows you're in town." She got up and put two sandwiches on a plastic plate. "Here, take him this. If he wants anything else, he'll have to come in." To Zoey she said, "He got so good at making fancy knives and other stuff that he sold his boat to open up his little shop. So now I got my man around the house all winter and summer, too. A mixed blessing, I'd say." She winked and the birds cackled in her throat.

Zoey followed Thomas out the back door. They walked past a patch of rhubarb plants and a tangled mass of raspberry bushes to a small shed. Thomas knocked, and a deep voice from inside growled, "If you're not a king salmon, I hope you at least brought something better than peanut butter!"

Zoey looked at Thomas as if to ask, "Are you sure we want to go in there?"

12

Captain

Thomas pushed the door open.

"It's suppertime, Captain. We brought sandwiches."

Zoey followed Thomas into a tiny workshop. Shards of light fought through a gritty window at the back. A small black-and-white TV balanced on a wooden crate in one corner. Dozens of small tools, most of which Zoey didn't recognize, hung on the walls.

Captain sat at a table covered with more tools and lit by a gooseneck lamp. Two plastic lawn chairs were the only other furniture. He looked up and smiled, revealing several missing teeth. As he maneuvered his heavy body from behind the table, his plaid wool shirt hung open. Underneath was a faded T-shirt with a frayed collar.

"Thomas, what brought you into town?"

Captain reached out a big arm and put a hand on Thomas's shoulder. Teeth weren't the only thing he was missing. The last two fingers of his right hand were just stubs.

"Every time I see you, you look more and more like your dad." He studied Thomas's face for a moment, then turned. "Who's this?"

"That's Zoey. Her mom's boyfriend is hauling fish for us this summer over on Halfmoon."

"Well, hello there, Zoey. Where you from?"

"We live in Anchorage now, but I'm really from Colorado."

"Traffic is terrible in Anchorage, and I hear Colorado's dry as a desert." His laugh ended in a deep cough. "How do you like the Bay?"

"Fine, I guess," said Zoey. "We just got here." Thomas and Captain stayed silent. They wanted to know what she really thought.

"It's so flat! That's the biggest difference. And the light is different here. It seems like it comes from everywhere at once instead of just from the sun."

"Good," said Captain. "That's a good start."

Thomas turned to Captain's worktable. "What are you making?"

"I got knife orders, but I'm getting tired of those."

Captain pulled three big hunting knives from a drawer and held them out. Carvings on two of the handles showed dog teams. The third was decorated with beluga whales. *What tiny details!*

"I started these little masks." He sat down and placed a white disk against a rough wooden board clamped to the tabletop. "Captain carves ivory," Thomas said.

Captain was silent as he pressed a tiny chisel into a delicate face framed by a carved hood. The scratch of the metal tool was faint against his heavy breathing. Thomas and Zoey moved closer. Thinly etched lines became wispy fibers that joined together into a fur ruff around the edges of the hood. The moon face had wide-apart eyes that seemed to grow from the surface like petals on a flower. Below them, sharp cheekbones, a small nose, and partially formed mouth.

How does he carve such delicate lines with only three fingers?

Thomas turned his head toward Zoey. His face, only inches from hers, radiated warmth and Zoey smelled the faint odor of gasoline from the boat. She felt herself flush a little, tossed her bangs, and stepped back.

"What is ivory, anyway?" she asked. "Where does it come from?"

Without looking up, Captain continued. "It grows out of the mud. Just like the blueberries."

"The mud?"

"Come on, Captain," Thomas said with a hint of laughter in his voice, "tell her."

Another breath. "This stuff is fossilized ivory. Mostly from woolly mammoth tusks."

Zoey stared at him in disbelief.

Thomas laughed. "Those tusks are all around here."

"Here? In Naknek?" Zoey asked.

Captain chuckled. "They keep showing up. This one came from down around Graveyard Point where the bank wore away. It stuck up out of the sand. Sometimes people find 'em when they're fishing or berry picking. Took about three people to get this one in a skiff."

"Wow! A real prehistoric tusk."

"Only Alaska Native people are allowed to carve fresh ivory from the walrus. But anyone can carve the fossilized stuff." He reached into a drawer and handed Zoey a couple of small knives with short blades. One blade was straight. The other hooked at an angle.

"I got a piece of alder you can try if you like. Alder's a good thing to start on, right Thomas?"

Thomas nodded. "Softer than ivory, and if you make a mistake, there's always more."

Zoey looked up at Captain. "Really? I can try it?"

He lumbered over to the edge of the table, reached in a cardboard box, and slid a weathered piece of driftwood toward her. It was a little shorter but much thicker than Zoey's arm and had a natural bend to it. A root maybe.

Zoey sat nervously. Thomas moved next to her. He took the piece of wood in his hands. "You have to hold it for a while and look at it, right Captain? Pretty soon you see something, something living inside. It wants you to cut away the extra parts and let it out. No two people see the same thing. If you're quiet, it talks to you."

Captain smiled. "I taught him back when he could hardly hold a knife. Made him count his fingers after every lesson. His mom was afraid he'd leave one lying around. . . ." He held up his hand briefly. "This isn't from carving—it's fishing that'll get you."

Thomas crossed the cabin floor to the windowsill and brought back a wooden replica of a small open-deck sailboat.

"I made this last year for Captain's birthday. He learned to fish on a double-ender just like this. Everybody used them. See, it comes to a point at the bow and the stern."

Zoey took the model boat and turned it gently in her hands. She ran her finger over the smooth sail, which was not made of cloth, but was carved from a separate piece of lighter-colored wood. The sides were made of three slats of wood that gently curved to where they came together at either end in a V. The tiny craft looked like it could sail away. *Thomas was good!*

Captain leaned back in the shaky chair and crossed his arms over his chest. "When I was your age, Zoey, it was against the law to use motorboats. It's tricky to sail and fish at the same time. Lots of fish though. Sometimes they'd jump right into the boat."

Zoey could see Captain sailing his fishing boat out in the Bay just as if it were a movie.

"Captain knows a lot," Thomas said.

"I just tell you what you like to hear." The old man smiled.

"Thomas likes the stories about his dad. He was a good fisherman. A highliner."

Was?

Zoey balanced the piece of driftwood in her fingers, turning it over and over. She saw that a branch growing at one spot had left a bump that came almost to a point. Thomas put his hand over hers to guide the knife. "Here, try to keep your hands soft. Feel the wood."

His hand was warm. Smooth in a way, and strong. Zoey made her own fingers relax. Then, as though she knew just what to do, she began to take thin shavings from the wood with the straight knife. Thomas withdrew his hand, and she heard a laugh from Captain.

"I guess we got ourselves a carver, Thomas. I'll show her how to hold the knives, but you better help her when the fishing's slow out there. Here." He handed Thomas his empty plate. "Mind taking this back to Rose?"

Thomas took the plate and headed back to the house, but Zoey kept her attention on the carving. Captain watched her.

"You're wound up like a driftnet on a drum. What's up?"

Zoey was deep in concentration. Without thinking about it she said, "Oh, my brother was real sick. That's why we came to Naknek, to the clinic."

"But he's better now?" Captain heaved himself out of his chair to get a closer look.

"Yeah, thanks to Thomas."

"Good. So. What else?"

Zoey stopped carving and looked at the floor. Should she tell this total stranger what was really bothering her? Something about him made Zoey feel like she had known him for a long time. He made her feel like she could do almost anything—even carve with a knife that was so sharp it could lop off a finger. She stopped thinking and just started to talk.

"My mom and dad got divorced last year, and my mom's new boyfriend made us come out here. I was just getting used to Anchorage. But I guess we need the money. I need money too, so I can go back to Colorado to see my dad. But I haven't heard from him, so I don't know where to send my letters. Still, I'm going to find him."

Captain let her words settle before he answered. "Money, yes. Money can help solve problems. But there's usually more to it than that. Kind of like the carving. Sometimes it takes a long time to see what's right in front of you."

Zoey showed Captain what she had done so far to the alder branch. "What does this look like?"

Captain smiled. "It doesn't matter what it looks like to me. What do you see in there?"

Zoey looked back down. Yesterday she would have said it was just a piece of firewood. Today, she was sure it could be something more, but she wasn't sure what. She knew she wanted to learn more about carving. Something in the wood wanted to get out, just like she wanted to get out of Bristol Bay. But there was more to it than that.

13

A Gift

The next morning, Zoey helped Rose make French toast while Eliot watched cartoons. Sweet bacon smells teased Zoey's nose while she laid forks and spoons on a green and white vinyl tablecloth. The pattern matched the café curtains hung around a picture window that framed a big mountain ash tree in the yard. The branches of the old ash swayed in the wind. Beyond were the brown bluffs on the far shore of the Naknek River.

Eliot took a thermometer from his mouth and handed it to his mom. He coughed weakly.

"Ninety-nine." She rubbed his forehead. "That's a lot better, and those blotches are nearly gone."

"Mom, shhhhh!" said Eliot, without taking his eyes off the TV screen.

Zoey's mom smiled at her. "Eliot is Eliot again."

After breakfast Zoey helped Rose dry dishes while the old woman talked.

"Captain's my fifth husband. They say I love 'em to death. First one was cancer, second was a snowmachine accident and the third a hunting accident. Then my last husband was in a plane crash coming in from Kodiak. A foggy day, real cold. He called me twenty minutes out. Last I heard from him. The plane ran right into the ground. Couldn't tell the difference between the fog and the snow. It happens around here."

"That's terrible," said Zoey's mom. "Do you have kids?"

"There they are." She swept her arm stiffly around the room.

Zoey turned her head as she stacked a dry bowl with the others. She had noticed all the photos but hadn't looked at them carefully. Now, she saw kids of all ages, many holding up fish for the camera.

Rose continued. "Three girls. All grown and married. Seven grandkids, and that's just so far. That's the tribe there." Zoey followed her finger to a big, professional-looking photo.

"Most of them help with the setnets. But not near Halfmoon. Our fish camps are along this side of the Bay. Not far from the river. You maybe saw them on your way in."

Zoey wondered what it must be like for Rose to lose so many husbands. All those people in the photos. They had all lost a dad, a stepdad, or a grandfather. Some more than once. All those families didn't really exist anymore, at least not the way they were in the pictures. But from what Rose said the ones that were left stuck together. At least they still fished together every year.

There was a knock at the door. Lee Roy and Thomas were back from a trip to the store.

"You guys ready to go?" Thomas put a bag of groceries on the table for Rose. "We should head out if we want to catch the tide. Otherwise we'll be here another night, and Mom'll kill me."

Thomas stuffed the celery, onions, carrots, and potatoes Carolyn had asked for into his backpack.

Lee Roy sat to watch the cartoon with Eliot, but Thomas pointed to his watch, and Lee Roy pulled himself away. He draped an arm around Rose. "Well, Sis, I better get these folks back to their boat."

“Thomas, say ‘Hi’ to your mom for me.” Rose crossed the kitchen and took a loaf of puffy, homemade bread from the breadbox, wrapped it in a dry cloth, and handed it to Thomas. “Give her this, and don’t you dare eat it on the way.”

Zoey smiled.

When Rose hugged her, Zoey surprised herself by squeezing back. She liked the sturdy feeling of Rose’s arms around her. She seemed like someone you could count on.

Zoey was planning to stop by Captain’s workshop to say good-bye, but before she got to the door Captain walked in and handed her a cloth bag.

“Something to keep you busy out there.”

“For me?” She untied the leather strings. In the bag were two small carving knives. Tiny etched salmon swam up the wooden handles. Zoey knew they were salmon by the humps on their backs. The humps meant they were ready to lay their eggs. It seemed like every gift shop in Anchorage had pictures of spawning salmon in the window. Next to the knives lay the piece of wood she had worked on the day before.

“Just to get you started.” Captain gave Zoey a wink. “Thomas, you keep an eye on her. Keep track of those fingers.”

“Wow, thanks, Captain,” Zoey said. “What should I make?”

Captain was already headed back to his shop.

“I know. Whatever’s in there trying to get out!” Zoey called after him.

Captain waved without turning around.

Lee Roy started the truck. Eliot sat in front with their mom, so Thomas and Zoey once again jumped in the open cargo bed. Zoey pulled her hat down over her ears. Forty-five degrees, the TV weather had said. It would be even colder out on the water. As Lee

Roy turned the truck around, Rose waved, then disappeared as they turned the corner onto the main road.

On the way back across the Bay, with the engine humming and Thomas steering, Zoey felt more at home in the skiff. The return trip seemed much faster than when they had come, and before long, she could make out their campsite on the far shore. As they neared it, Thomas explained that even though commercial fishing season wouldn't open until at least Saturday, he had to hurry home and help his mom. Nearly every family in the Bristol Bay region was already busy gathering fish to smoke and freeze for their own use. Those fish, plus the moose and caribou they hunted in the fall, would be their main food during the winter. "Subsistence," Thomas called it.

Zoey remembered her dad doing a kind of subsistence too. Every fall, he would bring home trout and deer, sometimes an elk. He would cut up the meat and wrap it in plastic, then in brown paper. He would have loved to catch salmon in Alaska, Zoey thought, and she felt a hollow ache in her stomach.

Thomas slowed the skiff as they approached the beach.

Zoey worked her way to the bow and grabbed the rope, ready to jump off when they hit the sand. Patrick stood on the shore, waiting, while next to him Lhasa wagged her tail so hard Zoey thought the dog might fall over. As soon as the boat was secure, Zoey leaped out, kneeled, and flung her arms around her old friend. Eliot joined her.

"Oh, Lhasa, I missed you." Zoey rubbed her face in the dog's neck.

"Kraak, kraak," cried Eliot, running around flapping his arms.

"Apparently, Raven Boy survived," laughed Patrick. He picked Eliot up, mid-flap. "Hey, Buddy, I was worried about you. Glad you're okay."

"Kraak, kraak," Eliot didn't stop flapping, and Patrick put him down again.

Patrick turned to Thomas and gave him a little salute. "Thanks for taking care of them." He peeked at Zoey's mom, who was still in the boat gathering their stuff. "I didn't sleep much last night. If you hadn't made it back on this tide, I was going to get in the plane and come after you."

"Well, I'm glad you didn't do that," Zoey's mom answered, "but you sure picked the wrong time to disappear off to Dillingham." She tossed a sleeping bag at Patrick, a little harder than she needed to, Zoey thought.

Thomas looked out at the Bay. "I'd better get back to camp. Seen my uncle around anywhere?"

"Not since I brought him out yesterday," answered Patrick.

Zoey's mom reached for Thomas's shoulder. "Why don't you come and have some lunch at least."

Thomas shrugged. "The tide's going out, so I could just leave the skiff here and pick it up tonight. Can't stay long though. There's a lot to do before the season opens."

Eliot galloped ahead. Zoey was happy to see him running again. It was almost as if yesterday's illness had never happened. "Thomas, come on and I'll show you where Zoey and I sleep. It's really cool."

Does he have to show Thomas everything?

Later, when they all sat together in the big tent, Patrick said, "Thanks for leaving the note. That raven of yours was my only welcoming committee when I got back from town."

"You saw Midnight?" asked Eliot.

"Well, I don't know if it was Midnight, but a raven kept coming around pecking on your tent platform."

"Did it have a gray feather on its tail?" asked Thomas.

"You know about that too?" asked Zoey.

"Yeah. He hangs around our place sometimes, but I haven't seen him much lately."

"That's because he's been here!" Eliot flapped his arms a few times. "Visiting me, Raven Boy! Kraak, kraak!"

Zoey's mom set a plate of peanut butter and jelly sandwiches on the cable-spool table.

"I didn't notice any gray feather," said Patrick, "but I didn't look real close. Anyway, I'm glad the weather cooperated and you're all back safe and sound."

Zoey swallowed a big sticky bite and asked with some difficulty, "What will I do when everyone starts fishing?"

Patrick wiped crumbs off his chin. "There's more than enough jobs to keep us all busy around here, if you're up for it."

"So you and mom dragged me out here, and now I'm supposed to do slave labor?" Zoey could feel herself getting tense.

"No, Zoey, I'm talking about a *job*, where you get paid. You keep saying you want to earn money this summer."

This was news to Zoey. Suddenly, she was interested.

"What job could I do?" Her mind began calculating—how long would it take to earn enough to get to Colorado?

"Well, that's up to the Gambles."

"Me too. Me too!" said Eliot.

"Maybe you too, Raven Boy."

Zoey wolfed down the rest of her sandwich and hurried to the little tent. She wanted to walk Thomas home, but first she had to get out of yesterday's clothes. She had just pulled on a clean turtleneck and was about to unzip the tent flap when she heard a noise.

Ping, ping, ping.

Midnight!

14

Patrick

Zoey peeked out through the flap just in time to see the big black bird hop twice then fly down the beach toward their old fishing boat. No time to follow because just then her mom called.

"Zoey, come on. We're walking Thomas home."

Zoey noticed her hairbrush in a corner of the tent and made a quick attempt to calm her wind-tangled hair. Curly as it was, the boat ride had made grooming nearly impossible. She put it up with a hair tie instead, threw on her jacket, took a last look in her hand mirror, then zipped up the tent flap and ran to catch up. Thomas was already hiking down the beach with Eliot. Patrick and her mom followed.

Once they crossed the creek, Kenai bounded up to meet them. He growled at Lhasa and she turned sideways letting Kenai know, in the ancient language of dogs and wolves, that she knew he was boss.

As they got closer to the Gambles' fish camp, Thomas disappeared behind the Quonset hut and a man about Patrick's age emerged. Beyond him, rows of salmon strips hung drying on a rack capped with a blue-tarp roof.

"Don't worry about Kenai. He's part wolf, but he's a sweetie.

He'll get used to you," said the man, who wore a wool jacket and tall rubber boots. When he got closer, Zoey saw that his baseball cap said "Peter Pan Seafoods" over a picture of a silvery salmon. Under the brim, brown bangs covered his forehead. He was about Thomas's height, but stockier.

His eyes smiled but not his mouth.

"Hi, Harold," said Patrick. "Getting settled in?"

Harold nodded. "Sure. Hey, Patrick, didn't want to say anything coming in yesterday, but you think that old Cessna'll make it through the season?" This time he actually gave a half-smile.

"The plane's gonna do fine, Harold. Didn't think the fish would care about the paint job." Patrick's grin faded. "Hey, I heard about your brother. I'm real sorry."

Zoey realized they were talking about Thomas's dad.

"Comes with the territory," said Harold stiffly.

She froze. She had thought Thomas's parents were just divorced, like hers. But now she realized it wasn't that. It was much worse. Maybe the worst possible thing. There was so much that could get you around here.

"So, who's the sick kid?" Harold changed the subject.

Eliot gave a dramatic fake cough.

"That's my son Eliot, and I'm Alice," Zoey's mom broke in.

"You went all the way to Naknek for some cough drops?" Harold gave Eliot a full-blown grin. His teeth were shiny white. "Last time I had to go to that clinic was 'cause I managed to kick the fillet knife, and it stuck right in my foot. Couldn't get there for three days, though. Fishing was too good to leave."

Thomas walked up just in time to add, "His foot looked like a spawned-out salmon: all green and purple. They were about ready to chop it off."

“What can I say? A fisherman’s gotta fish.” Harold winked at Eliot. “That health aide had to chase me around the parking lot to sew that foot back up. I had enough of those guys.”

Zoey shuddered. She didn’t want to see any more health aides either. She noticed that Harold and Thomas had the same bright dark eyes.

Thomas turned to her. “Zoey, this is my Uncle Harold.”

“Hello there, miss.” Harold grinned at Thomas. “How’d a nice little city girl like you get stuck in a fish camp in Bush Alaska?”

Zoey frowned. She just couldn’t escape being the “city girl.” She started to tell Harold she would rather be just about anywhere *but* Bush Alaska, but Patrick stepped in.

“Actually, Harold, Zoey and Eliot want to work for you this summer, if you’ve got anything for them to do. Right guys?”

Zoey looked down. She needed to earn money, but she had no idea what kind of job Harold might have for her. Three days ago she hadn’t even known what a setnet was.

“I can do it,” said Eliot. “Zoey, you can too.”

Eliot sounded so grown up. Zoey wanted to throttle him.

“Well, they’re both kind of pint-sized, but I think we can keep ’em busy.” Harold’s eyes crinkled. “Women and kids used to run the setnets, you know, while the men went out in the boats. Lots of families still work the beach. Young kids just like you.

“In fact,” Harold went on, “if you guys and Thomas can handle most of the day-work, then I can take the night shift. That would be a big plus.”

“Hear that, Zoey?” said Patrick. “Thomas here can teach you all about it.”

Zoey felt her cheeks get hot. She did not look up.

"Sounds good, Harold," Patrick continued. "We'll be over first thing in the morning. Then I'll fly into town."

"Hold on." Harold turned toward the Quonset hut. "I've got something for you." He returned with a lumpy plastic bag. "Since you're about the only ones in this part of the Bay who aren't set up to catch your own fish, thought I'd take pity on you." He held out the bag. "Try the best take-home dinner in the world."

Patrick peeked inside. "Bristol Bay sockeye! Hey, thanks. We've been talking about salmon for weeks, even had a little smoked salmon before we came out here, but I don't know if the kids have ever eaten fresh sockeye before."

Back at their camp, Zoey's mom complained of a headache. "I need to lie down."

"No problem. Get some rest, babe." Patrick stroked her hair, and she curled up in the sleeping area.

Fat raindrops drummed against the canvas ceiling.

Patrick put some rice in a pot and fried up the salmon on the Coleman stove. Zoey wasn't thrilled with the way dinner smelled, but when she tasted the fish, she liked it. She couldn't remember Patrick making anything but sandwiches at home.

Before they were half done eating, Zoey's mom was sound asleep. After dinner, Zoey got out the carving knives and the piece of driftwood Captain had given her. Eliot tried to watch her, but his eyes kept closing. It had been a long day for all of them.

"I tried that once," Patrick said. "I wanted to make a bentwood box."

"What's that?" Zoey got out her pencil.

"The Tlingit in Southeast make them. It's a wooden box with no nails. Cedar, usually, and carved on top and the sides. They're beautiful, real works of art, but I was hopeless. I think it takes years to learn that stuff."

He took a knife from Zoey and tested the edge, then handed it back. "Careful with that. It could do some damage. Beautiful handle. Your Captain knows his stuff."

"Yeah, he showed me this: the straight one is for making lines and the hooked one is for scooping out," Zoey explained. "But first I have to draw on the wood. I think that's the way you're supposed to start."

"You're the artist. Hey, Raven Boy," he said to Eliot. "The faster you get to bed the faster you'll get better." But it was too late: Eliot was already asleep, hunched over with his head on his arm. Patrick picked him up, as if he were no heavier than a pillow, and carried him out to the other tent.

When he came back, he put some radio parts on the table across from Zoey and started assembling them. "Hope I can fix this. The one on the plane works fine but it's good to have an extra. Only way pilots can communicate. Communication's important, don't you think, Zoey?"

Zoey concentrated on drawing. What she saw in the wood, she decided, was a raven. That little bump near one end looked like the beginning of a beak.

If I were a raven trying to get out of something, I'd push with my beak first. Let's see, what comes next?

"You miss your friend in Anchorage?"

Zoey wasn't ready to answer. She squinted her eyes and held the piece of wood out at a distance. Sometimes that helped her see what to draw.

"Bet you miss your dad, too."

Zoey still didn't answer.

"Life deals out some tough cards sometimes," Patrick continued. "I don't talk about it much, but I was a little younger than you when my mom took her own life. Pills, I think. They never really told me."

Zoey looked up, startled. "What? I didn't know that."

The sound of the rain pressed in on the tent. Zoey fiddled with her pencil, then outlined a wing.

"One day she was there cooking dinner for my big sister and me, the next day she wasn't."

"You have a sister? I didn't know that either."

"Yeah, in California. And I had an iguana, too. Diego. A real cool one. Big. Maybe two feet long." Patrick tightened a tiny screw in the back of the radio.

"I guess I never thought of you . . . as a kid, I mean. I'm sorry about your mom." She drew the start of an eye just above the bump, wet her finger, wiped it off, then drew it again.

Lhasa sighed, stood up, turned around twice, then dropped down next to Zoey's foot. Zoey put down her pencil and stroked the dog's head.

"I don't talk about it. It's just I hope we can be friends. Everybody has some holes in their life, and we have to help fill 'em up for each other."

The rain beat steadier, louder. They sat silent for a while, but it was a comfortable silence.

Zoey yawned. She was tired, but she wasn't ready for bed yet. She drew the raven's feet. How many toes does a raven have?

"Do you like it out here, Patrick?"

"I like big spaces. Lots of sky overhead. I feel kind of hemmed in in the city. All those cars and people seem to suck the air out of everything. How about you?"

"Anchorage is okay." She yawned again. "But I like Colorado better."

"What do you like about Colorado?"

"It's dry there. And shiny."

"Shiny?" Patrick asked.

"Yeah, in the winter the snow falls and everything looks shiny. Here everything is about water. The bay, the rivers, and the clouds full of rain!" She smiled up at the ceiling, where the rain was still pounding. She actually didn't mind the rain so much.

Patrick nodded. "I know what you mean about the rain, but stick around. It'll snow here, too, you know." He smiled gently.

"You'd better get to bed, Zoey. Don't want you to get sick, too."

Zoey put her wood in the carving bag and stood up.

"Goodnight, Zoey."

"Night, Patrick." She lifted the tent flap. "Come on, Lhasa."

As she unzipped the little tent, she heard her mom cough. A loud one. The air outside felt raw from the cold rain. She crawled quickly through the opening and let Lhasa in behind her. Eliot hardly stirred. She tucked the carving bag into a corner of the tent down near her feet. When she slid inside her sleeping bag, the icy lining made her shiver. She realized the side next to Eliot was warmer and moved as close as she could without disturbing him. Lhasa crawled up on her other side, making a warm sandwich, with Zoey in the middle.

She felt too confused to sleep. Patrick tried to be nice to her, and he really did seem worried about Eliot, but she didn't want to like him. She remembered all the late-night talks she'd had with her dad. She would talk and talk for hours and he would always stay up and listen to her. He gave pretty good advice, too. But where was he now?

Zoey wasn't feeling so tired anymore, so she reached for her stationery box.

June 22

Dear Dad,

I miss our late-night talks. Are you okay?

Eliot got really sick. He had asthma so bad we had to take him in a boat to a place called Naknek—all the way across Bristol Bay! I was really afraid. But he's fine now and we're back at our camp and I'm snuggled in my sleeping bag and he and Lhasa are right next to me sound asleep.

Guess what?! I think I might have a way to make enough money to come and see you. I'm not giving up!

Oh, one other thing . . . I decided Patrick isn't so bad even though he's still kind of a know-it-all.

Do you miss me, Dad? Sometimes it's hard for me to remember what you look like. Isn't that weird? You better send me a picture.

Your homesick daughter,

Zoey

Zoey put the letter away and burrowed back down into her sleeping bag. Her thoughts swirled as she lay there, one arm around Lhasa. The sound of waves rushing up and down the beach made her feel like she was rocking in a boat out on a wide sea. But which way was she going? And was anyone steering?

15

Fishing Begins

The next morning, Patrick prodded Zoey to get up. She groaned and stretched without getting out of the warm sleeping bag. Patrick explained in a low voice that her mom was still sick and Eliot needed to rest another day, so it was just the two of them. Thirty minutes later they headed down the beach toward the fish camp.

"What does Harold want me to do? He didn't act like he thought I could do much. What if I can't do it, whatever 'it' is." Zoey had to hurry to keep up with Patrick's long stride.

Patrick slowed a little. "No one's forcing you, Zoey. But I'll let you in on a secret."

Zoey caught up.

"Since Thomas's dad died, the Gambles are short-handed. Money is tight, and I think they were going to try to get by without hiring another hand. You won't be that expensive, so if you hold up your end, they will be more than fair with you."

"So he did die. I wasn't positive about that. What happened to him?"

"I don't know, Zoey. I don't think they want to talk about it."

"No. I guess not."

Zoey couldn't think of anything else to say, and they walked in silence for a minute. Then she let her thoughts turn back to questions of work. Maybe she would just show Thomas what a city girl could do. And Harold too. And maybe, just maybe, she could earn enough for a plane ticket out of here.

Rain still peppered the flat ocean and the air was swollen with mist. Zoey was happy to be wearing the once-dreaded rain pants and was adjusting her hat when she saw Thomas on the other side of the creek.

When they caught up to him he said, "The first opening started at five AM. It was on the radio last night. They didn't need to wait till Saturday. I guess they got enough escapement."

"Escape-what?" asked Zoey.

"It's complicated, but you know how the salmon need to swim up into the rivers and streams to spawn, to lay their eggs?"

Zoey nodded.

"Well, Fish and Game has people who keep track of how many fish make it upstream in all the different parts of the Bay."

Patrick added, "It's called 'escapement'. Right now, they must think there's been enough in our area so we can fish. Later they might tell us to hold off for a while."

Zoey wasn't sure she really understood.

"Don't worry about it right now," Thomas said. "All we really need to know is that it's okay to fish. Harold already picked the net once, but it's a lot for one person to handle. My mom said if you help me, we can give Harold a break and she'll pay you, just like the rest of us."

"There you go, Zoey," Patrick grinned. "Think you can handle it?"

Zoey wasn't at all sure she could handle it. But she was ready to give it a try. Fishing must pay at least as much as babysitting. If she made enough, she could get back to Colorado and find her dad.

Zoey wanted him to explain why he had disappeared. Then maybe she could convince him and her mom to get back together. Anyway, she couldn't let Eliot be the only fisherman in the family.

They were almost to the fish camp when Carolyn banged out of the Quonset hut door, arms full of heavy-duty fishing clothes.

"Zoey! So glad you're here. I heard you might join the crew, so I got these ready just in case. Here, try on some of this old stuff. You don't want to get your nice rain gear all covered in mud and fish slime."

Patrick held up a pair of neoprene waders with attached rubber feet. "These oughta do. Try 'em on. I gotta get going. Still need to put braces in the back of the plane to hold the fish totes. You guys might have enough fish by the end of the day to make our first load for Dillingham."

With a wave, Patrick loped off down the beach toward the airplane.

Zoey pulled on the waders one leg at a time. They came up almost to her chin. The oversized suspenders fell around her sides so Carolyn cinched them up from behind. She chuckled. "Well, they are a little long but next summer they ought to fit just fine."

Next summer? Could she be serious?

Then she handed Zoey a pair of rubber boots. "These go over the neoprene. Give you a little better footing, and you won't ruin the bottom of the waders."

Zoey tried not to make a face as she replaced her own boots with a pair that was at least two sizes too big. She rummaged through the remaining fishy-smelling rain jackets and picked out what looked like the smallest. She slipped her arms in. Hmmm, she thought. Perfect for a small elephant.

"I'll go get the truck." Carolyn disappeared over a gravel bank beyond the Quonset hut.

Harold walked up the beach from the edge of the water where he had been working on the net.

"Thomas, your crew's got the next set. You can show Zoey the fine points of picking fish. Use the raft. It's out behind the house. I'm gonna try to get a little sleep, and then I'll come and check on you."

Before Harold disappeared into the Quonset hut, Zoey saw him look at her and shake his head. He didn't think she could do it. Was he right? She would soon find out. Carolyn motored down the beach toward her in an ancient, rusty pickup with the name "Power Wagon" written on the side. Thomas walked up with a big inflatable raft on his shoulders.

He set the raft down and hooked a fat cable from the winch on the front end of the truck to a metal ring at the top of the net, which stretched out into the water. Then he grabbed a big bag made of canvas mesh from the back of the truck and spread it out in the bottom of the raft. Finally, he tied a line from the raft around his waist.

"Follow me," he said, pulling the raft behind him.

Thomas waded into the shallow water and Zoey followed behind. Her boots immediately filled with water. It felt a little cold but the neoprene feet of her waders kept her dry. Half walking, half sliding through the mud, she picked her way behind Thomas. Her foot hit a rock and she lurched forward. Thomas grabbed her arm.

Why did she always have to look like an idiot around Thomas?

"You don't want to swim in that outfit if you can help it," he said with a tiny smile. "In fact, those boots'll pull you under if you fall in deep water, so make sure you can kick them off if you need to."

Pull you under? What had she gotten herself into? She took off a glove and trailed a hand through the water. It was like ice. She quickly dug her hand back into the glove.

When the water reached Zoey's knees, she could see salmon caught in the net, all silvery and some still moving!

She was surprised at how big they were. Each was as long as her arm, right out to her fingertips, and nearly as big around as the thickest part of her leg.

Zoey watched carefully while Thomas moved to the nearest fish and slipped two fingers under the sockeye's gills. He twisted his arm so his palm faced the sky and the fish's weight hung from his fingers. Then he eased the fish smoothly out of the net and tossed it into the canvas bag, which took up nearly the whole inside of the raft. It looked easy enough.

Zoey focused on the ones still in the net. "I thought they were supposed to be red," she said to Thomas because that was what she'd seen in the magazines.

"That doesn't happen until much later." Thomas checked the rope tied from his belt to the raft that drifted alongside them.

"Once they've made it past our net and everyone else's, and fought their way up the stream, that's when they really change. They'll turn bright red. The females will lay their eggs and the males will fertilize them. Then, in a couple of days, they'll die."

"That doesn't seem fair."

"I guess lots of things aren't fair. But what are you gonna do?" He looked up at Zoey and shrugged his shoulders. "Your turn."

Zoey reached one hand into the icy water and grabbed a salmon's head, then pushed two fingers of her other hand under its gill. Through the glove she could feel the thin membrane under the gills give way. The heavy fish shook twice.

"It's wiggling!" Zoey yelled, yanking her hands away from the fish. It fell back into the net, shook for a few seconds, then stilled.

"That's what we want. We don't like 'em to drown in the net. And we want to keep the net as empty as we can so the new fish don't get scared away."

That made perfect sense. What was she afraid of anyway? Zoey was determined not to look like a helpless city girl. She wasn't afraid to touch fish. Her dad had taught her how to kill trout by hitting their heads on a rock and how to slide a knife smoothly up their bellies to the gills and then to pull the insides right out of the opening all at once. But she had to admit, those trout were nowhere near as big as these salmon. And they were *not* still moving.

"Those teeth look sharp."

"You just have to be careful. And work fast."

Zoey tried again. This time she managed to get her fingers all the way under the gill cover. She twisted her arm the way she'd seen Thomas do it, and she discovered her fingers hooked naturally inside the gills. Unfortunately, she also discovered the salmon was too heavy to lift out of the net with one hand.

"Now grab just in front of the tail with your other hand."

She yanked on the heavy salmon a couple of times with both hands, and finally heaved it up out of the net.

"Hey, not bad," Thomas said, smiling.

Zoey was staring at the fish. Even on this overcast day, the sides of her salmon shimmered silver all the way from its nose to the end of its tail. The upper part of the salmon was darker, greenish-blue and kind of metallic.

At that moment, the salmon thrashed wildly in her hands. Without thinking, she jerked away. The enormous fish flopped back into the dark water, outside the net this time, and disappeared.

16

Rulers of the World

Don't worry," Thomas said with a laugh. "There's plenty more where that came from. But don't let Harold see you do that."

Zoey gritted her teeth. When it was her turn again, she slid two fingers under the gill cover, twisted, and held the fish solidly. Then she clamped her other hand just above the tail. *This fish was not going anywhere but into that raft!* Ignoring Thomas's gesture of help, she managed to press the fish between her chest and the raft. Then she rolled and slid it up the side of the raft and in. It wasn't pretty, Zoey knew, but it was in.

Thomas reached over and pushed the fish into the canvas bag that lined the bottom of the raft.

"Why do you have that big bag in there?"

"It's called a brailer. If you leave 'em loose in the raft, they tend to disappear."

"How long have you been doing this?" Zoey stood with her legs far apart, like Thomas. Immediately she felt more stable.

"I guess I was out here as soon as I could walk."

By her fifth salmon, Zoey was finally able to get the fish out of the net and into the brailer without any disasters.

The sticky mud sucked at her boots. With each step, she struggled to keep them on her feet.

After about twenty minutes, Thomas raised his arm and shouted to his mom on the shore, "Okay, it's ready."

The old Power Wagon moved backwards and the empty net in front of Zoey slipped through the water toward the beach. Carolyn stopped the truck and a new part of the net was beside them, full of fish.

"Oh, I get it," said Zoey. "The net is attached to the truck, and when your mom backs up, she pulls the net with her."

"Cool, huh?"

They waded into the new supply of salmon.

An hour later, they had reached the end of the net. Carolyn pulled the truck forward and the net slid back out to its original position.

Dozens of small floats along the top of the nylon mesh stretched out toward the deeper water. Zoey figured the net could reach from one end of the big gym at her school to the other.

She watched the small white buoys. "What keeps it from floating away?"

"My dad set it all up years ago. The net is attached to a bunch of ropes and pulleys. Those two big stakes anchor it to the beach. Those are the deadmen. Like you saw in Naknek. Remember?"

Zoey nodded her head and thought of Thomas's joke about the dead fishermen. Between the mud, freezing water, heavy net, and thrashing fish, it seemed all too easy to become one of those.

"Wow! You said Fish and Game was complicated, but this net is *really* complicated."

"That's only part of it," Thomas laughed. "Those white floats hold up the top of the net. And a string of weights called the lead line pulls down the bottom under the water. That holds the net open so the fish can swim into it."

Zoey tried to make sense of all this new gear, but felt like her head was beginning to swim, too. Then she noticed Carolyn had unhooked the net and moved the truck to a spot on the beach near them. Carolyn waved, turned, and walked up to the Quonset hut.

Zoey and Thomas lugged the raft as close as they could to the truck. The cargo bed was full of gray plastic crates like the ones her mom stored winter clothes in, but bigger.

Thomas pulled a crate down and opened it. "These are fish totes." He began to toss fish from the raft into the tote.

"Come on, Zoey. Here." He tossed a fish to Zoey. It slipped out of her hand and onto the sand where it flopped before she picked it up and slid it into the tote.

"Hey, you're learning. We gotta fill every one of these. Soon as we get a full load, Patrick'll fly them into Dillingham to the processor."

Zoey picked up another fish from the brailer and heaved it into the tote.

"That's it." He spun around and threw another salmon like it was a piece of firewood. He ran around behind Zoey, "Think quick!"

Zoey turned just in time to grab at another flying salmon. This time she caught it but as soon as she steadied herself, Thomas ran up and pretended to guard her as if they were playing basketball. He grabbed the fish right out of her hands and threw it overhand into the tote.

Zoey caught a glimpse of Harold up behind the generator shed. Thomas must have noticed too because he quickly got serious. "I guess that's enough 'fish ball' for now. You like basketball?"

Zoey shook her head.

"I used to play with the JV team. Didn't stick with it though. People around here get pretty crazy about basketball. It's a long winter. There's not much else to do."

Zoey wanted to ask him if he had played with his dad but changed her mind. Instead she said, "How much salmon do you think we got so far?"

"The totes hold about a hundred and fifty pounds each."

They continued tossing salmon, gentler now, until the raft was finally empty. They had only filled two of the totes. At least twenty more were still stacked in the truck.

"Now we get to start all over again." Thomas turned toward the water.

"Come on, let's see what we caught while we were standing here."

Zoey followed him back out into the water and, sure enough, more salmon were stuck in the net. It had taken nearly two hours to pick the first wave of salmon, get them into the totes and reset the net, and she was ready for a break, but apparently that wasn't how it worked here in Halfmoon Bay.

By the time they had filled the raft a second time, the tide was out and most of the net lay limp on the mud. Zoey was done in. Every muscle in her body felt sore, especially her forearms. Her fingers were stiff from clamping down on flapping salmon tails, so she was glad Thomas didn't try any more "fish ball." She didn't think she could lift one more sockeye.

"Okay, Zoey, not much more we can do until the tide comes back in." Thomas nodded toward the house, and they headed in for a break.

Carolyn had been right to warn her about fish slime. The bulky clothing felt even heavier and definitely stinkier as Zoey shrugged herself out of the grimy rubber pants and let them fall on the ground near the door.

Thomas looked at her without speaking. Zoey sighed and

gathered up the smelly pile. She hung her jacket and pants on a hook by the door. Thomas rinsed off their boots and then the rest of the rubbery gear with a hose attached to a pump powered by the generator.

Inside, Carolyn gave them peanut butter sandwiches and hot tea. Zoey wondered if people ever ate anything besides fish and peanut butter in Bristol Bay. Today, though, she had no complaints, especially when Carolyn produced a bag of Oreos.

After lunch, Zoey sank into a tattered chair in a corner and entertained herself looking at pictures in a magazine printed three years before she had been born. Thomas and his mom went out back to check on the drying salmon that would be part of their subsistence fish, food for the family when winter came. Zoey was asleep when Carolyn shook her gently to say the tide was rising.

It was time to pick the net again.

This time Zoey didn't lose as many salmon and was quicker at untangling them from the net. She took her gloves off to push her hair out of her eyes.

"Thomas, did you know Patrick last summer?"

"Not really. I saw him around Dillingham, but he didn't haul for us last year. We used the Power Wagon to drive the fish along the beach to Etolin Point. It took too much time though, and just about ruined our truck. We didn't make much money that way. Patrick'll cost us, but we can sell a lot more fish, so it should be worth it."

Zoey nodded.

He looked at her with an intensity that made Zoey squirm. "You seem really mad at him sometimes."

She was surprised he had noticed. "I don't know. Until my mom met him, we had a pretty normal life. But that wasn't good enough for Patrick. He had to drag us out to 'the real Alaska'." She said the last three words with an edge that shocked her.

"It's the only Alaska I know," Thomas said quietly.

"Haven't you ever wanted to live somewhere else?"

Thomas just shrugged.

Zoey was about to ask Thomas how his dad had died, but at the same moment she lost her balance in the mud. She struggled to stay upright, but her feet went out from under her and she fell backwards. Instantly, she felt the heavy, cold water press in on her body. Icy rivulets leaked in through tiny holes in her waders. She held her breath, squeezed her eyes shut, and braced herself.

Just before she went completely under, something tugged on her suspenders. Thomas had her. His grip steadied her until she was able to get her feet underneath her again. She jammed her boots into the ground, grabbed Thomas's arm, and pulled herself up. Without thinking, she looked directly into his eyes.

She wondered if she'd ever find her balance again. "Thanks."

"No big deal. You might have to do the same for me sometime."

Zoey doubted that would ever happen, but it was nice to hear. She was thankful for the borrowed fishing gear. Without it she would be soaking wet.

By the end of the day six totes full of salmon sat side by side on the beach. *Almost a thousand pounds to sell!* Harold met them as they came in. He looked pleased. "Another week, you'll more than double that, but it's okay for a start. Hard work, huh? When Thomas was little I told him it would make him a man. Seems to be working!" He threw an arm over Thomas's shoulder. "Don't you worry, Zoey, we'll break you in slow." He laughed.

Harold was joking, but Zoey felt a stab of fear. If this was slow, fast would be crazy! She had never worked so hard in her whole life and everything ached. Her arms. Her fingers. Her neck. Even her legs ached from tramping through the endless mud. Still, though she would never have admitted it to anyone, she liked knowing she had done as much as her body could do.

After carefully watching how Thomas did it, Zoey rinsed her rubber gloves with the hose while they were still on, then removed them and slapped them together to get off more of the sticky fish scales. Her pruney hands looked about a hundred years old.

When she looked up, she saw Eliot hurrying toward her along the beach.

"How did it go? Did you get lots of fish? Mom was going to come with me but she made it to the creek and said she felt sick. I'm supposed to come get you. I'm not sick anymore."

Zoey could tell. She pointed to the full totes of fish, then waved her shriveled hands at her brother.

"I'm Crab Woman." She teetered toward him, her arms outstretched. "Look out Raven Boy or I'll throw you in the chowder with the salmon."

Eliot shrieked, ran a few steps, then stopped and giggled. "Raven Boy and Crab Woman. Rulers of Bristol Bay!"

"Rulers of the world!" Zoey cried as they shook their fists in the air and ran down the beach toward their own camp.

17

Bag Balm

That night, carrying the jug of water from the stream to camp was almost more than Zoey could manage. Her raw hands hurt just gripping the handle.

Patrick cooked up the rest of the salmon Harold had given them. Zoey tried to eat, but fish eyes kept staring up at her from the plate. She only got down a few bites. Eliot ate every morsel. He was still full of energy, and except for a runny nose, he showed no sign of having been sick.

In the end, Patrick cleaned Zoey's plate for her. "Never waste wild fish or game. It's not respectful."

Zoey was not in the mood for another lecture from Patrick, but she had never thought about showing respect for her dinner. "What's so special about fish? I'd trade it all for a 7-Eleven."

"It's an old custom in the real Alaska and a strong one."

Zoey knew by now the "real Alaska" meant "not Anchorage."

"People who live in Bush Alaska depend on fish and caribou, berries, and other wild food. The custom is to show respect for the animals—never take more than you can use."

Zoey felt something slip inside. Before she could think, it popped out. "You know, you're not the only animal expert in the world, Patrick. My dad fishes and hunts with a bow and arrow. He shows more respect than you ever could flying around in your little airplane."

Zoey's mom called from the sleeping area, still sick. "Can't you guys be friends?" She walked shakily to the Coleman stove and put the teakettle on.

"We're fine," Patrick answered. "How do you feel, babe?"

"I think I'll live. But I want you all to double your vitamin C dose. Too many weak immune systems around here. How are things over at the fish camp?"

Zoey held up her wrinkled hands. "They still hurt."

Her mom sniffed. "Even with my stuffy nose I can smell that. Did either of you wash your hands before dinner?"

Eliot had already left the table and was rolling on the floor with Lhasa.

"You and the dog outside," she said. "There's not enough room in here for you and your new-found energy."

Eliot grabbed his jacket and opened the tent flap. His mom picked up his wool hat and threw it to him.

"Run around the tent a few times, but don't go far," said Patrick.

Zoey sighed. "I'm taking my fishy hands to bed, and if anyone has a problem with that, too bad."

"It might not be a problem now," Patrick said, "but when a big grizzly bear tries to share your sleeping bag because your hands smell like dinner, you might change your mind."

Zoey sighed again. One more way to become a dead fisherman. Even going to bed was a hassle in Bristol Bay.

"Wait a sec, and I'll give you some warm water to wash with." Her mom poured from the teakettle into a metal bowl. "Here, take this."

Patrick grabbed his backpack and began pawing through it. “And come back in when you’re done. I have something to make your hands feel better, if I can find it.”

Outside, on the edge of the tent platform, Zoey put down the bowl, sat, and eased her hands into the warm water. She closed her eyes in appreciation. For the first time all day something actually felt good. When she rubbed her hands with soap, her skin stung, but she kept washing, testing every few seconds with her nose.

Once the smell was mostly gone, she went back inside, patting her hands lightly with a paper towel. Patrick handed her a small jar.

“Bag Balm?” she said. “You’re kidding, right? This is what they use on the *cows* back in Colorado. See, here’s a picture of a big udder right on the label!”

Patrick opened the jar and rubbed some of the gooey stuff onto Zoey’s hand.

“Cows, sheep, horses, dogs . . . and Alaskan fishermen. This is the best stuff to have between your hands and those fish.”

“It’s got lanolin in it, honey,” said Zoey’s mom. “Put it on every day and it will keep your hands from getting cracked.”

“Fish slime loves to get in those cracks and cause infections,” said Patrick.

Without looking at Patrick, Zoey stretched out the other hand and let him apply more of the sticky stuff. His hands were huge compared to hers, but his touch was gentle.

“I feel like a postage stamp,” she said. “If I touch the side of the tent, someone’s going to have to peel me off.” But the truth was the salve immediately soothed the stinging stiff feeling. She opened and closed her fist.

Ahhh. Better.

A while later, when they were settled in their sleeping bags and Eliot was asleep, Zoey blotted her still-sticky hands with more paper towels and took out her stationery.

Even though she still didn't have her dad's address, she wanted to write to him again. In another couple of weeks, it would be her birthday, the first one since they had left Colorado, and she was sure there would be a card from him. She hoped it would have a return address.

June 23

Dear Dad,

What a place Bristol Bay is!!! I had no idea there could be this many fish all together at once! And I definitely do have a way to make enough money to come see you. I got a job. A real job where I get paid, just like the grown-ups. I worked all day picking salmon out of a setnet. My hands are all raw. It's stinky, hard work, but it's kind of cool to see the big totes full of fish when we're done. And the fish are so beautiful when they first come out of the water.

I work with this boy named Thomas. Even though he is older, I am sort of friends with him. At first I wasn't so sure, but now I think he's nice.

Dad, you would love it here because you like to fish so much. The salmon are MUCH bigger than trout. My arms are sore from lifting them all day.

Where are you, Dad? How come you haven't written? Mom said she left a forwarding address with the post office. When you write to Anchorage, your letters will go here. Or send them to General Delivery, Dillingham, Alaska, 99565.

I wish you could see me now. I feel like I'm much older than when we left Colorado. I'm almost a real teenager. I haven't gotten paid yet, but I might have enough by the end of the summer. But right now I'm having a hard time writing because my hands hurt so much from the fishing. More later . . .

From your not-so-little-anymore daughter,
Zoey

Zoey folded the letter and slipped it back in the box. She tried to picture her dad reading the letter, but it wasn't working.

18

A Cake in the Coleman?

It seemed like Zoey had just put her head on the pillow when she awoke to find Eliot pulling on her.

"Hey, cut it out."

"Everyone's already gone. Mom's all better. She said to get you up."

And that's the way it went for the next couple of weeks. Zoey rushed to get ready. Then she rushed to the fish camp where she rushed to pull fish out of the net. She felt like she was caught in some kind of current, pulling and pushing her life along, but she didn't know where to. She wondered if the salmon knew where they were going or what would happen when they got there.

She thought about Naknek and how just about everyone else around Bristol Bay must be busy with fishing. People doing jobs that hadn't existed three weeks before: picking, packing, or cutting strips to smoke or dry for the family freezer.

Harold said Eliot was too young to wade out in the mud. He got to pick up fish that slipped out of the raft onto the beach, but mostly he and their mom helped Carolyn prepare the subsistence fish the Gambles would need in the winter. Carolyn taught them how to split the fish for drying and smoking. It was a complicated and precise process she said she learned from the elder women in Naknek.

Carolyn split the fish with a special knife she called an *ulu*. It looked like a half-moon with a handle stuck to the flat side. And it was sharp! She started by cutting all the heads off. Then she cut the fish in half the long way almost to the tail, but not quite through. She pulled out the backbone, then made careful slits all the way down the meat on both sides almost to the skin, but not quite. Zoey's mom hung the fish by their tails on the horizontal poles of the fish rack. A tarp roof kept the rain off.

Carolyn was also the official Power Wagon driver, always on call to reposition the net. Thomas and Zoey did the picking during the day, then Harold took over for night shifts. Thomas sometimes helped Harold as well. Sleep was a precious luxury in Bristol Bay during salmon season.

For Zoey the days of fishing flowed together. It seemed like the thick schools of salmon would never stop. Sometimes she watched Eliot from the water while she picked the net. He would walk up and down the beach, suddenly morph into Raven Boy or maybe a giant eagle and swoop down on a helpless fish. He also delivered snacks with a proud grin from Carolyn's kitchen to the crew, which now included his big sister.

Everyone had some sort of job. Zoey's mom often went with Patrick on his flights to Dillingham, leaving Zoey in charge of Eliot. Sometimes she took a big bag of stinky clothes with her to wash.

Thomas and Zoey picked fish, fish, and more fish. Just as Harold had predicted, the catches were much bigger than the first week. Now they were getting two hundred wild sockeye in the net from just one set, and filling about twenty totes on a good day.

Sometimes, when the tides were right, Harold would work well into the night. Patrick helped too. "If *we* don't catch 'em, someone else will," was Harold's favorite line of encouragement. Luckily Zoey's mom put her foot down at the idea of her children working the night shift.

Even so, Zoey worked harder than she thought possible. This wasn't just busy work, people were counting on her. She didn't want to let them down, especially Thomas. Plus, although she hadn't seen any yet, there was the money.

Harold still teased her. If she complained, he reminded her that these were "puny" sockeye salmon. "They only weigh six or eight pounds. Now kings, they're something else," he said as they tossed the fish from the brailer into the totes. "Some of those king salmon are bigger than you."

Still, the sockeye seemed plenty big to Zoey. Her arms ached, and in spite of the Bag Balm, her hands remained rough and chapped.

The best part of the day was the hour or so after fishing and before dinner. Once the last tote was filled, Zoey and Eliot hurried along the beach to the old fishing boat to hang out, sometimes with Thomas, sometimes with Midnight, always with Lhasa. On the way there, Zoey would collect interesting shells for her growing collection. At the boat, they played and talked about what they would do when the fishing slowed down. Zoey wondered if that time would ever come.

The longest day of the year, the summer solstice, had long since come and gone, but as they entered July, the mornings still stretched magically into afternoons and well into the middle of the night. From one dawn to the next, the sky never got completely dark. A few hours of deep twilight were the only sign that tomorrow had come. Harold told them to "enjoy it while it lasts 'cuz winter will be here soon enough."

Winter! To Zoey, it didn't feel like that long ago when the snow had drifted over her bedroom windowsill in Anchorage.

Even with light in the sky, Zoey fell asleep well before her sleeping bag could warm down to her feet. She occasionally worked on her carving, but made little progress. Writing her dad wasn't happening either. She just couldn't stay awake long enough.

One afternoon, after five hard sets, Patrick and Zoey's mom took fifteen hundred pounds of sockeye to Dillingham in one trip in the shaky old plane. When they returned, Zoey's mom asked, "How about a party for your birthday?"

Finally! Zoey was going to be a teenager!

"We could invite the Gambles, and I think I can bake a cake in the Coleman."

"Really, a cake and everything?"

It wouldn't be much of a party without Bethany, but it was better than nothing. Zoey wished her friend could come and visit. She would show her how to pick the nets, they could play together on the old fishing boat and meet Thomas. But Bethany's mom couldn't afford a jet trip to Dillingham.

Zoey knew she would at least get a card from Bethany, and she was sure her dad wouldn't forget her first teenage birthday either.

"How can you have a birthday party in a tent?" Zoey asked. But she knew it could be done. Nothing was easy out here in Bristol Bay, but you could make things happen if you put your mind to it.

19

Blue Skies and Brown Bears

The next morning Zoey woke with a start. A woman's voice in the other tent, and it wasn't her mom. Carolyn! What was she saying?

"Harold saw her. A big female. She had her head inside a fish tote. He shooed her away by banging on a gas can, but she might still be around. Usually, they stay up the rivers and don't bother us, but it means trouble if they get in the habit of nosing around camps. Sometimes we have to shoot them. No choice. Maybe with no fishing today, that grizzly'll head off somewhere else."

A grizzly? Here in camp? And no fishing?

"We'll be on bear alert. Appreciate the heads up," Zoey heard Patrick say.

"Okay. See ya tomorrow then." Carolyn's voice faded.

Zoey dressed quickly and slipped from the tent without waking Eliot. She watched Carolyn walk away down the beach. She had a rifle strapped over her shoulder. Then Zoey noticed Patrick at the tent door.

"You got a day off."

"What happened?" Zoey entered the big tent. She could see her mom still in her sleeping bag.

"No fish."

"No fish? How can that be? And what's this about a bear?"

"Shhhhh. Don't wake your mom. Sometimes the wind can churn things up so bad the fish don't come near shore. Or maybe there's a break in the run or the fish just move around. Nobody really knows. It's okay for a day or so, but you know how everyone here depends on those fish."

"But there were millions yesterday." Zoey rubbed the sleep from her eyes and sat on the log chair.

"What's going on?" Eliot came in. His hair stuck straight up in the back where he had slept on it.

"No work today. No fish," Patrick said without looking at them. "I guess you two have a day off. But we'd better hope they're back tomorrow or we'll leave Bristol Bay as poor as we came."

Zoey could see the trouble if the fishing didn't start again soon, but she was ready for a break from the grinding work of fishing.

"And what about the bear?" Zoey asked.

"There's a grizzly bear nosing around."

Eliot jumped up and down. "Yeah! A bear! Yeah!"

"Shhhh! Eliot. Your mom's asleep. " Patrick brought his finger to his lips.

"Eliot, are you crazy? Bears are dangerous," said Zoey in a loud whisper.

"I just want to see one."

"That bear is a serious matter," Patrick said. "Don't you two go anywhere by yourselves as long as it's around. Not even to the latrine. And stick close together, even in camp. Do you hear me?" Patrick looked like he meant it. He reached up to the highest shelf in the tent, pulled down his rifle, and checked it. "Good, loaded and the safety's on." Then he put the gun back on the shelf.

Lhasa's loud barks erupted from somewhere not too far away.

They all fumbled into their boots and jackets and rushed outside. The barking came from near the old fishing boat. Patrick raced toward it, the rifle under one arm.

"Back in the tent!" he yelled. "If Lhasa's onto our bear, I don't want you outside. Go in and tell your mom what's happened. I'm going to see if I can find that dog and get her back before she gets us all into trouble."

"But Lhasa might not come for you," Zoey was frantic. "She hardly knows you. She knows *me*."

"Do what I told you. I don't have time to argue." Patrick disappeared around the grassy hill.

Zoey was furious.

"Come on, Eliot, let's go."

"But Zoey, Patrick said it might be dangerous!"

But Zoey was already running in the direction Patrick had gone. Eliot followed, but he couldn't move as fast as Zoey and quickly fell behind. Zoey passed the boat and rushed through the tall grass that marked the end of the sand, then onto the tundra beyond. She stopped short, stunned by the vastness of it. She had never come out this far before. The great plain of Southwest Alaska swept out before her for miles and miles, until it melted into the horizon. The land was nearly flat, except for patches of scrubby green and brown shrubs, sprinkled with tiny bright purple, blue, white, and yellow flowers. The sky above was Zoey's favorite shade of paint, cornflower blue.

She could see Patrick's head and shoulders above some bushes in the distance, but not Lhasa. Patrick did not move, and the barking had stopped. Eliot caught up with Zoey and together they walked as quietly as they could toward Patrick.

When they were perhaps a hundred feet away, they could see

that Patrick was kneeling and holding Lhasa's collar while the dog stared intently at something beyond them. Zoey could make out a small pond, and on the far side of the pond two little bear cubs pawed each other playfully. They were round, almost fluffy looking, and as cute as puppies.

Her eyes widened. An enormous rock beside the cubs suddenly stood up and stretched itself into a huge brown bear. Zoey's heart pounded. The mother bear rocked on her hind legs waving her nose in the air. She sniffed in their direction and then turned and stared straight at Zoey and Eliot.

Zoey held her breath. Everything began to play like a movie in slow motion. The bear huffed, came down on her front paws, and lumbered toward them. Zoey's eyes were locked on the enormous animal as it moved closer and closer. She saw its golden fur rippling in the sun, its body hulking and graceful at the same time. The bear moved around the pond at a speed Zoey would never have thought possible. The slow motion sped up.

Patrick was still kneeling, but now he had the rifle aimed at the mother bear.

Zoey and Eliot stood transfixed, unable to move, breathe, or even blink.

He's going to shoot the bear! Zoey thought. *The cubs will be all alone. They'll die.*

Zoey closed her eyes. She couldn't watch.

An explosion cracked across the tundra. Then two more, so loud they hurt Zoey's ears.

Zoey dove to the ground and pulled Eliot with her. She didn't want to see it, didn't want Eliot to see it.

That was the gun. Patrick killed the bear. Did he shoot the babies, too?

Afraid to look, but more afraid not to, Zoey lifted her head and peeked out. She glimpsed the mother bear as it ran away from them, the cubs close behind her. They disappeared in the brush beyond the pond.

"Back to camp. Now!" Patrick yelled as he stalked toward Zoey and Eliot. Zoey and Eliot stood, and even from that distance she could see his face was dark and twisted. She had never seen him this mad before.

"What were you thinking, Zoey?" he yelled when he caught up to them. "You *have* to listen to me when I tell you things out here! You almost got yourself and Eliot killed."

Zoey took a deep breath and then threw her arms around Patrick.

"Thank you, thank you, thank you for not killing that bear! I thought you shot her and the babies, too." Zoey squeezed him hard before letting go. "I'm sorry we followed you. It was dumb, I know it was dumb. But I was so worried about Lhasa."

All the thunder seemed to evaporate from Patrick. His mouth dropped open and he shook his head as if in wonder. After a moment he recovered and said, "We can't talk now. We need to hurry. Sometimes a bear will circle around and come after you.

20

Swallowed a Lead Line

AS they got closer to camp they heard Zoey's mom.

"Zoooooooey, Ellllliot . . . Where are you?"

Eliot got there first and ran into her arms. Zoey, Lhasa, and Patrick gathered around.

"What happened? I heard gunshots. I woke up and you were all gone. Where were you? Why didn't you wake me?"

"Slow down. One thing at a time." Patrick hugged her and smiled. "I'm glad to see you're up. Come on, let's talk inside."

They trooped into the tent and little by little the entire bear story spilled out.

"And then I was sure Patrick killed the mama bear and even the babies. I was so mad, but then I was so happy that he didn't."

"That was a close one," Patrick said. He looked more relaxed as he fired up the stove and filled the coffeepot. Then he went to the tent door and carefully surveyed the beach and the grass beyond.

"She could just as easily have kept coming after us. I could have shot her, but then I would have had to shoot the cubs, too. They would starve on their own. Plus it's no simple thing to kill a grizzly that size. The skull is so tough a bullet can bounce right off. Shoot anyplace but the heart, and all you do is make a very angry bear."

He took a long sip of coffee. “Let’s hope that’s the last we see of them. Sows with cubs don’t usually come around people. That might have been the one that was into Harold’s fish totes earlier, but she won’t put her cubs in danger like that again soon.”

That was a long speech for Patrick. Zoey realized he was just as wound up as they were.

Zoey’s mom shivered. “And to think how close you two came to being that bear’s breakfast. Zoey, do you understand now that you have to listen to Patrick out here? He knows this area. You have to listen.”

Zoey’s eyes shifted down. The worst thing was that she had put Eliot in danger. She hadn’t trusted Patrick to save Lhasa, but in the end, he had saved all of them, even the bears.

Zoey stared at the tent floor. “I’m sorry, Mom, Patrick. I know. I got carried away.”

“Forgiven,” Patrick answered quietly. “Come on now, I bet you’re all starving. How about some pancakes?” Zoey’s mom went to the shelves and began gathering ingredients.

A couple of hours later, after a longer-than-usual breakfast and a quick cleanup, Patrick took his rifle and walked Zoey, Eliot, and Lhasa to the old boat. Finally, they had some time to fix it up, and Patrick had volunteered to be bear guard. As they approached, they heard pounding, and when they rounded the hill, Thomas looked up at them, hammer in hand.

“Hey, what’s up?” asked Zoey.

“What’s it look like? Just patching up some of the biggest holes with this old plywood. Think she’ll float?” He grinned and put down the hammer.

“Probably not,” Patrick laughed. “But it’s a nice thought. You guys should be fine in the boat, but stick together and make plenty of noise. Bang that hammer around. I'm going to go a little way out on the tundra and see if I see anything."

"We met the bear," Zoey explained. "It had cubs!" She and Eliot told Thomas the whole story, interrupting each other the whole time: "You should have seen her." "She was beautiful! I'm so glad Patrick didn't kill them."

Eliot finally changed the subject. "Are we really going to launch the boat?" he asked.

Thomas laughed, "I wouldn't go that far." He stepped back to examine his work. "But this should keep out some of the rain."

"When we get it all fixed up, we can bring everyone here and surprise them," said Eliot as he disappeared back into the boat cabin.

Thomas found a sunny spot, sat down in the sand, and leaned back against the side of the boat. Zoey sat cross-legged nearby.

"Are you coming to my birthday party?" Zoey asked Thomas.

"We're bringing the ice cream."

"Ice cream! Is there a grocery store around here that I missed?"

"We have a freezer hooked up to our generator. Mostly it's for fish, but Harold always stocks up on ice cream. We have frozen pizzas, too."

"Harold would give up his ice cream for my birthday?"

"He has plenty, and he's pretty impressed with the way you've been helping us."

Zoey remembered some good news. "Hey, guess what? My mom said she's baking a cake on the Coleman stove! I never thought that would seem like such a big deal. You really notice what you don't have out here. Which is mostly everything."

Zoey picked up a small stone and started to plow little

grooves into the sand next to her. "Even though it's only been three weeks, it seems like we've been here a lot longer. Sometimes I can hardly remember Anchorage."

"What do you miss most?" asked Thomas.

"I miss my friend, Bethany. She has about a million freckles. We tried to count them once and gave up. And I miss my bed. I didn't have my own room at home, but at least I didn't have to sleep right *next* to Eliot."

"I don't have any real friends in Naknek right now," Thomas said. "I mostly stopped hanging out after my dad died."

Zoey's sand grooves deepened into canals. "What happened to him?"

"Accident."

"Something with fishing?" asked Zoey.

"Yeah." Thomas looked away and quickly said, "Hey, let's clean up the rest of the inside. I brought an old broom."

Zoey let go of her questions and followed Thomas up the slanting deck and into the cabin. They shooed Eliot back outside and Thomas began to sweep the floor.

The sweeping brought an idea to Zoey that completely surprised her. She had always thought of Thomas outdoors, fishing, playing on the beach, or driving the boat. Now, with his broom, he looked like he might be cleaning up an apartment in any normal city. Without thinking, she put herself in the scene. Yes, they had friends coming over for dinner. She would put the food in the oven and then arrange flowers for the table.

She giggled, but another thought stopped her. What would he be like as a boyfriend? Zoey had never had a real boyfriend. And not that she wanted Thomas to be that. Still, she couldn't help wondering. Who would they hang out with? And where? In Naknek?

Just a few weeks ago Naknek didn't even exist for Zoey. Neither did the idea of a boyfriend!

There wasn't room for Zoey in the cabin while Thomas worked, so she sat on the side deck with her back against the cabin wall and her feet up against the curved wooden plank that ran around the edge of the deck. When Thomas was finished, she would go in and decorate. She watched Eliot playing nearby, and tried to imagine what might have happened to Thomas's dad and how Thomas must feel about it.

Zoey wondered if Thomas got that twisting in his stomach. Like you were almost going to be sick, but you never were, but the feeling wouldn't go away. An empty feeling, but heavy, too. Like a big weight inside you, as if you had swallowed a lead line.

How weird to know what a lead line is.

Zoey realized she hadn't had that stomach feeling in a while. She had been so busy. Now something about her birthday brought it back. Her dad.

She heard raven clucks. Midnight was standing on the ground, and Eliot knelt just a few feet away, his hand outstretched with a piece of cracker. The raven cocked its head one way, then the other. It hopped two steps closer to Eliot.

When did Eliot learn to be that still? He was frozen like a statue. The raven hopped closer. Eliot could have touched it.

Eliot whispered between lips that didn't move, "Get Thomas. He's gonna do it."

Thomas emerged from the boat, unaware that anything unusual was happening. He set the broom down.

"Pretty clean anyway."

In one quick motion, the raven swiped the cracker, bounced twice, and flew away.

Eliot jumped and shouted, "Raven Boy, Ruler of the Birds!"

"Whoa! I never got him to do that," said Thomas grinning.

Midnight circled back and landed on the bow. He watched Zoey, cocking his head and making strange clicking sounds.

Zoey bent over the side and whispered down, "Eliot, give me a cracker."

Eliot sighed. "Zoey, he won't come to you."

"Just let me try."

Thomas shook his head. Eliot passed a piece of cracker up to Zoey. She extended her hand just like Eliot had. Midnight looked at her and bounced a little closer.

I'm going to stay here as long as it takes.

Lhasa came running toward them, and the raven flew away.

"Lhasa!"

A cloud swallowed the sun. From where she sat on the bow, Zoey watched the Bay darken. On the horizon weird lines of dark gray formed.

"We better get going, Eliot. Come on."

Zoey zipped her jacket. Then to Thomas she said, "Don't forget my birthday tomorrow."

Next time she came out to the boat, she would bring her paints.

21

Dancing with Mosquitoes

In the morning, Zoey yawned then sat straight up. She was thirteen, a teenager! She peeked through the netting on the tent. Brilliant light washed the wet gravel. The sky was deep blue, and the cold wind that had been with them every day so far was gone. Yes! Clothes flew out of her duffel as she dug for her white summer shorts. A bright pink shirt, fuchsia actually, completed her birthday outfit.

"Zoey, hurry up," hollered Eliot.

"Hey, Birthday Girl, I wouldn't go far from the tent in those shorts," her mom said at breakfast.

"It's the first day since we've been here with real sunshine."

"Trust me. Long pants. And here, Mom's Deluxe Bug Dope. Sure to keep all those pesky insects away. It even has lavender oil in it."

Zoey rolled her eyes and stuffed the homemade insect repellent in her pocket.

On her way up the beach toward the fish camp, she shook her head. How old do you have to be before your mom stops dressing you? She would have to put on the fishing gear when she got to Carolyn's anyway. Lavender oil. Whatever . . . Eliot clumped along beside her, and Lhasa raced ahead then circled back to walk with them. Before they reached the camp, even the wispy morning breeze died away.

It was then that Zoey understood what her mom had been trying to tell her. With no wind to keep them grounded, every mosquito, fly, and no-see-um in Alaska seemed eager to get acquainted with Zoey, and not in a nice way. The no-see-ums were the meanest. They might be tiny, but boy, you knew they were there! Zoey lathered up with the oily bug dope but it didn't help much. Wherever they bit, Zoey itched like crazy afterward. The bugs didn't bother Eliot at all. Apparently Raven Boys were immune.

Zoey was surprised to see Harold walk up the beach toward them.

"Hey you two, fishing's still slow. Fish and Game stopped the opening. Tell Patrick we don't need him again. Good news is I hear it's someone's birthday today." He smiled a little. "You guys go have fun. See you tonight."

Zoey waved her hand around her head at the invisible cloud of insects. "Okay, Harold, but when will the fishing start back up?"

"It better start real soon, but that's up to Fish and Game now."

"Okay, thanks. Come on Eliot, let's get out of here." Zoey could see Harold was worried. Patrick would be, too. But it was her birthday. Her first teenage birthday. Her dad would never have let her work on her birthday. He would have planned something fun.

They ran for the tent. Lhasa trotted in front. Zoey couldn't wait to put her long pants and sweatshirt on, and she wanted to get her paints. She had an idea for the inside of the fishing boat.

A few minutes later, she and Eliot were both armored against their pesky new friends. Zoey tucked the paint set into her backpack and shoved the bug dope into her back pocket. Then she and Eliot each grabbed one side of the bucket of shells Zoey had collected and started up the beach toward the boat. Eliot's pack held crackers, a water bottle, and his Legos. Fully equipped for a day of freedom.

At the boat, Zoey climbed up the stern and into the cabin while Eliot went back to his digging project in the nearby hillside.

"It's going to be the best fort ever," he said as he dragged a loose piece of driftwood along behind him.

The cabin smelled like wet wood, but it was fairly clean from Thomas's sweeping. Zoey placed seashells wherever she could fit them on ledges around the walls. Then she organized other shells into circular designs in the corners of the floor. Lhasa lay on the deck outside the cabin door. Finally Zoey got out her paints.

She sandwiched the brush between her third and ring fingers and clamped her thumb on the back side, the same way she held pencils and pens. Mrs. Jones, her second grade teacher, had tried to get Zoey to write like everyone else, but her own way had always worked better.

Zoey maneuvered the brush across the rough walls in fine even strokes. Her hair was down today, just like in the teen magazines, more grown-up looking. But it kept getting in her eyes. She sighed, took out a rubber band and tied the strands back in a ponytail. She tightened her lips with concentration as she filled in the spaces and tossed her head sideways periodically for a better look.

Eliot came inside.

"The no-see-ums found me," he said.

"Do you want some bug dope?"

After he was lathered up, he poured his Legos onto the floor then stopped.

Tap, tap, tap.

Eliot's eyebrows rose. He got up, grabbed a few crackers, and slipped out the door.

Zoey turned back to the cabin wall. Already an ocean of color! Prussian blue, ultramarine, viridian green, and cadmium yellow. Zoey painted in a salmon with alizarin crimson. The fish leaped alongside a butterfly that hung close to a blue-green stream.

She set her brush down and wiped her face with a corner of her sweatshirt. The sky needed some clouds. She outlined places for them, then sketched in a sun that would eventually poke through. A mosquito found a hole in her jeans.

"Ouch!" She pulled her oversized wool socks higher.

The rest of the world fell away. The painting became a stage and the brush danced: touching down and leaping again. Zoey was no longer in a wrecked hull on mosquito-infested tundra. She was a crimson salmon, her tail thrashing the icy water. She was the sun-streaked butterfly tossed in a rush of air from nearby fins. She was a blade of dewy beach grass, bending with the breeze and springing back toward the sky.

Captain had said you have to look inside the piece of wood. See what's in there that wants to get out. Zoey had known he was right, but could not have said why back there in Naknek. Now she understood. It was just like painting. You didn't make the painting. You found the painting. Or the painting found you. She knew that, because, even though she had been drawing and painting for a long time, she could never say exactly what would come out next.

Zoey was five when she won her first art competition. It was for the environmental group Greenpeace. She had used crayons to draw a picture of a breaching whale under a rainbow sky. Since then she had won several more awards and a scholarship to the summer fine arts camp. Each time she felt a little braver about her painting. She could sense there was something inside her that didn't need teachers or parents or even friends. It just needed a chance to come out.

She looked around the cabin. The inside of the boat was beginning to have its own personality. Even though the painting was far from finished, Zoey felt satisfied. She breathed in the salty beach air, the mustiness of the old boat, and the familiar smell of paint.

There was a crunch in the sand outside. Thomas peered in the doorway. "Hey. Happy Birthday."

"Thanks! I'm excited about the party. What do you think about the fishing being stopped?" she asked.

"If it doesn't pick up again by tonight or tomorrow, it will be hard for people to catch up."

"It's been pretty good so far, hasn't it?"

"Yeah, but it costs a lot of money to get all the gear ready for the season. And to get the tenders, the cannery workers, and the pilots like Patrick here. If the season gets cut short, everything we made so far will just go to pay expenses. We won't have anything to live on in the winter except the salmon we've already stored."

"So even when people are ready and willing to fish real hard, sometimes they just can't? What a place this is."

"Yeah. Quite a place." Thomas had stopped looking at Zoey and was staring at the walls of the cabin.

"What's with the pictures? They're really cool! Did you do all this?"

"Yeah."

"Amazing! So these are your paints."

"Yup. I won these, but Mom's been getting them for me since I was little."

"And the butterfly?"

"I thought about painting a no-see-um with a stake through its heart, but decided to go with butterflies."

"But I mean, it looks like it might not make it. Torn wing and all that water around it."

"It's in a tight spot. I'm not sure yet."

"Maybe this will cheer it up." Thomas pulled a boom box out of his pack.

Zoey clapped. She went to the cabin door and hollered, "Eliot, come in and see what Thomas brought."

As Zoey stepped on deck, Thomas snapped in a tape, and music pulsed through the sticky air. Zoey recognized it right away: "The Tide Is High" by Blondie.

Lhasa scrambled up the deck, poised for adventure.

Eliot appeared from behind the boat. He waved his arms in the air, dancing a kind of two-step on the sand to the rhythm of the music. He tripped over Lhasa and nearly fell.

"Come on, you guys," he shouted.

Thomas set the boom box on the side of the boat, and he and Zoey leaped down and followed Eliot with Lhasa right behind them.

"Raven Boy loves rock and roll!" Eliot did a ballet leap while flailing at a mosquito. He landed on both feet, but his body was still moving, and he somersaulted in the sand.

When he stood up unharmed, Thomas laughed and Zoey applauded.

Thomas led them to the side of the boat. "See, it's almost done."

Zoey followed his finger to the name carved into the side of the boat, "Sockeye II." Underneath the letters was a jumping salmon. Thomas had managed to make the curving fish look like it was just about to shake free of the boat's side.

Thomas trimmed a sliver from the salmon's tail and put his knife in the sheath on his belt.

"Wow, I didn't even see it before." Zoey traced the outline with her finger. "That first time we were here, we saw that you had started to carve, but we didn't know what it was then."

"Sorry I didn't stick around longer that day. I didn't know you then."

"You're a really good carver," said Eliot as he examined the planks more closely. Then, unable to be still with the music blaring, he spun around in a way that looked like real dance steps. Zoey joined in and Lhasa barked. Thomas grinned, took out his knife again, and continued carving.

After a while Zoey stopped and asked, "Can I try your knife?"

"I don't know. A knife is like a dog. They know their owners and no one else is really safe around them."

"Oh, come on. Captain said you're supposed to help me."

Thomas handed her the knife, handle first. Zoey bent down and made the start of a line near the letters.

Midnight landed on the rail, bounced twice as always, and flew a few yards away.

"It's so cool that we have a pet raven!" Eliot jumped up and down, waving his arms to the beat of the music. "Kraak, kraak!"

"You know, Eliot," said Zoey, "ravens say a lot more than just 'kraak, kraak.' A guy who does bird research came to our school and said ravens make more sounds than any other bird in Alaska. And they use tools. Like sticks and stuff to help them get food."

But Eliot was busy trying to get the bird to come closer. Zoey went back to her carving. Thomas watched. The song on the boom box ended and a slow one started.

"You sure hold a knife funny. Good thing you don't operate on people." He smiled and put his hand over hers. "Remember to slice, not scrape. You want a sharp line." Zoey tried to follow his directions, but she was distracted by his hand, and she could feel his breath on her neck. Her stomach flipped. He let go of her hand and Zoey turned and looked at him. Those coffee-colored eyes. There was always something like a question in the way he looked at her. What was he looking for? Or was he asking her something?

Thomas took a step back. "Where did you guys learn to dance like that?"

"My mom taught modern dance classes back in Colorado." Zoey breathed in and changed position so she could carve a swirl above the top of the S. "She sang with us a lot too, and I used to love it when she danced with Eliot and me. In the winter we would play this game called 'Movie.' We turned on the lights in the living room so the big window would show our reflection. It made us feel like we were on a movie screen. We would make up stories, and Dad would always put on the same music, called 'Scheherazade.' Mom had a dancing dress that was pink and silky. I had a pretty dress, too, with yellow lace around the collar and a full skirt that twirled around. Sometimes Eliot would wear Mom's scarf as a turban."

She stopped carving and laughed.

"Dad was the audience. He would clap at the end and yell, 'Bravo, Bravo, Encore!'"

Zoey bent her head and concentrated hard. She began to turn her line upward into a stem that she could top with a flower.

"My family never did anything like that. At school once we had to folk dance. They make you stand in a square and follow directions that don't make any sense. My mom took us to play Bingo a lot."

"Did your dad come?" asked Zoey.

"No way. He was too busy." Thomas slapped at a mosquito.

"He was always fixing stuff, either for us or sometimes for other people."

They were quiet a minute, both intent on Zoey's carving.

"When Patrick moved in with us, the movie game changed. At first he just watched. One day, he got up and danced with my mom, hugging her and stuff. It was stupid after that, so I quit doing it, and pretty soon Mom stopped too. It made me mad. I told Mom Patrick didn't belong there, but she just said, 'Oh, Zoey, give him a chance.'"

"He doesn't seem so bad. At least he's around."

The boom box was silent. The tape had run out.

22

A Not So Happy Birthday

The smell of baking met Zoey and Eliot as they approached the tent later that afternoon. Thomas had gone back to his place and promised he would see them soon with his mom and Harold. The wind had returned. It's chilly dampness promised rain. Zoey hoped the weather would hold long enough for Patrick to get back from Dillingham with the latest mail.

As they pushed through the entry flap, they heard the familiar airplane noise overhead and their mom's voice, "It's about time. Go, both of you, and get washed up. Thomas's family will be here any minute."

When Zoey finished washing, her mom gave her some balloons to blow up. She and Eliot had just finished the last of them when they heard the Gambles.

"Knock, knock," a woman's voice floated through the tent flap.

Zoey greeted Carolyn, Thomas, and Harold. They shooed Kenai and Lhasa outside and all sat on the driftwood rounds that circled the makeshift table. Harold produced a six-pack of Coke, and Carolyn gave Zoey's mom the promised ice cream.

Harold roughed Eliot's hair. "Hey, make a muscle. Whoa! He's going to be a mean fish hauler." He turned to Zoey. "And your sister's gonna be up to a full crew share in a year or two if she keeps it up. What do you say, Carolyn?"

"Well, I've noticed Thomas seems to work harder when she's around." She winked.

"That's our Zoey." Patrick entered the tent carrying grocery bags.

"Did you check the post office?" Zoey asked immediately.

"Oh, yeah." Patrick handed Zoey a big envelope and a smaller one.

She smiled as she took them, but the smile froze. She stared at her nana and papa's return address, and then at Bethany's.

"That's it?" she said.

"If you were expecting something from the Queen of England, it must have been delayed," said Patrick with a grin.

Zoey turned away.

"Well, what is it?" asked her mom as she hung the balloons from a string over the center of the tent.

Zoey opened the card, and a twenty-dollar bill drifted to the floor. "Nana and Papa."

She opened Bethany's. A long letter with "Happy Birthday" written all around the margins.

"I'll read this later."

Harold lifted his glass. "Three cheers for the birthday girl. Hip hip hooray!" Everyone lifted glasses but Zoey. Her cheeks burned, and tears welled up in her eyes. She forced them away.

Her dad had said, "You'll always be my little girl." Well, she wasn't so little anymore, and she would be all grown-up by the time he noticed. Maybe he had a whole new family by now. Maybe he just didn't have time for her.

Everyone joined Zoey's mom singing "Happy Birthday" as

she put something that was pretty definitely a cake on the table. “Happy Bday!!!” was written on top in raspberry jam. Zoey closed her eyes tight and made the same wish she had made a year ago and just about every week since. She opened her eyes, blew the thirteen little flames out in one breath, and they dug in.

It was their first real dessert since leaving Anchorage. Each gooey bite should have tasted like heaven, but Zoey had to swallow hard to get it down. Everyone ooohed and aaaahed over the ice cream. Harold said what they really needed was some *akutaq*—Eskimo “ice cream.” Harold pronounced the word “a-goo-duk,” and said it was made with berries, whipped fat like Crisco or seal oil, and fish! He swore it was delicious. Eliot’s eyes got wide at the suggestion, but Carolyn said they would save it for another time.

Zoey sucked the cold, smooth strawberry ice cream off her spoon. It helped the cake go down but it didn’t change how she was feeling. This wasn’t how she thought her thirteenth birthday would be, with all these strange people, no friends, no dad.

Back home, Bethany would have spent the night. They would have made popcorn and rented a movie. Instead, she was stuck in Bristol Bay with the rain, the bugs, the bears, the slimy fish, and these people she hardly knew.

Patrick tossed something on her lap. A Frisbee.

“Maybe you can teach that raven to play ‘Fetch the Frisbee’—or Lhasa, anyway.”

“Thanks.” She ran her hands over the bright red saucer.

Her mom set a box down in front of her. The wrapping was decorated with fat, orange butterflies.

“I hope it fits.”

Zoey carefully unwrapped the package and pulled out a pink, hooded sweatshirt. She held it up so everyone could see the design.

It said “Alaskan Summer” and had a beautiful, leaping salmon above the words. The fish looked a lot like the one Thomas had carved on their boat.

“Patrick and I found it in Dillingham. Hope you like it.”

Zoey’s eyes filled up again. This is getting to be a habit, she thought. Her mom gave her a big hug. “Happy Birthday, Zoey.”

Zoey pulled the sweatshirt over her head. It was a little long, but it fit. Carolyn reached in her pocket and took out a small, folded bundle. She put it on the table next to Zoey.

Inside was a soft knit hat with a border of purple and lavender fireweed flowers. Zoey marveled at the tiny stitches.

“You made this? It’s so beautiful. I didn’t even know you could do this.”

“Oh yeah. Been crocheting since I was your age. I can show you sometime if you want.”

“One more,” said Zoey’s mom, and she plunked a small, gold box on her lap. It glittered. Zoey took the lid off and inside was a silver necklace with a bright red stone!

“That’s a real ruby for my real grown-up teenager,” explained Zoey’s mom. “It’s your birthstone.”

Zoey lifted it out and held it up. She had never had a necklace with a real gemstone. Her mom helped her fasten it around her neck.

Eliot grabbed the Frisbee from Zoey and threw it to Thomas. It just missed Carolyn’s head.

“Outside with that,” said Zoey’s mom.

Eliot and Thomas quickly exited. Zoey, wearing her new sweatshirt, necklace and hat, thanked everyone and followed the boys.

“Don’t be gone long.”

Outside, Zoey took a deep breath. She could taste the coming rain, and the light streaming around the edges of the dark sky had a strange green tint, as if something nasty was hiding behind the clouds. She let Thomas and Eliot run ahead. A few drops splashed her face. What a crazy birthday! Nothing from her dad, but she loved Carolyn's hat, and the ruby necklace. She reached up and touched the jewel.

The waves crashed louder than usual into the sand and sent sheets of water far up the beach. Thomas threw the Frisbee at Eliot, who ran around the edges of the spent waves as they soaked into the sand. He grabbed the disc and tossed it back in Thomas's general direction.

Lhasa and Kenai zoomed after the Frisbee. Thomas ran after the dogs. He wrestled the disc away from Kenai, turned, and threw it to Zoey. She jumped for it but missed. Thomas laughed and let the dogs get it this time. He walked over to Zoey and held something out to her. A shell—heavy and as big as her hand, different from any others on the beach.

"Happy Birthday."

She took the shell and turned it over in her hands. Both sides were perfectly intact. Dark pink ridges lined the outside, each ending with a small hole the size of her little fingernail. Inside were streaks and swirls of shimmery deep blue and coral on a silvery-gray background.

"It's abalone," Thomas said. "The carvers like to use it for decoration. We don't find them around here. Captain traded one of his knives for some. He gave this one to me after I cut his firewood."

Zoey had seen pictures of Alaska Native masks with the same flashing shells shaped into eyes, teeth, and other features.

"Thank you, Thomas. It's beautiful." She slipped it carefully into the pocket of her sweatshirt and looked up at him.

Somewhere inside her Zoey felt something slip, and, like the rain, she couldn't hold back anymore. Everyone had been so nice to her. Why did she feel so hopeless? Before she could think, she pulled a handful of her sweatshirt to her eyes and sobbed into it. Thomas put a hand on her shoulder, warm and sturdy.

Embarrassed, Zoey pulled away. "Sorry." She wiped her runny nose and cheeks on her sleeve. "I don't know what's the matter with me."

"Me neither. Seems like you had a pretty nice party. What's up?" His face was inches from hers.

He was so nice and here she was acting so ungrateful.

Thomas wrapped his arms around Zoey and held her. Hot tears escaped down her face and dripped onto his jacket.

"Come on, why so sad? I know you probably feel stuck out here and you would rather be with your friends in Anchorage, but I wish you wouldn't be sad." She turned her head aside, but didn't move away.

"I just thought . . . well, I thought for sure there would be a card from Dad for my birthday. I just don't get it."

Zoey let out another choked sob.

"It's just I haven't heard from him at all since we left Colorado. That was a year ago."

Now Thomas backed up a little and separated himself from Zoey. He looked at the sky, then into her eyes. "Zoey, you gotta try and get over it. If he wants to find you, he will. If he doesn't, he doesn't. You can't control what he does."

She pulled away from Thomas just as Eliot tossed him the Frisbee. It smacked her in the back of the head. Hard.

Even Thomas doesn't understand! Nobody does!

She grabbed the Frisbee and threw it as far as she could. It sailed down the beach, away from them until she could hardly see it anymore. She wished she could float on the wind like that. Not caring and never coming down.

"I wish everyone would just stop telling me to get over it!" Zoey shouted. "I'm not going to get over my dad. It's not something you get over. It's something you fix!"

With that, she took off running full speed back toward the tents.

"I hate it here, I hate it here, I hate it here," she chanted all the way.

When she reached their little tent, she threw off her rain gear, zipped down the tent flaps, and thrust herself deep into her icy sleeping bag. She pressed her head into her pillow. She wanted to drown in the softness. Rain rattled the tent and soon the din blocked out everything else. Zoey rolled over and grabbed her stationery.

July 7

Dad!

How could you miss my 13th birthday? Don't you even care about me anymore? You were always my friend. Even when mom was mad at me, you stood up for me. HOW COULD YOU just disappear! You know two can play that game. Some day you will want to find me and you won't, because I just won't be there.

I'm not your girl anymore. I'm a teenager, no thanks to you.

Good-bye for good,
Zoey

She read the letter over, then crumpled it up, and threw it to the far end of the tent.

23

Payday

Bristol Bay is a big machine that churns out salmon, but it's pretty good at churning out rain, too. The clouds dumped water on their campsite all night and into the next day. Foggy mist sagged low over the tundra. It was as though the sky knew how Zoey felt.

And more than the weather had changed since yesterday's bright morning. One good thing was that the run picked up, and the Gambles' setnet once again bulged with thrashing fish. Patrick was back to flying 1,500-pound loads of fish into Dillingham a couple of times a day.

But for the next week Zoey and Thomas hardly spoke to each other while they worked, and Zoey avoided the old fishing boat. She sometimes disappeared into her tent and wouldn't let Eliot in. She worked on her carving, but she didn't want anyone to see it. She still hoped for a card or present from her dad, but every time Patrick flew to Dillingham there was nothing. Maybe it just got delayed in the mail.

One extra foggy afternoon, Carolyn called to Zoey and Eliot as they were about to leave the fish camp at the end of the workday.

"I have something for you two. Hold on." She disappeared inside and returned with her purse. She counted out four fifty-dollar bills and five twenty-dollar bills and handed them to Zoey. Three hundred dollars! Then she gave Eliot two twenty-dollar bills.

"We never really decided what your pay would be," she said. "But you two have been a big help to us. You earned this. There will be more in another week or two."

"Wow," Zoey said. She couldn't believe it. "Thanks a lot, Carolyn."

"Yeah, nice!" said Eliot.

"You deserve it. *And* you deserve a day off tomorrow. Harold and Thomas can cover things. See you in a couple of days."

She closed the door, and Zoey and Eliot headed toward their campsite.

"What are you going to do with yours?" Zoey asked Eliot.

"My bike at home is too small. When we get back to Anchorage, maybe I could get a new one. How about you?"

"I'm not sure. I have to think about it." But inside Zoey knew exactly what she was going to do. If her dad wouldn't come to her or even write her back, she would go find him. She would get some answers one way or another. The first thing was to find his new address.

Zoey noticed a salmon leap out of the water. She scanned the surface for something else.

"Hey, Eliot, do you think we'll see belugas while we're here?" They continued walking.

Eliot picked up a flat stone and tried to skip it across the water. "Maybe they just come at night or something."

"I really want to see them before we go back to Anchorage," said Zoey.

When they entered the tent, Eliot waved his money in the air. "Look, it's payday!"

“You’re rich, Eliot. Better put it somewhere safe.” His mom stirred the seafood chowder, and the sweetness of butter, onion, and potatoes filled the tent.

“When we came out here, I never pictured you two with jobs. Not bad, huh?” She put the pot in the middle of the table and asked Zoey to set out bowls and spoons.

“Sometimes yes, and sometimes no,” muttered Zoey.

“I like my job,” said Eliot, joining her.

“Hey, Patrick, did you hear we got the day off tomorrow?” Eliot asked between slurps of chowder.

Patrick chuckled. “Actually, I asked Carolyn for that because I thought you might like a change of scenery. If the weather is half-way decent tomorrow I have a little plan that involves a trip to town.”

Zoey thought to herself, if we’re going to a town, I have a little plan of my own. Time to find out how much a plane ticket costs.

24 Dillingham

"You about ready?" Patrick asked the next morning after breakfast. "We don't want to miss lunch at the Muddy Rudder." He said it with a big grin. Zoey wasn't sure she even wanted to go inside a restaurant by that name. Another one of Patrick's plans. But she had to admit, it was nice of him to offer to take them into Dillingham for a "personal tour." Whatever that meant.

Zoey was up for a change of scenery, but she wasn't sure she wanted to get back into the little airplane. And she wanted to be very careful with her hard-earned money. She might need every dollar.

When they reached the plane, Harold and Thomas had already loaded it with fish totes. Patrick checked the oil and fiddled with the radio. Zoey and Eliot would share the passenger seat because the back was completely full of fish. Patrick lifted Eliot in, and Zoey grabbed onto the wing support and pulled herself up. She strapped the seat belt around them both.

"I wish I was going with you," said Zoey's mom.

They had discussed all of them going, but they knew there wouldn't be room with all the fish. Peak season, fish took priority. And Zoey's mom had already been to Dillingham lots of times. It was their turn.

Zoey's mom blew them a kiss and then—*oh, brother*!—she tipped her face up and got a kiss from Patrick. Zoey was getting used to Patrick being around all the time, but seeing him kiss or hug her mom still made her feel creepy.

Patrick climbed into the pilot's seat and put on his headphones. He checked to see if anyone was close to the plane, then yelled, "Clear prop," and turned the starter key.

They sat there a minute while the engine warmed up. Patrick went through a checklist. All Zoey could see was a piece of it. He checked off "rudder," and "ailerons."

They taxied down the beach picking up speed. Zoey strained to catch a glimpse of Thomas, but he didn't seem to be around. Like that first takeoff in Anchorage, Zoey tried not to be scared, still she held her breath until the plane lifted into the air.

The little campsite shrank quickly as they rose. The last thing she saw was her mom waving. Just when she thought she wouldn't get to see him, Thomas came running out the door of the Quonset hut and waved too. As Zoey raised her hand to wave back, Patrick dipped a wing, and Zoey gasped. Instead of waving, she clenched the door post. The plane leveled off, then rose a little higher and steadied. They were on their way.

Patrick spoke into the microphone. The engine was too loud for Zoey to hear him, but he had told her earlier that he usually called the flight service station to check the weather.

She relaxed a little and watched out the window for bears or anything else interesting. Patrick pointed ahead. Several caribou, heads down, grazed on whatever they ate out there in the tundra. Their antlers were huge, branching in all directions, but so graceful. Eliot stayed awake the whole way, even though it was hard for him to get his head high enough on the window to look down.

Zoey thought about the crazy summer so far, her summer in Bristol Bay. Just over a year ago she was still with her dad in Colorado. Bristol Bay didn't even exist for her then, and neither did Patrick and his airplane. Zoey sighed.

Sooner than she expected, Patrick pointed out the window on Zoey's side of the plane and shouted, "There's the Nushagak River."

The plane made a left turn, and a minute later Zoey could see the airport landing strip stretched out near the bank of the wide river. Nearby was a large boat harbor, mostly empty, and a string of long buildings at right angles to the water's edge. Those must be fish processors, like in Naknek. Several fishing boats plowed their way up the river, their bows pushing white waves toward either shore.

Patrick had been talking through the microphone all the while.

The plane dropped abruptly and Zoey gripped the door post again.

"Just air pockets," Patrick said, "nothing to worry about."

He leveled the plane off and brought it smoothly down to the runway. "Slick as a banana peel," Patrick said, grinning at Zoey and Eliot.

They pulled in near the tiny terminal building, and Patrick stopped the engine.

Eliot pointed to the microphone. "Can I try it?"

"Sure. I probably should've shown you this before we took off. Out here this VHF radio is a lot more useful than a telephone. See that little button? You push it if you want to talk and take your thumb off to listen. I'll switch it off for now though. We wouldn't want to give a false alarm." He flipped a switch on the dash. "If you ever need to use the radio, the first thing you say are the numbers on the side of the plane. Those are our call numbers. See, I wrote them here on the instrument panel when I first got the plane so I wouldn't forget. You do it like this."

He pushed the button down with his thumb. "This is Cessna N53079. Then you give your location, like five miles east of Dillingham. If you don't know exactly, just say near Dillingham or Halfmoon Bay." Patrick handed the mic to Eliot.

Eliot held it and smiled at Patrick.

"Go ahead. It's okay."

"This is Cessna N5 . . . what is it?"

Patrick said, "N53079."

Eliot repeated the number then added, "This is Eliot."

"That's right. Now you say 'Over' and lift your thumb off the button and listen to see if someone answers."

Eliot said, "Over."

"I want to try," said Zoey. Eliot handed her the mic.

"This is Cessna N53079. Can you hear me? Over." She grinned at Eliot. "What is it they say in the movies when they're in big trouble, like about to crash?"

"Mayday, mayday," Patrick answered. "That's the pilot's code for 'help.' You never say that unless it's a real emergency."

"Mayday, Mayday. I'm being held prisoner at the Muddy Rudder. Save me! Over."

Eliot laughed.

"There's another radio, by the way, a little handheld that doesn't have to be hooked to the plane. I keep it in the pouch behind my seat for emergencies," Patrick explained. "And while we're at it," he put his hand on the steering wheel, "even though this thing helps steer the plane, it also raises or lowers it. It's called the control yoke. Got it?"

Zoey nodded and added another new term to her mental dictionary. Lead line, "real" Alaska, deadman control yoke, there seemed to be no end to new words out here in Bush Alaska.

After Eliot had another turn with the radio, they climbed out of the plane and Patrick walked them to the side of the terminal. They were met by two bearded, long-haired men who looked like they hadn't washed in weeks.

"Hi, John, Mike." He nodded at them. "Zoey and Eliot, these guys will take the fish to the processing plant."

The two men backed a nearby van up to the plane to transfer the totes. Patrick led Zoey and Eliot to the parking lot where they boarded an old gray pickup truck.

"Where'd you get this?" asked Zoey.

"It's the Gambles'. It barely runs, but they leave it here for when anyone comes into town."

They had driven only a few minutes when they reached a long, low building with a big sign that said "Peter Pan Seafoods." Outside one end sat several huge trucks. Patrick pulled up at the other end near a big opening like a barn door, and they got out.

The smell of fish was strong, but not unpleasant. The noise was deafening. They all put fingers in their ears. Inside, long lines of people dressed in rubber aprons, boots, and gloves worked over conveyor belts. Patrick pointed to a belt carrying box after box full of glistening orange fish eggs. The sides of the boxes were marked with Asian symbols. Farther back in the enormous room, Zoey could see huge iron tanks lying on their sides.

"Those fish eggs are called *ikura*. They are the most valuable part of the fish, and they're headed for Japan," Patrick shouted so they could hear over all the activity.

Zoey remembered the trout eggs in Colorado. Their dad said it was roe and used it for bait, but sometimes he fried it in batter.

She and Eliot called it "fishy popcorn" even though it didn't taste at all like fish or popcorn. It was one of her favorite snacks.

"And back there, those big tanks are called 'retorts.' They're like big pressure cookers. After they put the salmon in cans, the cans get cooked in there so they are ready to eat when someone opens them."

Zoey couldn't believe it took all these people and all this equipment to make those little cans of salmon.

"Why is everything so big?" Eliot asked.

"Because they have to can tons and tons of fish in just a few weeks. It won't be long and all this will be closed down until next year. Those salmon come when they're ready, and then it's over."

"What happens to all the cans after they're cooked?" Eliot asked.

"They put them in boxes and put the boxes in big container trucks like the ones parked outside. The containers go on ships that travel all over the world."

Patrick cocked his head and moved toward the door.

Outside, Zoey said, "So when we catch fish at the Gambles, this is where it goes?"

"This is it. There are other canneries and fish processors in Dillingham, and you saw the ones in Naknek. They're in other towns, too. But it works out best for the Gambles to sell their fish here."

They got back in the truck, and Patrick drove through the main streets of Dillingham. The town was a lot bigger than Naknek, more buildings and more roads, but otherwise it wasn't that different. They pulled into the parking lot of N&N, the Dillingham general store.

Zoey patted the money in her pocket. Three hundred dollars plus the twenty from Nana and Papa and twenty more she had brought from Anchorage. She had never had this much money at one time. It really might be enough for an airplane ticket to visit her dad. Across the parking lot, she saw it.

A pay phone.

They got out of the car and Zoey said, "I'll catch up. I'm going to call Bethany. I have enough money."

"Hope she's there. We'll see you inside." Zoey raced to the booth and grabbed the phone book that hung inside . . . Alaska Airlines . . . There it was. She dialed the number and waited. After several announcements and a few holds, a woman came on the other end.

"Alaska Airlines. How may I help you?"

"How much is a one-way ticket from King Salmon to Denver?" Zoey knew the only way she could get back to Dillingham was with Patrick, and that would be tricky. But she might be able to get Thomas to take her to Naknek. And from there to King Salmon was only a few miles of road.

That was Zoey's plan. If she could get to Denver, she could find Uncle Rob, her dad's brother. She had his address. She could stay there, and they would know where her dad was.

"You would have to change planes in Anchorage and again in Seattle, but there's a daily connection that leaves King Salmon at ten forty. I can tell you how much that would be. Just a moment please."

Zoey's mind raced. She'd never traveled alone on a plane before but she was sure she could figure it out.

"That would be three-hundred fifty-seven dollars, if you buy the ticket on the same day you travel," the woman answered.

She almost had enough! "Great. Can I buy the ticket there in King Salmon?"

"You can buy a ticket at the counter there, and they can book you all the way through."

"Thank you." Zoey hung up.

Next payday would do it. Now she just had to figure out a way to get back to Naknek. She walked into N&N and an immense feeling of power took hold of her. Time to reward herself for all her hard work. She could spare enough money for a small treat. Something to remind herself that there was a world out there waiting for her. A world that didn't smell like fish.

She smiled. She was going to see her dad!

25

So Many Fish

Inside N&N were shelves and shelves of fishing gear, clothes, groceries, and toys. While Patrick gathered supplies, Eliot picked out a red Tonka truck. Zoey started to reach for bubble bath, then realized there was no place to use it. She finally found some pretty barrettes for her hair and then decided they needed a pack of Uno cards for the rainy evenings.

When they all met at the cash register, Patrick asked, "Did you reach her?"

For a moment Zoey didn't know what he was talking about. Then she remembered: Bethany. "Uh, no . . . she wasn't home." She wasn't used to lying and was surprised how easy it was.

"That's too bad. Maybe you could try again before we head back."

Zoey noticed Jiffy Pop on a display rack.

"Can we make popcorn on the Coleman stove?" Zoey asked.

"I don't see why not." Patrick dropped two containers in the cart.

The lady at the cash register smiled at Zoey when she gave her the change for her purchase. She was wearing a baseball cap and rubber boots, like just about everyone else Zoey had seen in Dillingham.

Back outside, Patrick said it was time for lunch. Then they'd have to get back. There might be another load of fish.

The Muddy Rudder looked like a cross between a warehouse and a grocery store. But when Zoey stepped inside, it smelled a lot better than either of those.

After devouring the meal, Zoey decided her hamburger was the best she had ever had. On their way out, the waitress said, "I have something for you two." She reached into a bowl near the cash register and pulled out two little plastic figurines. "These are *billikens*. Rub their bellies and you'll have good luck. Extra good luck for you because they're a gift." She placed one in Eliot's hand, another in Zoey's.

It was kind of a baby toy, with a shock of plastic hair on its head and oval eyes that made it look like a goofy version of a Buddha statue. Still, Zoey wanted to be polite.

"That's really nice of you. Thanks."

Eliot chimed in. "Yeah, thanks!"

"Nice kids you got there." The waitress waved at Patrick as they pushed out the door.

Zoey had to stop herself from explaining to the waitress that she and Eliot were not Patrick's kids. Patrick was not her dad. She was not here by choice, and soon she was going to do something about all of that.

Patrick encouraged Zoey to try her phone call once more. This time she really called Bethany, and Bethany really wasn't there.

After they were all strapped in the airplane, but before he turned the engine on, Patrick spoke to the tower again.

"Dillingham Radio, this is Cessna N53079 with a flight plan. Over."

He listened through the headphones then spoke again.

"Dillingham to Halfmoon Bay, one hour en route, three hours of fuel, and three souls on board. Roger 079, copy flight plan."

When they were airborne, Patrick took a different route so they could see all the activity out on the water. They followed the Nushagak River down to the mouth where it met Bristol Bay. All along the riverbank, Zoey could see setnet sites just like Thomas's. Beyond where the river emptied into the Bay in a wide, muddy fan, what seemed like a hundred fishing boats jockeyed for position. Patrick cruised low enough for them to see the white floats of the nets strung out behind the boats like long tails.

A half hour later, Zoey recognized their beach below. It was hard to believe this was their home. The little camps looked so tiny and unimportant. Once more her stomach flipped like a pancake as they dropped lower. A few seconds later they landed on the beach, and Patrick taxied up to the place beyond the Gambles where he always parked the plane. He shut the engine off, and they sat there a minute.

"Did you see all those driftnetters out on the Bay?" asked Patrick.

"I couldn't believe how many there were," Zoey said.

"According to the Fish and Game reports, last year they caught more than two million sockeye each day in Bristol Bay at the peak of the season. More than any other place on the planet."

"I can't even imagine that big a number," said Zoey.

"You think that's big, some years they catch more than forty million fish in a summer."

So many fish!

Zoey wondered out loud, "What if they catch too many salmon, and there aren't enough to get up the river and lay eggs?

I know you said Fish and Game keeps track of the escapement, but I don't get how they do it."

"That's the biologists' job. They have people actually counting fish in the streams where they know they spawn. They watch those escapement numbers real close. Not enough salmon makin' it upstream? No fishing allowed."

Eliot piped in, "How many fish does it take to cross the road?"

"I don't know, Eliot," said Patrick. "How many?"

"Too many!" Eliot laughed as if it was the funniest joke in the world. For Zoey and Patrick it was, and they all laughed together. For a moment, all of Zoey's problems disappeared. She realized that, except for a few times with Bethany, she hadn't really laughed all year.

Later that night, after Eliot had gone to bed, Zoey stayed in the tent with her mom shuffling the new Uno set. Patrick was already asleep.

"Zoey, what are you going to do with your money from this summer? You might end up with five or six hundred dollars."

"I'm still thinking about it."

"Maybe you should think about saving it for college. Or maybe art school, if you want."

"How much are you and Patrick going to make?"

"Enough to pay the rent all year and then some. Maybe we can go for a little vacation before school starts. We could go see Nana and Papa in Juneau."

Zoey shuffled some more. "Mom, what if you and Patrick break up?"

"What a thing to say! Why would we do that?"

"You broke up with Dad."

"That was different."

"Why did you make us leave Dad? All you ever told me is that you fought. But everybody fights. I don't get it."

"Honey, I don't talk about it because it hurts, and because I want you to have a good image of your father."

"C'mon, Mom. I'm old enough. I can handle it. What really happened?"

"Some things are better left unsaid."

"Yeah, well, what goes unsaid doesn't explain anything and I need to know. I'm a part of your decision, you know. It's affected me."

"Okay, fine, Zoey. The fact is, he couldn't keep his hands off other women."

Zoey's mouth dropped open. She tried to speak but nothing came out. She couldn't even breathe.

Finally, she squeaked, "I don't believe you. Dad would never do that."

"This is exactly why I didn't tell you before. I figured when you were old enough to understand we would have this conversation. I don't think you're old enough yet."

"Do you know where he is? Why doesn't he ever write?"

Maybe she was hiding his letters. Maybe she didn't want Dad to find her.

"I wish I knew. Last I heard he was staying with your uncle in Denver."

Zoey's pulse quickened, but she didn't let it show. She was right. She just had to get to Denver and then she would find him.

"Honey, I know you love him, but it just wasn't meant to be between us."

"Are you saying all this just to get me to like Patrick? So I'll give up on Dad?"

Zoey could see she was pushing too hard. Her mom had that

squinty look again, and her own eyes were getting all watery. But, it was too late to hold back.

"I don't care what horrible things you tell me about Dad. Patrick will never be my father. Never!" Zoey stood and put her hands on her hips. "I just want a normal home like other kids have, with a *real* mom and a *real* dad. Not some pathetic pilot who expects us to live in a tent while he follows his stupid salmon halfway around the world."

Zoey turned and blasted out of the tent. In her own tent she got into the freezing sleeping bag and lay there silently. Eliot snored lightly with Lhasa curled around him. She squeezed back her tears.

"Lhasa," Zoey whispered. But the dog kept her head on Eliot's shoulder. Zoey couldn't blame her. Who would want to be friendly to an angry teenager with a big mouth.

The sleeping bag warmed up, and little by little, she relaxed. She didn't feel like writing to her dad tonight. Instead she reached for the carving bag and the flashlight. She needed the extra light inside the tent for her nighttime carving.

Zoey aimed the flashlight's beam on her driftwood and wrapped a hand around the straight-bladed knife. Slow down. Breathe. Pressure the knife firmly but gently. One fine line after another. Together the lines were becoming a wing. She blew away the shavings and examined her work. Cut away more wood on the neck so the bird's head could cock to the side, like Midnight's. When the figure was done, she would paint it ebony black, with a gray feather. But now she was too tired—her hands wouldn't cooperate anymore. She reluctantly put the wood and knife away and sank into her sleeping bag.

She dreamed that rivers of bright silver salmon swam over

her, thousands of them. She tried to push up through them to breathe, but they kept coming and coming. She did not dream, however, that Bristol Bay was about to bring her a new adventure. One that would change everything.

26

Midnight

Fishing resumed, and Zoey struggled once again to get slippery, fat salmon out of the net. But much harder than that was getting some friendly words out of Thomas. Ever since her birthday, things had been different between them. She knew it was her fault. She was the one who had pulled away that night on the beach when he was just trying to help. She felt miserable.

Plus, if she was going to fly to Colorado, she figured she would need Thomas's help to get to the airport.

One morning, Patrick and their mom flew off early with a load of fish, leaving Zoey and Eliot to work at the Gambles. Soon after, though, the wind kicked up so much that all work on the nets stopped. Zoey and Eliot headed back along the beach to make castles in the wet sand along the bank of the creek, where it wasn't quite so windy. Overhead, the sky darkened as angry black clouds spread across the Bay like tentacles.

They had just begun to pile sand into a mound when Zoey was surprised to see Thomas walk up.

Eliot waved him over. "We're building a giant sand castle. Want to help?"

"I don't know." He glanced at Zoey. "Depends on your sister."

"Sure, if you don't mind hanging out with a city girl. I'm not used to being out of my limousine, you know. I usually have my driver build the sand castles." Thomas looked her in the eyes for the first time in days and saw her teasing smile.

"Hey," Eliot interrupted, "Lhasa found something!" On the far side of the creek, farther up from the shore, the dog had her nose pressed to the ground. Her tail wagged furiously.

They couldn't see what it was from where they were standing, so they waded across the stream to get a closer look. There it was: a black lump in the sand.

A raven.

Zoey's heart sank. No blood or anything. Nothing out of place. But she could tell it was dead. Thomas rolled it over with a stick. The gray feather—Midnight.

Eliot knelt and reached his hands out toward the body, but Thomas stopped him.

"Don't touch it, Eliot. We don't know what was wrong with it."

"I'll touch Midnight if I want to," Eliot said in a surprisingly firm voice.

He picked up the dead bird and Thomas didn't fight him. Instead he knelt down and watched Eliot stroke the raven's head as if it were a baby.

"What happened, Midnight? You were the best thing about this whole place," said Eliot in a shaky voice.

Zoey crouched alongside her brother and put her arm around him.

"Maybe he was really old . . . maybe it was just time for him to go."

They stared at the animal that had delighted them with its antics nearly every day since they got here.

Eliot was in tears now. "He was getting so tame. Eating right out of my hand. I think we were his only family."

"That's true. We never saw any other ravens with him," Zoey added and reached out to touch him too.

Zoey looked up at the dark sky. Out toward the horizon it was even blacker. She said in a quiet voice, "The sky looks like something out of a horror movie. I wonder if that had anything to do with it."

They sat in silence for a while, staring at the eerie sky, until Eliot said, "What should we do with him? We can't just leave him here to get eaten by eagles." He stood up, and wiped his face.

"We should bury him. Right here." Thomas began to dig a hole with his foot.

Eliot pursed his lips and stood firm. "No. Up by the boat where he used to find us. We should bury him up there."

There was no arguing with Eliot. The urgency in his voice was something Zoey had never heard before. They agreed and followed Eliot to the old boat. Nearby, was a small shrubby bush. Eliot stood in front of it.

"I hereby name this Midnight's Place."

They all found sticks and dug the hole. Lhasa helped.

When the grave was finished, Eliot kneeled down and carefully laid Midnight in the hole. They took turns covering the bird with sand. Thomas found a flat rock and placed it gently on top.

"Now what?" asked Eliot. "Should we say a prayer or sing a song or something?"

Thomas leaned back on one knee. "You know, Raven is one of the Native spirits with special powers. The elders used to tell us lots of Raven stories. They called him 'the Trickster.' Raven could change into anything."

Eliot looked up. "You mean Midnight was magic?"

Thomas smoothed the mound of sand. "I don't think anyone really knows."

"What kind of stories did they tell?" Zoey asked, hoping to get him to say more.

Thomas thought for a moment. "My favorite was the one about how Raven changed into a piece of down. You know, like the little feathers in your sleeping bag."

"Why would he do that?" Eliot asked, his attention already captured. Eliot loved a good story.

"You have to let me tell it," Thomas continued. "A long time ago there was no light in the world. Everyone lived in the dark. But Raven got tired of the dark, and he knew an old man who kept three glowing boxes of light all to himself."

"What was in the boxes?" Eliot interrupted again.

"I'm getting there. Raven was also curious about those boxes, so he spied on the old man. He saw that the man had a beautiful daughter who went to a creek every day to get water. So, Raven changed into a tiny piece of down and floated on the water. The next time the daughter came, she scooped the down up with the water and drank it. Magically, she became pregnant and gave birth to a Raven Boy."

Zoey laughed and Thomas gave her a grin. "The old man loved his grandson, the Raven Boy. He spoiled him and let him do anything he wanted. It didn't take long for the Raven Boy to trick the old man into letting him open his special boxes. When he opened the first one, all the stars escaped into the night sky."

"Cool," said Eliot, "Raven Boy made the stars!"

"But he wasn't finished yet. When Raven Boy opened the second box, the moon soared out and joined the stars. Finally, Raven

Boy opened the third box, and the sun flew up into the sky, bringing daylight into the world. In the end, Raven Boy turned back into a raven and flew up into the sky with the sun."

Eliot was quiet, but smiling.

"Guess I better keep my eye on *our* Raven Boy," said Zoey looking hard at Eliot but with a big smile on her face. "I better not catch you opening any of my boxes."

Eliot looked at Thomas. "I knew Midnight was special," he said quietly.

Zoey glanced out at the Bay. Whitecaps covered the surface and there were no fishing boats in sight. She could see dark sheets of rain moving in.

"We better get back. Thanks, Thomas."

Thomas pulled Zoey's hood back over her head. "Sorry about Midnight. I told Harold I'd help him mend the net this afternoon, if this wind settles down." He turned and trotted away down the beach.

"Good-bye, little raven." Eliot raised his hand then turned away.

As they bent into the wind, Zoey cinched her hood tighter. The sand swirled around them forcing them to close their eyes. Good thing they knew the way home. This wind was stronger than anything Zoey had felt in Bristol Bay before. She would be glad when her mom and Patrick returned. She was worried about them flying in a storm.

As they approached the tent platforms, Zoey could tell something was wrong. She could see one of the lines that held down the big tent's awning had snapped loose. It flapped wildly and slapped the support poles angrily. If she didn't do something fast, the whole thing might collapse. But getting hold of it without getting hit was the challenge.

The loose line smacked the tent platform. It looked and sounded like a bullwhip, and the business end was flying right at them.

"Eliot, watch out!"

27

Japanese Typhoon

Zoey yanked Eliot back and the line whizzed past, missing their heads by inches.

Great! she thought. *Why is Patrick always gone just when we need him?*

But she knew she couldn't wait for her mom and him to return. In this wind, she figured the whole tent could collapse if she couldn't get it tied down right. Zoey slipped out of her jacket and waited for her chance between gusts. When the line went momentarily slack, she rushed forward. Using her jacket, she pressed the loose end of the line into the corner of the tent and held it there. Then she retied it to the stake using a knot Thomas had shown her called a clove hitch.

The tent secured, she held the flap open for Lhasa and Eliot, then followed them and tied that line down to the platform. Inside, the wind whistled under the floor. Lhasa stretched herself out with her head on her paws, but her ears twitched with every creak and groan of the tent.

"What should we do?" Eliot said, jumping on the sleeping bags.

It was chilly in the tent, so Zoey put her jacket back on. "We just need to wait here until Mom and Patrick get back. How about we write letters?"

Zoey found her mom's stationery and she and Eliot settled around the table. The sides of the tent snapped in and out. Zoey hoped her knot was holding, but she didn't want to go outside again to look. She could hear the waves crash loudly on the beach, and she wondered again if it was safe enough for Patrick to fly in this kind of weather.

As if reading her mind, the tent quaked like a giant kite trying to leave the ground. Eliot made one of his "Oh boy, this is cool" faces and said, "Wow, big storm."

"It's okay, Eliot. I bet it blows itself out real soon."

Zoey hoped it was true. To keep herself from worrying, she started a letter.

July 21
Dear Dad,

Sorry I haven't written in so long. It's hard to write letters that I can't send. If you'd write just once, I would have your address and then I'd know you were listening. Don't worry. I'm saving them for you. Maybe I'll just have to bring them when I finally come to visit.

We've been really busy out here. I'm still working on the setnet, and Eliot is still helping to pick up stray fish and deliver food. It's really windy today, so there is no fishing, but we . . .

Suddenly, the tent made a strange sort of buzzing noise. Zoey wondered if it was possible for it to rip off its foundation and fly away with them inside like Dorothy's house in *The Wizard of Oz.*

. . . are safe inside the tent. Don't worry, Mom and Patrick flew to Dillingham this morning with a load of fish, but they should be back any minute.

Oh, I don't think I told you about our pet raven, Midnight. He was really cool. Eliot even got him to eat out of his hand. But he died. We found him just a little while ago on the beach. I am really sad he's gone. This place won't be the same without him.

By this time the wind was blowing so hard, Zoey couldn't hear the waves crashing anymore. She wished it would be over. She tried to concentrate on her letter.

Fishing hasn't been much fun lately. I liked it when Thomas and I could joke around, but now everyone's worried about money and we have to catch every last fish and Thomas and I kind of got into a fight...

The sound of ripping fabric cut through the wailing wind. It started low, then got louder. *woooOOOOOOSHHKHKHKHKHKCH!*

Eliot grabbed Zoey's arm. She dropped the letter and they both jumped up and ran for the doorway. Zoey unzipped the door and pulled the flap back just in time to see their pup tent cartwheel up the beach toward the tundra and disappear in a squall of swirling sand.

Before she could react, a huge gust tore the tent flap out of her hand. It thrashed in the wind and slapped the side of the tent so hard that Zoey was afraid the big zipper would whip back and hurt them.

Eliot tried to hide behind her. "Help!" he shouted.

Just outside the opening, the awning shook even harder and then the front poles on both sides buckled and collapsed. All around her, shelves of food crashed to the floor. Lhasa barked as a ketchup bottle burst open and splattered the cooking area red.

"We have to get out of here!" cried Eliot.

"Maybe we can make it to Thomas's camp," Zoey screamed back. "I can hardly see out there."

She felt like they were trapped in the middle of a hurricane. *Were there hurricanes in Alaska?* They couldn't stay, but she was worried about leaving. *Was the wind strong enough to pick them up?*

And no one was around to help. They were alone.

Eliot squeezed Zoey's hand. "Zo, are we going to die?"

Zoey looked at him and knew what she needed to say. "Of course not, Eliot. We're going to be fine. We just have to stay calm and get to the Gambles' place." But what she really wanted to say was, *Yes, Eliot! Yes, we are going to die because our mother abandoned us and flew away with her stupid boyfriend.* But she knew she had to keep her cool for Eliot.

She held on to her little brother with one hand and pushed his rain jacket toward him with the other. "Put this on. Right now."

Then their boots and her own rain gear. She grabbed the little clothesline they used to dry gloves and hats over the stove and tied one end around her waist and the other around Eliot's.

"Okay, Eliot, we're going," she screamed. "Stick with me. Hold on to this rope and don't let go!"

She nodded her head up the beach. Without a glance back, they abandoned what was left of their little home. Lhasa quickly took the lead.

Zoey could hardly stand in the wind. It felt like a giant hand trying to push her over. And the sand was like a million tiny knives pricking her face. The smell of the ocean engulfed her. What she had thought was rain was mostly spray from waves crashing on the sand. The ocean was just a few feet from the tent!

When did it get so close? Will it flood our camp?

A sound like a gunshot startled Zoey and Eliot as they pushed their way through another wall of wind. When they turned toward the noise, they saw that a seam on the big tent had given way and one entire side had blown out. The loose fabric flapped wildly like a tattered flag surrendering to the storm.

Zoey crouched as low as she could and pushed ahead. But to where? She couldn't see more than an arm's length ahead of her. She thought they should be to the stream by now, but it was nowhere in sight.

"Heeeeeeeelp!" Eliot's scream was lost in the fury of wind and water. Where were they?

28
Refuge

If they couldn't find Thomas's place, what then? Maybe they should just try to dig a hole in the sand and take shelter. But the second she thought it, Zoey realized she wasn't standing on sand anymore. The ground at her feet was covered with grass.

They had somehow made it all the way up the beach to the tundra. Zoey was shocked. She had no idea how they had ended up here, but it didn't matter now.

She could just make out the outline of something tall and dark through the blowing sand and rain. What . . . ? She pulled Eliot toward the shape. Then, she knew. It was the old fishing boat! This was the lucky break they needed. Now she just had to get them inside. She stumbled down the side of the hill and Eliot crashed into her at the bottom. When they got to the boat, Lhasa put her front paws up on the stern and they shoved her up. Then Zoey and Eliot crawled up the deck. Heavy raindrops splashed around them.

The cabin door banged wildly. Lhasa wouldn't go near it until Zoey shoved her body against it to hold it steady and block the wind. When they were all through, she pulled the door shut. A soaking rain blew in through the empty window frame. They crawled past Zoey's painting, down the ladder, and into the hold, where they huddled together against the thick planks of the hull. Lhasa curled up next to them.

"What's going to happen to us, Zoey?" Eliot wiped at his nose with the back of his hand. He looked cold and scared. "Maybe the ocean will come all the way up here and take our boat and we'll float away and. . . ."

"Shhhhh. . . . that's not going to happen, Eliot." But Zoey wondered if it actually could.

The wind sounded even angrier now, and the old hull twitched as though it too might blow away. Zoey knew someone would come to look for them eventually, but she also knew it was too windy for Patrick to fly. He and her mom would have to wait out the storm in Dillingham.

What happened to them now was up to Zoey. The wind and rain didn't care. Not about the tent, not about them, not about her screwed up family. Not about the boats or the fishing nets, and certainly not about pilots like Patrick in their bargain-basement airplanes who thought they could fly around this wild place whenever they wanted. The silly pilots who thought they were in control.

Ever since Zoey, Eliot, and their mom left Colorado and her dad, it had seemed as if their lives had been thrashed around like a blown up tent. And now Bristol Bay itself felt like it might get torn up and tossed aside by a force so powerful nothing could control it.

The old boat smelled of mold, rotting wood, and wet dog. A dreary light sifted through cracks in the planking. Water began to pool on the floor.

Eliot shivered and his lips looked purple. He found one of Zoey's shells on the floor and threw it hard. It hit the wall and smashed into tiny pieces. His voice was loud and angry. "It's not fair." Lhasa moved away.

“Who do you think lived on this boat?” Zoey asked, mostly to get Eliot’s mind off the storm. “Do you think they had kids?”

Eliot shivered again, but didn’t answer. She put her arms around him and tried to warm him up. Then she thought of something that might help even more. She got up, crossed to the other side of the tiny space, and brought back the paints she had stored there when she decorated the cabin. In the weak light, she began to paint on the wood planks beside them: a pair of big rubber boots, then legs, then a raincoat.

“See, Eliot, here’s the fisherman.” She painted a scraggly looking face.

“And this is his wife.” The next figure looked a bit like their mom.

“And here is their little girl.” She painted in two blonde pigtails.

“They all lived in the boat together. The little girl had a special boat-bed that hung on ropes so the waves would rock her to sleep.”

She dipped the brush in the burnt sienna and quickly added a little cradle.

“Her dad was extra careful when he drove the boat so it wouldn’t wake his little girl.”

Zoey squinted at the painting. “Do you want to add something?” She handed the brush and palette to Eliot.

It was working. Eliot stopped shivering, grabbed the brush, and painted a stick figure of a boy with messy hair. “The family *also* had a little boy.”

“Definitely,” Zoey said, taking the brush back. “And when that boy grew up, he got married and started a family of his own. And now they live a long way from here in a big . . . big . . . house.” Zoey finished a large, solid square and started on the roof.

“*Not* a tent,” Eliot said with a laugh.

The square took shape, and soon it looked a lot like their old house in Colorado. "And they never, ever, ever ate fish again," Zoey finished.

Eliot and Zoey were both smiling. Then Eliot drew out of his pocket the little *billiken* he had gotten in Dillingham. "Do you have yours, Zo?"

"Sorry, left mine in the tent. I guess we'll have to depend on yours. Remember she said to rub its belly for luck."

"I *know*, Zo." Eliot rubbed and rubbed.

"There. We're going to be okay," Eliot said confidently, tucking his good luck charm back in his pocket.

Zoey closed her paint box and sat in the driest corner she could find. Eliot joined her, and she patted the space in front of them for Lhasa. The dog curled up on their feet and put her head on Eliot's lap. Much warmer.

"Zo, do you think Dad knows where we are?"

"I don't know, Eliot."

"Why doesn't he write us or visit?"

"I don't think he's forgotten about us. He's probably just really busy. He doesn't know about everything that's happening here."

"He would tell Patrick to make a better tent, huh."

"Don't worry, Eliot. *I'm* going to tell Patrick to make a better tent."

"But how are they even going to get back and find us in this storm?"

"All storms end sometime, Eliot, and this one will too."

Eliot leaned on Zoey and stroked Lhasa's head. "I miss Dad."

Zoey made a sort of pillow out of Eliot's hood to cradle his head. "Me too. But we're going to be okay."

After a while, the moaning wind and battering rain felt

almost like a lullaby, and they drifted off to sleep—first Lhasa, then Eliot, then Zoey—all woven together in a knot of arms and legs and wet dog hair.

Early the next morning, a hand tickled Zoey's cheek.

She opened her eyes and saw Thomas sitting next to her. "Wasn't sure if you were really breathing," he whispered.

Zoey rubbed her eyes. The storm noises were gone. A few rays of sunlight broke through the cracks in the planking. She gently moved away from Eliot and closer to Thomas. "How did you know we were here?"

"The wind didn't seem too bad inside our Quonset but when I woke up and saw that Patrick's plane wasn't back, I figured they were stuck in Dillingham. So I went to check on you."

"How does our camp look?"

"Not so good. You better come back to our place and get dry while you wait for them."

Zoey looked at her sleeping brother. "Could we maybe let him sleep a little longer? He's been through a lot." She could feel Thomas's warmth seeping through her jacket into her chilled shoulder.

"Bet I don't look like a city girl today," she said, trying to smooth down her wind-blown hair.

Thomas just stared at her, surprise in his eyes. "You know, that 'city girl' crack I made was a long time ago. I don't think about you that way. At least not anymore." He looked down at the floor.

"And I shouldn't have said what I did on your birthday," he continued, "about 'getting over' your dad."

Zoey put a hand on his arm. "It's okay." Thomas looked at her again, softer this time.

"Hey, when I saw your camp, I was really worried. It's a mess. That wind must have been really strong. How'd you get up here?"

"We were trying to get to your place but we got lost, and we ended up here instead." She fiddled with the zipper on her jacket.

"Thomas, can I ask you something?"

"Sure."

"Do you still miss your dad?"

He was quiet for a long moment. "Yeah, all the time. When it first happened, I didn't talk to anyone for. . . ."

Zoey interrupted. "What was it, Thomas? What happened?" She paused.

"I understand if you don't want to talk about it but I've been talking all summer about my dad. So, it's really your turn."

Thomas gave her a sideways grin. Zoey felt like she could almost see an argument going on inside him while he tried to decide what he should say.

"Well, when you put it like that." He sort of shrank away from her then sat very still.

She waited.

"After all the years of going out in bad boats, bad weather, and everything, it was really kind of stupid. He wasn't even commercial fishing. It was the most important thing for him to bring food home for his family. Fishing, hunting. That's just what he did. Last spring he went over to Togiak for herring. As usual the weather was crappy. He was pulling in a set and the boat rolled or something and he got thrown over."

A long silence.

"He never surfaced. Divers brought him up the next day. Said he got tangled in the gear."

Zoey was speechless. She leaned forward and put her hand on his arm.

"He didn't have his knife with him, so he couldn't cut loose. It wasn't like him to not have it."

Another pause. "I always wear my knife now. Everywhere."

Zoey leaned closer to Thomas and moved her hand to the back of his. He didn't pull it away.

"It's taken me a while to get back into things. For a while I pretty much stopped talking to anybody. I spent a lot of time with Captain just doing the carving. It's a lot better now, but I just don't feel like hanging out with my friends from town like I used to. They just seem, I don't know, pretty young. Anyway my mom needs me."

He slipped his hand from under Zoey's and ran it through his hair. "So, I understand how you miss your dad. Patrick seems okay. But I know you have to do what feels right for you."

Zoey wasn't sure what she wanted to say, but the words popped out on their own.

"I hated it when we weren't talking. Picking the net was torture. Or maybe worse torture." They both smiled. "I like it better when we're friends."

This time Thomas took her hand and squeezed. A warmth rushed all the way down to Zoey's toes. She avoided his eyes and let a delicious feeling take her. For a long moment the boat was her whole world.

Then a new sound. Outside. Lhasa scrambled to her feet and her ears twitched. An airplane!

"They're back! Eliot, wake up! We've gotta go."

Thomas seemed about to say something, then he turned and ruffled Eliot's hair. "Hey, Eliot. It's morning."

Eliot sat up and rubbed his eyes.

"They're back, Eliot! Hurry! They won't know where we are and they'll be worried sick."

Zoey took a step toward the ladder, then spun around and kissed Thomas on the cheek. "Thanks, Thomas. For everything!"

She scrambled out of the boat and raced toward the beach. She could still hear the plane, and it was definitely landing. Thomas and Eliot would have to catch up.

29

After the Storm

Zoey wasn't even halfway down the hill when she saw her mom walking toward her. She sprinted the rest of the way, threw her arms around her, and squeezed. Her mom pulled her head back and looked her over carefully.

"Zoey," her eyes were extra big. "Thank goodness, you're all right! Where's Eliot?"

Zoey took a shaky breath. "Eliot and Thomas are right behind me. Everyone's fine. Eliot and I slept in the boat last night." She hugged her mom again. "I was so afraid, Mom. I didn't know what happened to you."

Then she remembered their camp. "The wind! It blew up our tents!"

Her mom squeezed her again. "I know, honey. But never mind right now. You and Eliot are safe. That's the important thing."

They held on to each other tightly, neither speaking for a long time.

Finally, they let go. The sun slipped out from behind a cloud.

"What happened to you guys?" asked Zoey. "Was it too windy to get back?"

"We were only supposed to be gone a couple of hours, but once we landed in Dillingham, they closed down the whole airport. No one could take off. I was beside myself with worry. The weather office called it a Japanese typhoon. Winds got to seventy miles an hour."

They walked toward the boat. The new day was blustery with puffy clouds, but no sign of the storm.

"Our tent just ripped right off the platform and blew away," Zoey told her.

"We saw the platform from the air. We parked in the regular place near the Gambles. Patrick went to see if you were there. I just took a chance you might be at the boat." She hugged Zoey again. "Mother's intuition." Her green eyes welled up. "I'm so sorry, Zoey. You kept telling me it was a mistake to come here, and you were right." She wiped at her tears with her sleeve. "I should have listened to you."

Before Zoey had a chance to think about how that news made her feel, Eliot ran up, Thomas just behind him.

Eliot and their mom hugged and then she checked him, too, top to bottom, for any ill effects of the adventure. Words poured out of Eliot as he told her about the wind, the tents, sleeping in the boat, and even about Midnight. Their mother listened to it all, stroking his hair the entire time.

Finally, as Eliot was winding down, she asked Thomas, "How did you ever find them?"

"Once I saw the tents, the boat was the only place I could think of to look. But I didn't really do anything. The storm was over by that time. Zoey's the one who got them there in one piece."

Thomas smiled at Zoey. "If you're not careful, she's going to turn into a Bristol Bay Girl." Zoey smiled back.

Together they walked to the forlorn campsite. Patrick soon joined them with Carolyn and Harold along to help. Carolyn invited the Morleys to sleep over until they figured out what they were going to do.

And the damage! Zoey couldn't believe it. The big tent lay soggy and limp across the platform. Everything that had been neatly stacked under the kitchen awning was either blown away or scattered across the beach. The sealed five-gallon totes of food had survived, but everything in cardboard boxes was soaked, and some things like books and the kerosene lantern were just gone. Washed away in the surf maybe. They found Patrick's rifle half buried in the sand.

They searched and they searched, but they couldn't find even a scrap of the pup tent.

Where is it? Did it blow out to sea?

Zoey hated to think that all her belongings—her carving stuff, her new sweatshirt, her birthday necklace—might be drifting slowly across the ocean toward Japan. And what about the letters she wrote to her dad? Zoey's stomach churned. Those letters were her only link with him.

They collected as much loose gear as they could carry and lugged it to the Quonset hut. It took most of the day hunting and digging in the sand to find the bits and pieces of what, just a day ago, had been their home. Late in the afternoon, hungry and tired, they made their last trek and returned to the Gambles. They ate a quick dinner, then Carolyn found enough blankets and sleeping bags for everyone. The guys would sleep out in the generator shed, and the women and Eliot inside the hut. Tomorrow they would search again for the pup tent and figure out what to do.

Meanwhile, Harold made sure to remind them, the salmon would be back soon and someone really ought to catch them and fly them into Dillingham. The salmon didn't care about the storm or the missing tent.

In the middle of the night, Zoey lay awake in one of the Gambles' old sleeping bags. It smelled . . . comfortable. But she couldn't sleep—too many worries flying around her head—so she listened to the sleeping sounds around her and thought about going back to Anchorage. Why wasn't she more excited about that idea?

She thought of Claudia in *The Mixed-Up Files of Mrs. Basil E. Frankweiler.* Claudia wouldn't go home until she unraveled the secret about Michelangelo. Zoey had a secret to unravel too, but hers was in Colorado, not Anchorage. Going to Anchorage wasn't part of her plan. In Anchorage she doubted they would let a thirteen-year-old buy her own plane ticket. But out here it seemed like no one really cared. There were too many bigger things to worry about. One way or another she was determined to get to Colorado, and her best chance still seemed like starting from Bristol Bay.

Zoey sat upright. She wasn't one bit tired. Instead of her problems being solved, they were getting more complicated. And she was running out of time. She would need to work a few more days to get the rest of the money for the trip. And to do that, she had to convince her mom to let her stay a while longer. If she could convince her, she was sure she could talk Thomas into another trip to Naknek, and from there she could find her own way to King Salmon.

It could work. It had to. If it didn't, her dad might be out of her life forever.

30

An Uncertain Good-bye

Kenai's wild barking and the yeasty smell of sourdough pancakes finally put an end to Zoey's fitful sleep. Then voices. Carolyn and her mom. Zoey kept her eyes closed but listened hard.

"You know, Carolyn, it's too late in the season for us to set up the whole camp all over again. Patrick's going to fly us into Dillingham where we'll catch the jet to Anchorage. Of course he'll stay as long as you need him."

"I certainly understand, but we'll sure miss you around here. You're welcome to move in here with us if you'd rather stay." Zoey's mom didn't answer, but blew her nose. *Was she crying?*

Zoey sat up in the middle of the unfamiliar floor. Her head felt stuffed with cotton. Eliot was already up and setting the table as Carolyn poured coffee. Their mom flipped pancakes on the gas stove.

Zoey wiggled a foot in the bottom of the sleeping bag feeling around for her pants. Just as Thomas walked in, she hooked the pants, reached down, and pulled them on without letting the sleeping bag slip below her chin. She was getting good at that!

"How's the hero this morning?" Thomas asked her.

"Happy to be warm and dry. I wasn't sure I ever would be again." Zoey looked Thomas in the eye and whispered so no one else would hear, "Mom wants Patrick to take us all back to Anchorage."

"Isn't that what you wanted all along?" Thomas whispered back.

Zoey sighed. "Anchorage seems like a lifetime ago. I miss Bethany, but she'll just want to hang out at the mall. For some reason, that doesn't sound so good anymore. Plus, if I stay here, I could earn some more money." But Zoey knew there was more to it than that.

"Money! That's all you women think about." Thomas pretended to cry.

Zoey laughed. "Does that mean you'll miss me?"

Thomas grabbed one of Kenai's old chew toys off the floor and began tossing it back and forth between his hands. If she hadn't known him better, Zoey would have thought he was nervous.

"Is making money the only reason you want to stay?"

"No fair, I asked my question first."

Thomas looked intently at the ceiling, as if deciding whether it might fall on their heads. "I suppose I'll miss you a little bit." He threw the chew toy at her. "Okay, I answered. Now it's your turn."

Zoey grinned, "No, money's not the only reason I want to stay."

She was rescued from saying more when her mom called out, "Come on, guys. Let's eat."

When everyone was seated, Eliot said, "Zoey, aren't you happy? Mom says we have to go home now?"

Zoey finished chewing. "Not really."

"Me neither," said Eliot, sticking another forkful of pancake in his mouth.

"Where are Patrick and Harold?" Zoey changed the subject.

"They're setting out the fishing gear," Carolyn answered. "They said they would look for your tent after they were done. The water is still pretty churned up from the storm, but the salmon will be back soon. Maybe a week or so left of the run." Carolyn shook her head. "It's gonna be a pretty lean crew without you guys." She smiled at Zoey. "It's been great having you here. Plus *this* one seems a lot happier." She nodded toward Thomas, who compressed himself into his sweatshirt like a turtle into its shell. Eliot giggled.

Zoey saw her chance. "You know, Mom, I don't really have to go back yet. I could stay and help Patrick and the Gambles. I don't mind sleeping on the floor for a few more days, if it's okay with them."

Carolyn jumped in, "We'd love that. And I was thinking, Rose's birthday is today. I was hoping Thomas would run into Naknek to take her a present I made her and also pick up some supplies. Better today than tomorrow, since the fish might be back then. He might like Zoey to go along and keep him company. I sure would—safety in numbers." She looked at Zoey's mom.

Zoey couldn't believe her good luck. Carolyn's suggestion was a complete surprise, but it was just the extra leverage she needed to win her mom over. She gulped down her last bite of pancake.

"Can I, Mom?"

"Today? Don't you think you need a day to rest?"

"Mom, I'm fine."

Zoey's mom held up both hands. "I know when I'm outnumbered. Have you guys been plotting this?" She laughed. "Anyway, I guess skiff rides are no big deal for Zoey anymore."

"I want to go! All I remember from last time is Zoey's drawing," Eliot broke in.

Zoey's mom grabbed Eliot by the shoulders and bent her face into his mussed hair. "Sorry, buddy, but I need you in Anchorage with me, and that's that.

"No fair!" Eliot made his best pouty face.

"Zoey, first I have to talk to Patrick and make sure it's okay with him. Come on, let's help Carolyn get this place cleaned up. Then we can head over to the campsite and start working."

"What's Rose's present?" Zoey rolled up the sleeping bag.

"Oh, just a scarf I crocheted." Carolyn reached in a drawer and pulled out a pretty white scarf. She handed it to Zoey.

Zoey slid her hands over the delicate blue flowers skillfully stitched into each end. "Wow! This is so cool! They look like real forget-me-nots, even the yellow center. Rose will love it."

"I still haven't had a chance to show you how to crochet, have I? Next summer maybe?"

Zoey thought about that. Where would she be in a year?

"Sounds good to me," she answered. She was tying the sleeping bag roll when the door opened and in stepped Patrick with a bundle in his arms.

The pup tent!

"Harold and I checked up beyond the old boat and noticed a tent pole sticking out of some bushes. Good thing the door netting was zipped up tight. A bunch of stuff was still inside, including this." He grinned and handed Zoey a slightly soggy sleeping bag. "Another good reason to keep your tent closed. Good job, you two!"

"Anything else in there?" Zoey grabbed the tent. The zipper was stuck so Patrick helped her. After a few tugs, it opened and Zoey felt around inside until she found what she was looking for. She didn't want to draw attention to either the rain-soaked letters or the little carving bag, so she smiled and said, "It's all here," before tucking them into her sweater.

Harold walked in looking rushed. "You are a lucky bunch. Can't believe how much you found. Sorry I can't help you set it back up. Quick cup of coffee and then I gotta go down and work on the next set."

"No problem, Harold," said Patrick. "I'm going to take the kids and their mom over to Dillingham to catch the jet home. Then I'll patch the tent and finish the season with you. Stay as long as you need."

"No fair!" yelled Eliot. He threw a sugar cube at Zoey. "You get to do all the good stuff." Then to Patrick he said, "Why does Zoey get to stay here if I don't?"

Patrick wrinkled his nose and knit his eyebrows. "Who says *Zoey* gets to stay?"

"Zoey wants to stay here with you and help the Gambles until the end of the season," her mom explained.

Zoey turned and faced Patrick directly. "I'd like to keep working if you say it's okay."

Patrick looked shocked, but let out a laugh. "Well, I guess I shouldn't be surprised when the 'I'm-not-going' girl says she doesn't want to go again."

"I won't take up much space," Zoey continued. "And I can help Thomas pick the net and maybe fly with you if you need company in the plane."

Patrick plucked a cube of sugar from the little porcelain bowl in the middle of the table and sucked on it.

"For that matter, with a little creativity, maybe everyone could stick around," he said. "Alice, I think I can salvage enough of the big tent to get us by for a while. As long as we don't get another storm."

Her mother put her hands on her hips. "You know, Patrick, honestly, I've had enough wilderness living for one summer."

"Mom, can't we please stay?" said Eliot.

"Oh, Eliot. It's more than that. If I can get back to Anchorage in the next couple of days, I can get an application in for a teaching job. That would pay a lot better than the piano lessons."

She went on, "Zoey, you're thirteen now, and you've grown up a lot since we got here. I'm proud of you. You've earned the right to finish out the season if that's what you want."

Thomas caught Zoey's eyes across the table, and Zoey felt her stomach tingle.

Patrick sipped his coffee. "Our food supply is pretty much gone, except for the canned stuff and a couple of bins, and I don't think any of the air mattresses are salvageable."

Zoey's mom stood and cleared her cup. "If you take Eliot and me to catch the jet, you can pick up more food at the same time."

"And you can eat your meals here, with us, for these last few days," Carolyn piped in.

"Thanks, Carolyn," Patrick said, "that will be a big help. We'll bring whatever food the storm didn't get over to your place. Okay then, I guess it's settled."

Eliot started to cry.

Zoey took pity on him. "Eliot, remember you wanted to use your money to buy a new bike," said Zoey. "Now you can get it before school starts and have time to break it in. And it's only one week. We both have jobs to do. I'm going to help catch the rest of the salmon and you need to take care of Mom."

"Yes, Eliot," said their mom, "I'm going to need a man around the house. You think you can handle that?"

"It's not fair," said Eliot.

"How about if Lhasa comes with us?" their mom offered.

Eliot crossed his arms and pouted fiercely, but Zoey could tell the battle was over.

"Wait a minute. I've got something for you." Carolyn sorted through some mail in a basket near the sink. She pulled out two envelopes and handed one to Eliot and one to Zoey.

They looked at each other, not sure what to do.

"Go ahead, open them. They won't bite."

Eliot ripped the envelope open and pulled out a twenty-dollar bill.

Zoey got another hundred and fifty. "This is too much Carolyn. I didn't do that much."

Carolyn waved her off. "You had a hard job and you did real good. I'd take you back anytime." She looked at Eliot. "And as for you, young man, next year we'll show you how to pick that net."

Both Zoey and Eliot thanked her and slipped the money in their pockets.

Outside the sky was clear. The only signs of the storm were a chill in the wind and a scattering of whitecaps on the bay. Zoey caught up with her mom, who wrapped an arm around her as Eliot sped ahead toward their old campsite.

"What time is Thomas picking you up for the run to Naknek?" Zoey's mom pulled Zoey's hat down over her ears.

"As soon as we get the camp sorted out and you and Patrick take off, I think." She pushed her hat back up. They watched Harold carry the raft down to the shore.

"Better get a move on if you're going to catch that tide," Harold yelled. "I'm expecting my work crew back tonight." He moved off toward the setnet, the raft bouncing with each step. Still facing the watery expanse of Bristol Bay, he called, "If you pick up some more ice cream, I won't complain."

Zoey smiled.

Later that morning, Zoey once again watched Patrick and her mom load the plane. Lhasa sat in the back with Eliot. Zoey would miss her. She'd miss Eliot and her mom, too. This time Zoey would be the only one standing on the beach waving good-bye.

She hoped she was doing the right thing staying behind. It was all happening so fast now. What would her mom think when she found out she'd taken off for Colorado? What would Patrick do?

But she couldn't think about that now. If she did, she might chicken out. And then she might never find her dad.

The engine whirred to life and she jumped up and down waving her arms in the air as the plane taxied down the beach and lifted off. The tiny yellow speck disappeared over the horizon. The storm clouds were gone. The sky was cornflower blue.

31

Dad

This time the skiff ride across the Bay seemed like no big deal to Zoey. Of course, the weather was better than their last crossing—not as rough, and, for now, no rain. Zoey was surprised at how many more driftnet boats there were. At least fifty within a mile or two, and she knew there were lots more she couldn't see.

But Zoey's mind was on other things. She had stuffed as much as she could into her little backpack, in case everything worked and she really did end up on a jet to Colorado. She had packed a change of clothes, her birthday sweatshirt, the hat from Carolyn, her carving set, and the dried-out letters. She patted her chest and felt her necklace under her shirt. Finally, she made sure Thomas's abalone shell was stashed safely in a pocket.

The skiff engine was too noisy for much conversation with Thomas, and they both kept their eyes on the water. But Zoey felt relaxed. Their silences didn't feel awkward anymore. What would it be like not seeing him every day? She hadn't really tried to imagine that.

The closer they got to Naknek, the more she wondered if she was doing the right thing. Ever since she, her mom, and Eliot had arrived in Anchorage, Zoey had focused all her energy on somehow recapturing their old life in Colorado. Now she wasn't sure if that was even what she wanted. She looked at the waves shooting from the skiff's propeller. They were big and intense at first, but they shrank as they rolled out toward the faraway shores, until finally, they melted into the vastness of Bristol Bay.

Zoey's old life was starting to feel like those waves. So powerful when she was back there in the middle of it, but slipping away now, smaller and smaller, into the past.

Like before, Thomas beached the skiff in front of Roy and Clara's. Only this time no one was around. "Probably in town," Thomas said.

He waved down a big truck that lumbered along the beach and chatted with the driver, obviously someone he knew. *Did everyone know everyone here?* After a minute or two he and Zoey climbed in the back and sandwiched themselves between totes of salmon. Zoey let herself lean lightly against Thomas's back and he didn't move away.

The driver pulled into the Naknek Trading Company and Zoey and Thomas hopped out. As Thomas took out his list, Zoey eyed the pay phone and told him she'd meet him inside the store. She still hadn't told Thomas about her plan. She was afraid he would try to talk her out of it, or maybe even stop her. She had decided to call her uncle before she bought the plane ticket. She wasn't sure if she would tell Uncle Ron she was coming, but she at least wanted to make sure he was home before she showed up on his doorstep. His house would be the best place to start looking for her dad.

Also, when the time came, she could tell Thomas that someone would meet her at the airport when she got to Colorado. That might help convince him.

Zoey dialed the number for information and waited.

"Yes, I need the phone number for Ron Morley please. In Denver." She waited. It was chilly in the phone booth. The wind had picked up and a little rain dripped off the roof.

The operator read the number and asked, "Would you like me to connect you?"

Zoey pawed through her pack for a pen and paper, but gave up.

"Yes, please."

"One moment."

Zoey's heart was in her throat. What would she say if some-one picked up?

"Hi," said a strange voice. It sounded like a little boy.

"Is Ron there?"

The boy hollered, "Uncle Ron, it's for you."

Zoey was puzzled. Who could that be? She and Eliot were the only kids in the family as far as she knew.

Zoey wanted to hang up. If she did, no one would know she had called. But she also wouldn't get the answer to the questions that had haunted her for so long. She resisted and held the phone tighter.

"Hello, Ron here."

"Uncle Ron?"

Silence.

"Uncle Ron?" Pause.

"Zoey? Is that you?"

"Yes, it's me! How are you?"

"Oh, about the same as always. But this is a big surprise. Where are you calling from? Are you in Anchorage?"

"No, we're in Bristol Bay now."

"Where in the heck is Bristol Bay?"

"Way out west on the edge of Alaska. Almost to Japan."

"Japan?! Well, that's a heckuva long ways away."

"Uncle Ron, I'm calling because I'm trying to find my dad. I haven't heard from him in a long time, and I thought maybe he's been trying to reach us but didn't know where we were."

There was a long pause on the line. "I guess your dad's been pretty busy."

"Busy? Like with work?"

"When's the last time you talked to him?"

"I'm not sure, but I think it was when we first got to Anchorage. . . ."

Ron cut her off. "Wait a minute. You mean my brother hasn't talked to you guys for almost year?"

Zoey was getting worried. Uncle Ron sounded mad.

"Hey, Zoey, I think you're in luck. Your dad's right here. I'll get him and he can explain himself."

Zoey heard her uncle call out, "James, it's for you. Get your butt over here!"

She heard muffled sounds, the phone changing hands. Zoey felt like her skin was stretched so tight around her she could barely breath.

Suddenly, Thomas was there, knocking on the pay-phone window. "Bethany?" he mouthed.

Zoey nodded and held up a finger for him to wait. At the same time, she heard the voice she had been waiting for all this time.

"H'llo."

He said it just the way he always used to answer the phone back home. Without the "e," like he was in a big hurry and didn't have time to say the whole word.

"Dad? Hi. It's me, Zoey."

"Zoey! Is that really you? What a surprise!"

The voice in the receiver was both familiar and strange.

Zoey felt the words she had thought about for so long pour out of her. "Why haven't you written, Dad? Or called? We moved to Bristol Bay and I was worried you didn't know where we were. . . ."

"Whoa, whoa, whoa. Slow down. I haven't talked to you in a long time. Back up. How are you? And what's this Bay you're at?"

But Zoey didn't want to explain all that now. "I told you all about it in my letters. I wrote you a bunch. But after the first one came back, I didn't know where to send the rest. But I saved them all so I can give them to you when I see you."

"Sorry about the mail. I moved a while back. Must not have given them the new address. But I'm glad to hear you're a better letter writer than your old dad. I don't write much. Never have. But there are lots of things I've wanted to tell you, Zoey. Things have really changed for me." Now he sounded excited.

"I got married! Katie's her name and she's got two kids about the same age as you and Eliot. That kid that answered? That's Spencer, my new stepson. Today's his seventh birthday. Everyone's over here having a party."

Zoey thought about her own thirteenth birthday party. Her dad didn't even send a card.

"And guess what? We've got another one on the way. A baby. You're going to have a little sister in September, Zoey! Can you believe it?"

No, she couldn't believe it. Zoey had gone totally numb. As if she had fallen under the icy water at the fish net. She couldn't move. Couldn't breathe. She felt like she might die. Why did she ever imagine her dad missed her? He would have figured out some way to write or call if he had.

"Zoey, you still there? Zoey?"

But Zoey still couldn't find any air to answer him.

"Hey, I'm sorry. It's just that everything happened pretty fast. I had to find a new job, and then I met Katie. I don't know where the time's gone. Zoey?"

"That's great, Dad," Zoey's own voice sounded foreign to her. There was no life left in it. "I'm really happy for you." But she didn't sound happy.

"You have to come visit us when the baby gets here. Eliot too. I'd love to see you and for you to meet Katie and the kids."

There was a loud cry in the background.

"Oops! Got a little crisis here. Gotta go. But hey, thanks for calling. Say 'hi' to Eliot for me. Give him a hug. I'll write soon. Just as soon as I can. Love you. Bye."

"Bye, Dad."

But he was already gone, leaving nothing but an angry dial tone. Zoey hung up the phone and stood frozen in place. She felt nauseous, like she was seasick on a lurching skiff.

Thomas pushed open the pay-phone door. "Was that your dad?"

Zoey nodded mutely.

"I thought you were calling Bethany?" He wasn't accusing her. She could see he was just confused. He took her hand and led her to a log next to the phone booth. They sat, and she buried her face in his sweatshirt. Almost immediately, she felt her shoulders shake and the tears start.

Zoey wanted to talk to Thomas, but she couldn't. Not yet. She couldn't face trying to explain her feelings. Or her stupid plan. They sat close together on the log and stared out at the Naknek River.

When the tears stopped, Zoey wiped her face with the back of her jacket sleeve and sniffed. Thomas found a wadded-up tissue in his pocket and held it out. "Sorry, it's all I have."

Zoey took it and blew her nose. "I'm just kind of in shock. My dad, he's . . . he's already married again! And his new wife has two kids just like Eliot and me. And now she's pregnant! I think he hardly remembered us."

She kicked at the gravel. "And the worst part is that I came here today because I was actually planning to fly to Denver to find him. How stupid am I?"

"Denver?"

"I figured I could get you to drive me to the airport in King Salmon. I have enough money for the ticket and I thought if I went there and found him—talked to him—he would explain everything and it would all make sense. And maybe he would even come to Alaska to be closer to us, or at least for a visit or something. I don't know. I didn't really get that far with the plan."

Zoey blew her nose again. "I'm such a mess."

"Fishing is messy work." Thomas winked at her.

Zoey didn't smile.

"Look, Zoey, you're not a mess. You've had a lot to deal with."

"Yeah, but so have you. You lost your dad too. You *really* lost him. But you don't go around crying and making crazy, stupid plans."

"You haven't known me that long. I've done plenty of stupid things since Dad died. When we talked about it before I didn't tell you, but in the beginning I was real angry. I thought it was so unfair. Why did it happen to me? What did I do? I got in the habit of punching things. Not people, just walls and doors and stuff. And I would yell at Kenai when he wasn't doing anything. I already told you I didn't want to be around my friends. I kind of lost it."

Silence.

Thomas shook his head. "It took me a long time to see it wasn't just about me. I wasn't the only one who lost someone. Mom, Harold, Captain, all Dad's friends. They all lost him and they all hurt."

Zoey didn't know what to say to that.

"You really punched a wall?" Zoey couldn't help but smile at the thought of a fight between Thomas and a wall.

"More than one. I was lucky I didn't break my hand," he smiled too, then flashed a full grin. He squeezed Zoey's shoulders and kissed her forehead.

"All right, enough moping. On your feet. Let's go give Rose her gift. Then we can hit the store and grab a little ice cream for the trip back. I'll call Captain and see if he can come and get us." He went to the pay phone.

A little later, Captain pulled up. But there was someone else in the front seat. It was Patrick! What was he doing here? She gave Thomas a look that asked him what was going on, but Thomas just shrugged. Then, as if he knew the rest of what she was thinking, he put two fingers to his lips and made a motion like he was zipping them shut.

Patrick was already out of the truck. "Hey guys! Didn't want to miss you."

"Hey, where'd you come from?" Zoey was surprised to find she was actually happy to see him.

Patrick hadn't come just for Zoey. He explained he'd landed in Naknek on his way back from Dillingham so he could meet with another fisherman to talk about using his airplane next spring for a different kind of fishing. They used planes to spot big schools of herring.

"I might make double what I made this summer in just a few days. There's big money in herring. The trick is to avoid collisions with the other planes. It gets to be a real zoo up there."

He put his hand out to help Zoey climb into the truck as if he were welcoming royalty. “Ladies first. See, Thomas, you have to be a gentleman with these city girls.”

“I guess you know about that, Patrick,” Thomas laughed. “But I haven’t seen any city girls around here in weeks.”

Zoey daintily deflected Patrick’s hand and pulled herself up into the cab, smiling back at Thomas.

Captain gave her a wide toothless grin.

“Hey there, Zoey? Got any carvings to show me?”

Zoey slid toward him across the big bench seat. “Actually, I do have my carving with me. Not sure if it’s any good though. I’ll show you when we get there.”

Patrick shooed her further over. “I think we can all squeeze in here. He motioned for Thomas to climb aboard.

Zoey sat back as the truck bumped down the road. It was not such a bad place to be, wedged into an old truck with good people on both sides of her, looking out at the big open spaces of western Alaska.

So her dad had a new family. Well she kind of did too. They were a little strange, but they were hers.

32 Crash Position

Zoey barely had time to be introduced to all the relations at Rose's birthday party before Patrick was shuffling her out the door. He had decided he and Zoey would head back to Halfmoon Bay together in the plane, and he was in a hurry.

"In Dillingham, I heard from another pilot friend that the fish were hitting hard along Halfmoon. I'm afraid Harold and Carolyn will get backed up if I don't make another delivery for them soon. I'm sure they could use your help too, Zoey. And I could use you in the plane to keep me from falling asleep."

Thomas needed to get back too, but Rose had a chore for him before he could go. The smokehouse roof had blown off during the storm and if Thomas didn't fix it, Captain would try to climb up there himself on some rickety old ladder, and Rose said she couldn't afford to lose any more husbands. Thomas didn't see any way around that one. He would take care of the roof and go back tomorrow on the morning tide.

Zoey delivered Carolyn's present, and on her way out the door she gave Captain a quick peek at her carving. The raven was almost finished, but it still needed eyes. She planned to use Thomas's abalone shell, but she didn't have any glue.

As they were loading back into the truck, Captain returned

from his workshop with a small jar. "This should hold that abalone on. You catch on fast, Zoey. I know guys that spend years, and still have to copy drawings out of books. But you—you can see what's in there." He reached out and rubbed the wings of her raven, appreciating each delicate feather. "These are real fine."

Zoey glowed all the way back on the short flight to camp. Harold and Carolyn strode down the beach to the airplane as Patrick and Zoey unloaded.

Zoey glanced at her watch. 2:30. Wow! A busy day, and it was only half over. Then she noticed the grim look on Harold's face as he approached.

He started in, "Well, I got some bad news and some good news. Which do you want first?"

Zoey had never seen him so serious before.

"What's goin' on?" Patrick asked.

He glanced over at the truck. "It's the Power Wagon. Transmission just up and died." He took a deep breath. "I can't even remember how many years we've been running that thing."

Zoey knew what he meant. She just assumed the old truck would continue to run forever. She didn't really know what a transmission did but whatever it was, it apparently wasn't doing it anymore. "Does that mean it won't run at all?"

Harold shook his head. "It's pretty much dead. Which means Thomas will have to help me haul that line in hand-over-hand every time we need to move the net. We can do it, just means we'll have to work a lot harder and it will take a lot longer. And just in time for the last big slug of fish we'll get this year."

Patrick took his baseball cap off and shook his head. "That really is lousy news. Of all the times for it to go out. Couldn't have waited one more week." He turned and gazed out at the fishing net.

"So, the fishing picked up?"

"That's the good news." He was excited. "They must have been waiting out there till the storm stopped 'cause the last set was huge. I couldn't even get the net all the way picked. Just trying to keep it from getting plugged. Carolyn's been doing your job, Zoey."

Carolyn stretched her back and groaned. "I forgot how much fun it is out there in the mud and the water and the flapping fish tails. Zoey, you don't know how happy I am to see you. Where's Thomas?"

"He's coming tomorrow. Has to help Rose fix the smokehouse roof."

Harol bent to lift a tote. "Better get these babies loaded."

It took everyone to haul the totes one by one up the beach to the airplane, more totes than Zoey remembered for a single load.

"How many pounds do you think we have?" she asked Harold as he tucked the last tote in and Carolyn walked up to the Quonset hut for a break.

"It's a big one. Maybe seventeen hundred pounds."

"Good thing it's a tough airplane. Handpicked for your operation, Harold. Not much of a ceiling, though," Patrick said studying the gray sky.

Zoey looked up. The shoreline was shrouded in mist.

Patrick saw her glance and continued, "Maybe three hundred feet to fly in between the water and the bottom of those clouds, but don't worry, there's nothing taller than Harold's Quonset to run into. Seriously, Zoey, we'll be fine."

Patrick patted the plane on the tail and opened the passenger door for Zoey.

"Come on, pardner, let's get this stagecoach movin'."

Zoey realized her backpack still held everything she had

packed that morning. She was glad she had her carving bag with her. If she had to wait around in Dillingham for the guys to unload and weigh the fish, at least she would have something to do.

She climbed into the plane, tucked the backpack behind her seat, and closed the door. She waved to Harold as he too disappeared into the Quonset hut.

Patrick opened the pilot's door and slipped into his seat, but didn't start the plane right away. Instead he looked at Zoey. "Well, what do you think, Zo? Probably won't be many more of these loads. It hasn't been such a bad summer, has it?"

"Not too bad after all," Zoey was surprised to hear herself say.

Patrick turned toward her. "Before we head out, I want to ask you something."

"Okay."

"Well, I've been thinking about this for a while, but wasn't sure when would be the right time to bring it up."

Zoey was curious. He had never acted like this before—so hesitant. "Patrick, what are you talking about?"

Patrick opened his mouth, closed it then blurted, "What would you think if your mom and I got married?"

Zoey let the words sink in. First her dad, now her mom? She had a million things she wanted to say to Patrick, but what came out was, "I thought you didn't want to live in Anchorage?"

"Oh, I'd keep on flying in the Bush. That's my job. But I love your mother, and you and Eliot aren't so bad." He smiled. "I'd be home quite a bit."

Zoey turned away. Her reflection in the passenger window stared back at her. She thought about her dad and the phone call. He was more like a thing she carried around in her mind. Like an idea for a carving, not something real. Zoey had dreaded the possibility that Patrick and her mom might get married, but that was because she had always expected her dad to come find them.

So what now?

It was too much to deal with in one day. She didn't want to think about it. She looked beyond the window to the edge of the tundra.

"Okay, okay. I can see it's not the right time. We'll talk about it later, okay?" Patrick poked his head out the door. "Clear prop."

The engine whirred to life, and Zoey watched the propeller disappear into a blur. After letting things warm up for a few minutes, they taxied down the beach. It took a little longer than usual for the plane to lift off with the heavy load, and because of the clouds, they weren't very high up when Patrick leveled off. Zoey watched for bear and caribou. Sometimes she glanced at Patrick, but she didn't want to talk any more right now. Besides it was too noisy.

Zoey tried to picture herself back in Anchorage. What was Eliot up to right now? She missed his happy chattering. She yawned as the warm air in the cabin enveloped her. *Don't go to sleep, don't go to sleep.* But her eyes had a mind of their own. The drone of the engine soothed her and she sank into her seat. She gave up resisting and drifted off.

She jerked awake. What was it? Some change in the engine noise.

There was no engine noise!

She heard it roar to life again, but it coughed and sputtered. Patrick pushed and pulled levers and buttons madly. Zoey had never seen him like this before. His body was rigid and his face dark.

Then the engine caught and smoothed out again. They were once more flying like nothing had happened. Zoey let out the breath she had been holding and leaned back in her chair. She barely touched the back when there was a sudden loud clanging, like someone was inside the engine beating on it with a hammer. *What could it be?* To her horror the propeller abruptly stopped. Once again, there was no sound but the wind rushing over the windshield.

Things seemed to move in slow motion. Was this like flying in a glider?

Patrick yelled into the handset: "Mayday! Mayday! This is Cessna N53079, twenty-five miles southeast of Dillingham. Going down."

Going down?

Every nerve in her body stood at attention. Forget the glider. They were being propelled at full speed into . . . but Zoey was too scared now to even look out the window. She looked at Patrick instead. He dropped the microphone and pushed the control yoke forward with both hands. The nose of the plane seemed to point straight at the ground. The green tundra rushed up at them until it was all Zoey could see.

"Crash position, Zoey!" he shouted.

"What?" she yelled back. They had never practiced that. She had no idea what to do.

"On the floor!" he shouted. He held the control steady and stared straight ahead.

Zoey unbuckled her seat belt, but her brain seemed unbuckled too. She froze, couldn't move. For a moment she saw herself from above sitting inside a battered old yellow plane. *This can't be happening.*

Then she was back in her body, which was pressing hard into the seat. She saw Patrick heave back on the controls, trying to level out the plane. Then with one hand on the control yoke he reached across and shoved Zoey forward with the other. She slid off her seat and down into the tiny foot-space between the floor and the bottom of the instrument panel.

Seconds later the plane plowed into the tundra with such force, Zoey's head slammed into the floor and then her whole body was launched up into the underside of the panel. The impact knocked the wind out of her. She tried to breathe, but she couldn't force any air into her lungs.

All around her, metal ripped and screamed.

The plane kept moving, bouncing then sliding.

A deafening screech pierced her ears as they plowed into something solid again. Zoey's face smashed into the floor. The plane lurched to a stop.

Silence.

Zoey struggled to inhale. Her chest felt trapped under a weight. With a desperate effort, she forced herself to speak. What came out was a croak, but she was able to gulp a bit of air afterward.

The breath cleared her head a bit. She gasped twice more before she could calm herself enough to take stock of her condition. She was wedged face down on the floor in front of the passenger seat. Her knees were folded up under her and her head faced the passenger door. The weight of her body pinned her left arm under her side. Her head hurt and she could feel something drip down her face. Blood?

She tried to push herself out from under the instrument panel, but her shoulders were pinned by something behind her. Maybe her seat. Did it get pushed forward in the crash?

A half breath.

All she could see was the gritty floor of the plane, bits of sand and gravel lined the aluminum surface.

Though she couldn't raise her shoulders, she discovered she could twist her head from side to side. Salmon were everywhere.

Some of the totes must have broken open. Heads, tails, fins . . . their bright silver bodies had flooded the cockpit. Now that she could breathe better, she realized she could also smell dead salmon and something she couldn't identify.

"Patrick, are you okay?" No answer.

In front of her Zoey could see the bottom of the passenger door. She knew that above it, just out of sight, was the handle. Could she reach it and get out? She tried stretching out her right arm, but something was in the way. She twisted her head a little further over her right shoulder and looked behind her toward the pilot seat, but her view was entirely blocked by a fish tote and a slimy mass of salmon.

"Patrick, can you hear me? Say something!"

Nothing.

Zoey had an idea. She stretched her right foot back toward Patrick's side of the plane. When she felt it hit the fish tote, she pushed hard, trying to shove it out of the way. It didn't budge.

"Come on, Patrick, answer me." She kicked at the tote again, mostly in frustration. She managed to roll onto her stomach. Now she could put both feet against the fish tote and brace her right arm against the door, to give her more leverage.

"Wake up! Wake up!" Her screaming exploded through the silence, as she pushed with all the strength she had.

The tote slipped a few inches toward the back of the plane.

"Yes!" Zoey screamed. From the pilot seat she heard Patrick moan.

"Patrick! You're awake!" *Yes, there was hope.* "Patrick, I'm stuck and I can't get these stupid fish out of the way. I need your help!" Another groan.

"Patrick?"

The smell Zoey couldn't recognize got stronger and filled the cabin. It was sharp and made her stomach churn.

Gasoline!

33

Mayday! Mayday!

"HELP! PLEASE SOMEONE HELP US!" Zoey was trying hard to stay calm, but she could feel panic right under the surface. She had to get them out of this plane, and quick.

If she could move the tote a little farther, there might be room for her to slide backward toward Patrick and she might be able to free her back and shoulders from whatever was pinning them down.

Push HARD, Zoey! Yes!

The tote moved a little farther. She was panting as if she had run a mile in her gym class.

Everything from her waist up ached, and her head throbbed against the metal floor. A cold, wet salmon slipped down next to her head. She wiped something sticky off her face with her free hand. Fish blood? No, hers! Zoey's fingers felt a gash near her temple. What if she couldn't get out? What if she bled to death? The blood kind of tickled as it oozed down her forehead, but it didn't hurt. Why didn't it hurt?

She couldn't worry about it now. The gasoline smell was stinging her nose and throat. She had to get herself and Patrick out of there.

She gave a deep grunt and pushed hard against the door with her one free arm using strength she never knew she had. Slowly her arm extended and her body moved backward, two inches, four inches. Two more. Finally, she could pull her shoulders and head up and out from under the instrument panel.

As she inched back farther over the seat, her feet sank into the sea of dead fish, but her head and shoulders rose up. She was free! She pushed again with her arms and was able to twist herself around so she was facing the rear of the plane.

It was a mass of shining sockeye, with blue totes cocked at crazy angles. Where the tail of the airplane had been, a hole the size of their tent door gaped open, surrounded by jagged aluminum.

Patrick groaned again and Zoey turned her head back toward him. She couldn't see his face because the fish totes had slid forward against his seat back and jammed him flat up against the instrument panel with the control yoke still wedged in his chest. His face was turned away from her and wedged into the far corner of the cockpit.

Zoey realized that if Patrick hadn't pushed her down off her seat, she would have been crushed by the avalanche of salmon that burst forward during the crash. Patrick had no way to save himself, though. He took the brunt of the load straight into his back.

Patrick wasn't moving and Zoey knew it was up to her to get them out of there. She searched frantically for an escape. The passenger door on her side was blocked by her seat back and more fish. The handle was buried in fish, but if she could get closer she might be able to push her hand down and find it.

She touched Patrick's arm, hoping to wake him. It hung at a strange angle. Broken, probably. He looked helpless, like a salmon in the net.

"Patrick, wake up! You gotta wake up!" Tears erupted and mixed with the blood from her face. She wiped her cheek. "Please, I'm scared. I need you!"

The odor of gasoline was overwhelming now. She had to get out, but how? She pulled her legs in toward her through the fish until they were underneath her. Then she pushed against the floor and launched herself out over the mess of fish. Before she could slide down into them, she used her arms to "swim" over the wet, slippery, salmon bodies.

She almost had it. A little farther and she stretched her hand down through the slimy fish and felt along the door. There was the latch! She grabbed it. With a click, the door sprang outward and a river of fish cascaded to the ground. Zoey was carried along by the waterfall of salmon and landed on the soft tundra.

She stood and looked around at where they had crashed. Tundra, with nothing but low shrubs as far as she could see. Where were they? She wasn't sure how long she had dozed before the crash, but they must be at least halfway to Dillingham.

Another whiff of gasoline reminded her she had no time to lose.

She walked around the plane and stood outside the door to Patrick's seat. If she could get it open, maybe she could get Patrick awake enough to climb out of the plane. She reached up and found the latch with her hand. It turned, but the door didn't move. *It must be jammed.* She banged on the window in frustration.

"Patrick, I can't get it open. You have to help me! There's gas leaking."

She twisted the handle again, but this time she leaned back and pulled with her full body weight, *POP!* The door exploded open and Zoey crashed back onto the ground. Several salmon plopped beside her.

She looked up. Patrick hadn't moved. His shoulder harness was holding him in his seat. With the plane door open now, Zoey could see thick trails of blood oozing from Patrick's head. Her stomach wrenched, but the wound would have to wait.

Zoey realized she wouldn't be able to get her hand on the harness buckle from outside the plane, because Patrick was wedged so tightly up against the controls. So she climbed in through her door and reached across Patrick. Farther and farther she stretched. There! She pulled the top of the clasp and it released.

His seat belt was unhooked, but Patrick still didn't move. Zoey jumped back down to the ground and went to his door again, plunging her arm in among the fish piled around his feet. She found first one pant leg, then the other.

"Okay, Patrick, I hope this doesn't hurt you any worse, but I have to get you out of this plane before it catches fire or blows up or something."

She grabbed the hem of his pants firmly in each hand and braced her foot on the nearby wing support. Then she pushed, hard with her leg, pulled with her arms, and lunged her whole body backwards. Patrick budged, but stayed in his seat.

Zoey pictured all the salmon she had hauled out of the water this summer, the muscles she had grown over the past weeks. She was not the same girl who had kept saying "no" to the whole idea of Bristol Bay. She was a full-blown teenager and a pretty tough one at that. She could do this. She twisted her strong hands deep into the loose hem material and concentrated intensely. Again she tried the grunt, just like an animal. It worked before. Raaaaaaaargh!

Two seconds later she was lying in a puddle of salmon with Patrick sprawled across her. Her chest hurt and her head hurt, and the blood on Patrick made her want to throw up. The gasoline smelled even stronger now, but at least they were out of the plane.

Zoey grabbed handfuls of tundra. She pulled and kicked and

finally squirmed out from under Patrick. Still he did not move. Taking hold of his pants again, she dragged him, a foot or two at a time, away from the plane. After twenty yards, she was so tired she could hardly make her hands grip the material. One more pull. There. She let go and fell to the ground. This would have to be far enough.

What next? She didn't know anything about first aid. And she had no idea where the first aid kit was, buried somewhere under a ton of salmon inside that gas-soaked airplane. Then she saw Patrick's eyelids flutter. His eyes were still closed, but he turned his head toward her.

"Pocket . . . radio," he whispered.

"Patrick! Oh, Patrick." She squeezed his hand. "Are you all right?"

"Don't use radio . . . in plane," he said, each word an extreme effort. "Electrical spark . . . fire. Use . . . emergency radio."

Zoey remembered! He had shown them where he kept the emergency radio that first time they all flew to Dillingham. It was behind his seat. She raced back to the plane and dug in the pocket on the back of the pilot's seat for the handheld radio. Found it! She was about to climb down when she noticed the top of her backpack poking through the tide of fish.

With the radio in one hand and her backpack in the other, she returned to sit beside Patrick, but she couldn't get him to talk again. She hoped he was only resting.

She stared at the radio. It was different from the one in the cockpit, but some of the buttons looked similar. How did she do it before? Push to talk, that was it. But which button? On the side, the one on the side.

Zoey pushed and held down the button. "Hello? This is. . . ."

How was she supposed start? Then she remembered what Patrick had said just before they crashed.

"Mayday! Mayday! This is Cessna. . . ." She had to look at the side of the plane for the numbers. "This is Cessna N53079. We had a crash landing and we are injured. Need help. . . . Over." She released the call button.

Static. No answer.

She tried again. "Mayday! Mayday! This is Cessna N53079. We are down somewhere between Dillingham and Halfmoon Bay. Please help us."

More static.

Zoey repeated the information several more times and listened hard after each transmission, but she got no answer. She knew the radio signal would not travel very far—Patrick had told her that much—but she was pretty sure that any airplane within a few miles of them should be able to hear her.

But what if I'm not transmitting right? She just had to hope it would work. What else could she do?

She stared down at Patrick, still breathing shallowly in and out. Big slashes cut a jagged line on either side of his face where his head must have struck the instrument panel. The bleeding had mostly stopped.

Zoey pressed her hands around the face that had once triggered so many negative feelings. "Patrick, it's me, Zoey. Can you hear me?"

Still he didn't move. "Don't die, Patrick. Please don't die. I'm sorry about all the mean things I said," she was sobbing now. "I wasn't really mad at you."

Patrick's eyes blinked open. Closed. Open again. "Zoey, don't cry. We'll get . . . out of this." His breathing sounded hoarse and shallow.

"Oh, Patrick, I'm so glad you're okay. I got the radio, the little one, and I tried a call, but there was no answer."

"Try . . . again, Zoey."

She pushed the button again. "This is Cessna N53079. We need help. We are down, southeast of Dillingham."

When she lifted her thumb off the button and stopped talking, she thought she heard something in the air. A hum? The sound of an airplane?

The radio sputtered in her hand. "This is King Air N34710 calling the downed Cessna. Do you read me?"

"Yes, yes! I read you." Through the clouds, not far away at all, was the nose, then the wings, and finally the entire airplane. "And I can see you!" Zoey shouted and waved. "I have an injured pilot down here. Need help. . . . Over!"

"King Air here; we read you. We can see your plane, but we can't put down there. The ground's too wet and rough for a safe landing. We'll radio Dillingham when we get a little closer and they'll get a helicopter out to you. Can you hold on for about thirty minutes? Over."

"I guess. It's Patrick, the pilot. He can't breathe right. Over."

"Hang in there. Helicopter will be there real soon. N34710, out."

The plane had already disappeared into the clouds.

The overcast sky turned to a steady rain now. Zoey pulled her hood up and sat closer to Patrick. She held his hand. She could see his chest rise and fall unsteadily. He wasn't talking, but he was still breathing. That was good.

She gazed out at the tundra.

How could her summer have ended up here? Her thoughts turned to her mom and dad. If they could only have found a way to work things out, her life would be so different now. But trying to stop two people from feeling what they feel is like trying to make the salmon stop swimming. Her dad had abandoned them—she couldn't think of any other way to say it—and she had spent most of the summer chasing after him, at least in her mind. And this man here, who tried to be her friend, who loved her mom, over and over she had pushed him away.

And then there was Thomas. He was so different from anyone she had known before. But so was everyone else she had met in Bristol Bay. She was beginning to see what Patrick meant by the "real Alaska." She wouldn't make fun of that anymore.

She heard the helicopter long before she could see it. She stood up and waved her arms. Gusts from the huge blades flattened the grass and rocked the downed airplane. Zoey kneeled again.

Patrick squeezed her hand. They were going to make it!

34

It'll Work Out

The rest of the day was a blur. The helicopter took them to Dillingham, where there was a small hospital. They wheeled Patrick into a back room, and Zoey slung herself into a chair in the waiting room, exhausted.

Almost at once, a nurse took her into a room and sat her on a plastic bed next to a table filled with lots of sharp, scary-looking instruments. As soon as the nurse left, Zoey closed her eyes and let her head sink into the pillow.

"That's going to need a few stitches." She opened her eyes to find a doctor sitting beside her, examining a gash on her forehead.

"Where's Patrick?" she asked. She wasn't sure how long she'd been lying there. A few minutes? A few hours?

"The pilot? Don't you worry about him. He's being taken care of. Time to get *you* fixed up, young lady."

Zoey tried to be brave when he gave her a shot that was supposed to numb her forehead. But he stuck the needle right into the cut, and it burned like crazy! Zoey held her breath and squeezed her eyes shut. Then nothing, no feeling at all. Just a little tug here and there.

Ten stitches later, with a big bandage over her right eye, she sat still while the doctor felt her arms and legs, poked at her belly, checked her breathing, eyes, and heart, and then announced: "Congratulations, no broken bones. Lucky girl. You'll be sore for a few days, though. I'll give you some Tylenol. If you're not feeling better by Saturday, come back in, okay?"

Zoey wobbled into the lobby and sat down to wait for Patrick. Exhaustion set in again. Her arms and legs felt heavy and her head throbbed.

She had been right about Patrick's airplane all along. Just an old rattletrap. Wait until her mom heard about this. None of it should be a surprise, though. Lots of the jobs in Bristol Bay were dangerous. If you got to be old with only a couple of fingers missing, like Captain, you were doing pretty well. Plenty of others never made it that far. She thought of Thomas. What a hard place to grow up.

She picked up an out-of-date movie magazine and flipped through the pages. Fancy dresses, shiny cars, perfect hairdos, and makeup. How strange and far away that world seemed now. Glamorous, but silly, too. What would those people do if they had to face a skiff ride in bad weather, a giant windstorm, an angry grizzly bear, or a plane crash? Zoey imagined what different movie stars would look like using the Jensen-Morley open-air latrine. She laughed out loud.

Patrick finally appeared with a fat bandage around his head. A nurse was pushing him in a wheelchair.

"Is this the girl that pulled you out of the plane?"

"Sure is. LuAnn, meet my guardian angel, Zoey Morley."

No one had ever called Zoey an angel, not even her mom. Zoey stared at the wheelchair.

"Don't worry, sweetheart, the chair is just a precaution in the hospital for anyone who's had a concussion. He'll be up and around soon enough. He's pretty lucky you were there. How old are you?"

"Thirteen."

"My goodness. Isn't that something? That reminds me, Terry over at the *Bristol Bay Times* called earlier. He wanted to know more about the crash. Especially about our young hero here. He's going to try to get in touch with you."

She turned to Patrick. "As for you, flyboy, you need to stay here overnight. Your sternum is cracked and you probably dislocated your shoulder, but it popped back in by itself somewhere along the line. You need to rest for a few days, then take it easy for at least a month. The concussion's the main thing we need to keep an eye on tonight. If you're feeling okay in the morning, with no dizziness, then you can go. But if your headache gets worse or you have any trouble seeing, you need to get your buns back here pronto. Got it? And you should get checked again in a couple of days, even if you feel fine."

The nurse turned to Zoey. "Honey, you'll need to take care of your dad for a while. Don't let him overdo it. He's not as indestructible as he thinks."

There it was again: your dad. But for the first time, Zoey didn't feel like correcting her.

"We have a room ready for Patrick and we'll make up the extra bed for you," LuAnn continued.

"I'm pretty sore, so I guess I won't argue," Patrick said. "Thanks for everything, LuAnn. Zoey, before we do anything else, we better call your mom and tell her what's going on."

It was an emotional call. Zoey's mom was ready to fly back to Dillingham to take care of them, but Zoey promised her they were fine, and Patrick said they would catch the jet in no more than a week. When he hung up, Patrick looked like Lhasa after she'd had been caught with her nose in the garbage. "Bad dog," her mom would scold, and Lhasa would look away, hang her head, and slink off.

When Patrick fell asleep, a zillion thoughts zoomed through Zoey's head. What if they had crashed in the water? What if the plane had exploded? What if the other plane hadn't come by? What will Thomas think about all this? She imagined his deep brown eyes and finally closed her own.

It could have been a lot worse. At least they were safe.

Light snores came from Patrick's bed, but Zoey still couldn't sleep. How come she wasn't tired? To get her mind off things she reached into her pack for her carving bag. She was almost finished with her raven. Just a couple of touches and then the eyes.

She took out the straight knife and rounded the top of the beak so it overlapped the bottom one just a tiny bit. It was an odd detail that she remembered about Midnight. Then she took out two discs, each about the size of a dime. Thomas had helped her cut them from the abalone shell with a tiny jeweler's saw he had back at the Quonset hut. She dabbed a little of the glue Captain had given her on the back of each disc. Then she carefully placed the discs into the indentations she had chiseled to hold the bird's eyes.

The raven was finished. Somehow, with its flashing abalone eyes, she half expected it to take flight.

She stroked the single gray feather she'd painted on the tail.

"Midnight, you're back."

A knock on the door startled her.

Zoey stuffed the raven carving into her pack, slid from the bed, and opened the door to a man carrying a notebook.

"Hi, sorry to bother you. I'm looking for a Zoey Morley." His sandy hair was brushed back like a movie star, and he spoke with a slight accent Zoey couldn't identify. "The girl who saved the pilot in the plane crash earlier today?"

"I'm Zoey. That lump in the bed is Patrick." Patrick didn't stir.

"No kidding. You're the hero?"

At that, Patrick opened his eyes and groaned.

"What do you want, Mister?"

"You're Patrick Jensen?"

"That's me."

"I'm Terry Holmgren from the *Bristol Bay Times*. Just wanted to ask you and your daughter a few questions, if you don't mind. When we heard about it, we thought it would make a nice story, since you both got out okay."

"What do you want to know?" Zoey asked.

Before long they had told him the whole story of their final flight in the taildragger.

"One more thing. Can I get a picture of the hero?"

Zoey couldn't believe it. Her picture in the newspaper! She looked at Patrick.

"Sure, she's definitely a hero. Probably saved my life." Patrick gave Zoey a sideways grin.

After the reporter left, Zoey crawled back onto her bed. While she had been talking to him a string of questions had been bouncing around in her brain, and now she fired them at Patrick. "What now? How do we get back to Bristol Bay? What about your plane? And what about the Gambles' fish?"

"Don't worry, Zoey, I have a plan."

Oh, boy. I've heard that before.

35

Ghosts in the Water

The next morning Patrick groaned a lot, made a few phone calls, and they were off. A call to someone at the cannery resulted in a ride back to Halfmoon Bay for Zoey on a fishing boat that was headed to Naknek. Patrick stayed behind in Dillingham to make arrangements to salvage his plane and to rent a new one, if he could, to finish out the season.

When Thomas, Carolyn, and Harold saw the gillnetter nose into their beach and deposit Zoey on the shore, they ran down to meet her with worried faces. After Carolyn gave her a big hug, they peppered her with questions.

Finally, when the initial excitement had passed, Zoey told them of Patrick's plan to lease a plane. She knew in addition to their concern about her and Patrick, they must also be worried about how they would get their fish sold for the remainder of the season. She assured them Patrick would show up tomorrow or the next day, though she wasn't all that convinced herself.

If Patrick couldn't find a plane, Zoey knew they would have to ferry the fish out to a tender in the skiff, which would take a lot more trips. It would mean higher costs, less fishing time, and lower prices than they got in Dillingham. Although she had not caused the problems, Zoey knew that

Patrick's crash and the dead truck were big setbacks for the Gambles.

For now, though, there was nothing to do but keep fishing. Zoey was too sore from the accident to help much, but everyone else plugged away, and by evening, four totes lay stuffed with sockeye, layered end to end.

Mid-afternoon the following day, work stopped while they all watched a bright red Cessna circle, then touch down and taxi up the beach. The prop stopped and Patrick opened the door.

"What are you all lookin' at?"

"Where'd you steal this rig?" Harold responded.

Patrick gingerly climbed out, wincing when the movement pulled at his ribs.

"It helps to know people. Only have it for ten days though. And they want it back with no stray fish under the seats. Think we can manage that?"

Harold grinned. Finally, some good news.

"I feel bad enough I dropped one of your loads on the tundra. Fortunately, insurance will cover all the lost fish."

"I appreciate that, Patrick," Harold said, "and luckily there's more where those came from."

Zoey still had the stitches in her forehead, but she felt mostly recovered. For the next few days, she settled into a routine of working with Thomas during the day, and eating dinner at the Gambles at night. Already Zoey could tell the sky was darkening earlier, a reminder the short Alaskan summer was beginning to slide into fall.

Patrick had resurrected their big tent, and one night Thomas walked Zoey back to their camp. Before, their conversations had been mostly about fish, fishing, and Bristol Bay. But now they talked about Zoey's family problems. And Thomas opened up a bit about his childhood, first in a village on the other side of the Bay called Egegik, where there were less than a hundred people in the wintertime, and later in Dillingham and Naknek.

"My ancestors have lived in this part of Alaska for thousands of years," he explained.

"Does that mean you're an Eskimo?" Zoey asked. "I know the Alaska Natives around Juneau are not called Eskimos. Sometimes in books they call them Indians, but they're not anything like the Indians around Colorado."

"That's because white people made those names up. There are lots of different Native cultures, and languages, too. And they all have their own names. I think of myself as Alutiiq, but I'm also related to some Russian fur traders, and who knows what else. There's just one thing you really need to know, Zoey. We don't live in igloos." He bumped shoulders with her to show he was teasing.

Zoey laughed. "I hate to tell you this, Thomas, but the truth is, that's what my friends in Colorado think." Thomas just sighed.

Talking about Thomas's life in Bristol Bay reminded Zoey her time here was almost over. What would Bethany think of Thomas? What would it be like to show him where she lived in Anchorage?

Fun, she decided.

The huge runs of salmon had thinned to a trickle. Finally one day Harold decided he needed Patrick for only one more delivery, and they would be done for the year. Carolyn insisted they celebrate the last night with a special dinner. Patrick and Zoey would take the last few totes to Dillingham the next morning and catch the jet back to Anchorage the same afternoon.

Patrick and Zoey hiked up the beach for their last dinner together at the Quonset hut. Thomas opened the door, and the delicious scent of cooked meat engulfed them. Carolyn and Harold were already at the table.

"Grab a plate," Carolyn gestured to the counter and gave Zoey a wink. "The restaurant's a little crowded, but there's room on the couch."

Carolyn speared a big piece of meat, spooned up a couple of potatoes, and handed the plate to Zoey.

"What is it?"

"Caribou," said Harold. "You like caribou?"

Zoey didn't know. She thought of the beautiful animals she had seen from the plane. But she was hungry enough to try anything, and she had learned to have faith in Carolyn's cooking.

Sitting on the couch next to Patrick with a plate balanced on her lap, she took a bite of the meat. The taste was intense—wild, like Bristol Bay—but good, too.

After dinner they played Uno until Zoey found herself nodding off.

"I better get Miss Zoey back to camp," Patrick said, "before I have to carry her."

As Zoey put her jacket on, Thomas asked, "Want to go for a paddle, Zoey? It's a full moon. Your last one in Bristol Bay."

Zoey felt her heart speed up. She glanced at Patrick, wondering what he would say, but he just raised his eyebrows like it wasn't his decision to make.

"Sure," Zoey answered, grinning.

Patrick grabbed his hat. "I'll meet you at camp, Zoey. Be careful in that raft. I gotta get you home in one piece or suffer the wrath of your mother. Or more wrath anyway."

Zoey and Thomas each carried a side of the raft down to the water. Neither had rubber boots on, so their feet got wet. The icy water tingled on Zoey's ankles. She sat at one end of the tiny raft facing Thomas and gazed out at Bristol Bay. Even though the sun had barely set, a dusky moon reflected from the water through a thin, low mist that rose no higher than the sides of the raft. The deep silence made the splash of Thomas's paddling seem like tiny explosions.

The mist swirled in the chilled air. Zoey was about to speak when she heard something a little like a squeaky door. She stared out over the gray water. Without thinking, she gripped Thomas's arm.

She heard the noise again, more clearly this time: a distinct warble sound and then a whoosh of what sounded like breathing.

"Belugas," whispered Thomas.

Minutes dragged by, the sound still present, but the maker invisible. Zoey scanned the water all around them. There! A ghostly white head rose and fell through the surface of the water, not more than three or four raft lengths away. Then another. And another. The whales swam closer, almost within reach. Zoey could hear their exhales mix with the strange warbling sound.

She felt dizzy. Belugas at last!

But what if they capsized the boat? The whales surrounded them, but not one touched their raft. Zoey relaxed.

"Looks like about twenty of them," Thomas whispered. "People call them 'canaries of the sea.' You think they sound like canaries?"

"Sort of, I guess," Zoey smiled shyly at him.

They sat, and watched until the belugas moved farther out and disappeared into the darkening mist.

"Thomas, I looked for them all summer. It's so cool I finally saw them." In her excitement, Zoey had risen to her knees and turned away from Thomas toward the spot where she last saw the whales.

Thomas leaned forward behind her and put a hand on each of her shoulders. Slowly and gently he eased her down until she was sitting with her back to him and leaning lightly into his knees. The little raft rocked softly.

"I better get you back now, or Patrick is not going to be happy." But he didn't put the oars back in the water. His hands stayed on her shoulders. He did not look at her.

"I was pretty down at the start of the season," Thomas said quietly. "I wasn't sure I could even get through it. When you and Eliot showed up, I just figured you'd stay at your end of the beach and we'd stay at ours. I never thought we'd spend so much time together. But I'm glad we did. I'm glad it worked out like this."

Then, as if it were the most natural thing in the world, he touched her cheek to turn her head toward him just a little and kissed her.

Zoey closed her eyes and held her breath. She felt warm all over. She kissed him back for what seemed like forever.

He pulled back first. "When will I see you again? Will you come back next summer?"

"I never thought in a million years I would want to come back here, but now I hope I do. There are no belugas at the mall in Anchorage. And no one like you either." She kissed him again, quickly and shyly. They both smiled.

The next morning, Zoey woke with that lead-line feeling inside. Leaving would be hard. While Harold helped Patrick load up the plane, Zoey and Thomas went to say good-bye to the old boat.

The first thing Zoey saw in the boat cabin was the mural she had painted. For a moment she was surprised by the feelings it brought up in her. She had forgotten how dangerously close to the water she had placed the butterfly.

"I think that butterfly is going to be okay," she announced.

Thomas laughed, then reached in his pocket. "Something for you."

He handed her a perfectly carved miniature replica of their boat, the *Sockeye II,* complete with the battered mast and a tiny version of the carving he had made on the bow. "So you won't forget."

She touched the sides. They were rough, just like the boat. It was perfect.

"I won't ever forget."

There was something Zoey wanted to give Thomas, and she was running out of time. She took an envelope from her pocket and handed it to him.

He opened it. Inside was about half the money Carolyn had given her. Zoey kept the rest for her college account. Her mom had drilled that one into her.

"I learned so much this summer, and your family took such good care of me. I really was a city girl when I got here. Now that I'm not wasting a whole bunch of money on a ticket to Colorado, I don't need all this anymore. Your mom and Harold can use it to get the truck fixed, because I'm not picking any more fish at Halfmoon Bay until they do!" She laughed. "Will you give it to them after I leave?"

Thomas closed the envelope and handed it back to her. "No way, Zoey. You earned this. We'll be all right. It wasn't such a bad season, and I'm going to skip school and go hunting in the fall like my dad would have."

"Sorry, Thomas, but I hate that plan. If you don't take it, so help me, I'll just sprinkle it all over Bristol Bay as we take off."

Zoey crammed the envelope inside Thomas's coat, dodged out the door, and took off running back toward camp. Thomas chased her as she zigzagged between the ridge of high grass at the edge of the tundra and the tongues of the waves that surged onto the shore. They reached the plane laughing and out of breath.

Patrick was waiting. "Time to go home, Zoey."

36

Home Again

And just like that, Zoey's summer in Bristol Bay was over. For the last time, the Gambles' Quonset hut shrank below her. Carolyn and Harold each shaded their eyes with one hand and waved with the other. Thomas stood apart. At the last second he raised one hand in a kind of salute. Then they were gone.

In the Anchorage terminal, Eliot nearly knocked Zoey over when he leaped on her. Her mom moved in behind him, a look of concern on her face. She hugged Zoey hard and whispered, "I'm so glad you're safe. We were so worried."

Next she was in Patrick's arms, but just as quickly, he backed away with clenched teeth.

"I'm afraid we'll have to just hold hands for a while." He rubbed his chest gently.

"Oh, Patrick. I'm sorry." She put her fingers to her lips, kissed them, then touched his chest. "I'm just so happy to have my family back."

Zoey realized then and there that her mom was right. Patrick, Eliot, Lhasa, and her mom were as close to a real family as she had. And the truth was, things could be a lot worse.

Zoey's mom reached in her bag and pulled out a newspaper. It was the *Bristol Bay Times*. There on the front page was a picture of Zoey at the hospital, a bandage over her eye, and Patrick in the background.

"GIRL SAVES PILOT IN FISHY CRASH!" blared the headline.

"Everyone's talking about you, Zoey. You're a hero!" Zoey's mom handed her the paper. "This came out the day after the crash, and the Associated Press picked it up. It's all over the country now. They've been reading about the Amazing Zoey Morley in Kansas City!"

"My sister's a star!" said Eliot with a grin.

Later that night, she felt strange back in her old bed. No waves, or seagulls, or eagles, no popping canvas or drumming rain. Just an occasional car driving by.

Zoey reached over to her bedside table for her stationery. She knew where to send this letter. Her Uncle Ron would make sure it got delivered.

August 5
Dear Dad,

I'm finally back home again. It has been an amazing summer. There was a Japanese typhoon, and a plane crash, and beluga whales and lots more. I can't wait to see you and tell you all about it. I am excited to come visit and meet my new baby sister. But that will have to wait until after the wedding. Mom and Patrick are getting married! I don't know when yet, but there will be a lot of planning and they're going to need my help. It seems like so long since we left Colorado. I feel like I'm kind of different, and that's OK. Pretty good, actually.

Your Bristol Bay Girl,
Zoey

PS I was in the newspaper. I'll send you a copy.

The next morning, after breakfast, Zoey found Eliot playing with his Legos.

"Hey, Eliot, I've got something for you."

She opened her backpack and pulled out a tattered paper bag.

"Close your eyes and hold out your arms." Zoey pulled the carving out and laid it in his hands.

Eliot opened his eyes. "Wow! Zoey. Did you make this?"

"Of course!"

Eliot ran to the bottom of the stairs and hollered up. "Mom, Patrick, come look at what Zoey made."

By the time they arrived, Eliot was galloping around the room holding up the sleek wooden raven with the flashing blue abalone eyes. "Kraak! Kraak!"

When his mom finally got him to stand still, they gazed in silence at the delicate feathers. They smiled at the cocky turn of the bird's head and admired its powerful-looking beak. Only the rings around the beak, where a small branch had once grown, gave it away as the lump of driftwood Captain had given Zoey back in Naknek.

Eliot placed the carving on his pillow. "It's Midnight, right Zoey? Midnight can live here with us now. Kraak, kraak!"

"Just for you, Eliot," said Zoey. "And I'll tell you a secret that it took me a while to figure out. Sometimes you lose the thing you want the most, but sometimes it comes back to you in a different way. If you just give it a chance."

The phone rang and Zoey charged up the stairs to answer it.

"Bethany! Yes, I'm home. The movies? Tonight? Let me ask Mom and Patrick."

Glossary

Alaska Peninsula Highway: The sixteen-mile road that connects King Salmon and Naknek.

Beluga whale: Easy to identify because of their small size, white color, and blunt foreheads, beluga whales are also known as sea canaries because of the whistles and bell-like sounds they emit for communication. In 2008, the National Marine Fishery Service listed the belugas in Cook Inlet, near Anchorage, as endangered under the Endangered Species Act. Belugas are plentiful in Bristol Bay.

Bentwood box: A cedar box made by Northwest Coast Indians from a single piece of wood that is steamed and bent to form its box shape. No nails are used in the process. It is often decorated with carvings and paintings.

Brailer: A large canvas or net bag with a draw cable at the top. Used to move fish from nets to travel totes or from boat to boat during their journey to the fish processing plant.

Bush Alaska: A term used by locals to describe the most rural parts of Alaska, which are not connected to North America's road network. Transportation in and around these areas is either by plane, snowmachine, boat, or dogsled.

Cable-spool table: Big wooden spools about three feet high and ranging up to six or more feet across that hold long lengths of communication or electrical wire needed for large construction projects. Once empty, the spools are often used by budget-conscious Alaskans for dining or patio tables.

Driftnet: A type of commercial fishing net launched and tended from the thirty-two-foot aluminum boats used in Bristol Bay. A driftnet can extend more than twice the distance of a football field. In the water, the net hangs from a string of floats and is weighted at the bottom with a lead line. When stored on board the boat, the driftnet is wound around a large aluminum cylinder or drum.

Escapement: The term used by Alaska Department of Fish and Game biologists for the number of fish with a given set of genetic characteristics that must be allowed to reach a spawning ground before commercial fishing is allowed.

Fireweed: One of the best-known Alaska wildflowers because of its bright magenta and pink-colored blooms on top of long stalks. In midsummer fireweed grows in large patches in open meadows and fields throughout the more temperate areas of Alaska. When the flowers begin to go to seed in the fall, it's a sign that winter is only a few weeks away.

Fish and Game: Alaskans use this shorthand expression to refer to the Alaska Department of Fish and Game, which manages commercial and sport fishing in Alaska waters within three miles of shore. Fish and Game also manages Alaska's wild game. The federal government is responsible for fisheries that operate beyond three miles from shore. The Fish and Game website, www.adfg.alaska.gov, is a wealth of information.

Halfmoon Bay: A small portion of the larger Kvichak Bay located at the head of the much larger Bristol Bay. Both the Kvichak and Naknek Rivers flow into Bristol Bay near Halfmoon Bay, making it an important area for hundreds of thousands of migrating shore-birds and, of course, all varieties of salmon.

Highliner: A very successful commercial fisherman.

***Ikura*:** A Japanese word for the eggs from the female salmon, called roe in English. *Ikura* is a delicacy often used in sushi.

Japanese typhoon: A type of violent sea storm that originates in the Pacific Ocean and can produce winds of more than 100 miles per hour. Japanese typhoons are characterized by high waves, strong winds, and heavy rain.

Kvichak River: The Alaska Native word *Kvichak* means "from or up to Great Water." It refers to Lake Iliamna, the headwaters of the river and the largest lake in Alaska. The Kvichak/Iliamna water system is renowned for great fishing, including the largest rainbow trout in the world and huge sockeye salmon runs.

Lead line (also, leadline): As it refers to part of a fishing net, the lead line is a long rope with small weights attached a foot or so apart and strung along the bottom of the net to hold it open as it floats in the water. In modern lead lines, the weights are sometimes encased in the rope itself.

Lower 48: An Alaskan term for the contiguous United States, meaning all the states except Alaska and Hawaii. Not to be confused with the "continental United States." Alaska is, in fact, on the same continent (North America) as the Lower 48 states.

Merrill Field: Anchorage's first airport. Now used mainly by small planes, Merrill Field was nevertheless the fifteenth busiest airport in the United States in 1984. It is located on the east end of Fifth Avenue near downtown Anchorage. Nearly 1,000 aircraft are based there.

Naknek River: A thirty-five-mile-long river that flows from Naknek Lake into Kvichak Bay. The town of King Salmon is at the head of the river, Naknek lies on the north shore, and South Naknek on the south shore at its mouth. Naknek Lake lies in the western-most part of the Katmai National Park and Preserve, famous for its volcanoes and large bears.

Retort: A huge pressure cooker used in large-scale fish-processing operations.

Setnet: A type of commercial fishing net that is fixed at or near the shore by an anchor or stake called a deadman. Used predominantly in Bristol Bay where the salmon often swim in very shallow water.

Skiff: A small, open boat powered by an outboard motor. In Alaska, skiffs are typically between sixteen and twenty-two feet long and nearly always made of aluminum. They are capable of carrying from four up to six or seven people and their gear.

Sockeye salmon: A species of Pacific salmon also known as reds or bluebacks, found in the North Pacific Ocean. The fry, or young, spend the first years of their lives in freshwater lakes. Then they migrate to the ocean where they stay for up to another three to four years before returning to their birthplace where they will die once they have spawned and the whole cycle begins again. When spawning, they change color from a sparkling silver with a bluish back, to bright red. They also develop a hump on their backs and a large snout. The average size of sockeye salmon in Bristol Bay, Alaska, is six to seven pounds. Bristol Bay is home to the largest commercial sockeye salmon fishery in the world, averaging approximately thirty million fish a year.

Southeast: A term used by locals to describe the southern panhandle of Alaska. Most of the area lies in the Tongass National Forest, the earth's largest remaining temperate rain forest.

Subsistence: A lifestyle that relies on local hunting, fishing, and trapping to provide food and other necessities. Subsistence activities are common throughout Alaska, particularly in the more remote areas.

Tender: A vessel fitted with machinery to load fish from fishing boats and transport them to a processor. Tenders anchor in heavily fished areas so nearby fishermen can sell their catch without having to travel all the way to an onshore processing plant.

Tote: A sturdy container used to hold and transport salmon and other seafood.

VHF radio: A combined transmitter and receiver-style radio used in Alaska and elsewhere by boats and small planes. VHF radios transmit and receive along a line-of-sight path and are capable of receiving marine weather reports and other information. Before the days of mobile phones, fishermen and others in remote areas made phone calls on their VHF radios by contacting a marine operator. The VHF radio is still a necessity in many rural areas where cell-phone service is unreliable.

Neoprene waders: Chest-high, one-piece neoprene overalls with feet attached. Fishermen typically wear another pair of rubber boots over the feet to give them better traction and avoid punctures. Commonly used for sportfishing and, especially in Bristol Bay, for setnetting.

Winch: A mechanical device with a rotating drum used to pull in or let out rope or cable, often used on a setnet. Winches can be as simple as a spool attached to a hand crank, or they can be motorized and capable of moving thousands of pounds. The drum used on a Bristol Bay gillnetter to retrieve and store the driftnet functions like a large winch.

Acknowledgments

My deep appreciation and gratitude to the following people:

My dear husband, the English major, Scott Miller, who cooked and sang for me and read, and reread the manuscript in all its fragmented iterations, offering invaluable ideas and suggestions.

My sisters, the Cheering Squad; Barbara, Linda, and Mimi for their immeasurable support.

My children: Heidi Liorah Wichser, for being the inspiration for Zoey, and for helping me see the world a little differently through her art. My oldest son Zachary, the inspiration for Eliot, who is still sweet and good-humored, and now an elementary physical education teacher, outdoorsman extraordinaire and, as always, a great support to me. Also, to my youngest, Spencer, and stepdaughter, Megan. Thanks for cheering me on!

Naknek residents Izetta Chambers, Violet Willson, and Trefon Angasan, who generously provided local knowledge and expertise.

Peggy Cowan, Superintendent of the North Slope Borough School District, and former Superintendent of the Juneau School District, and members of the Juneau School Board of 2009, Andi Story, Phyllis Carlson, Mark Choate, JoAnn Bell-Graves, and Margot Waring, who granted me a sabbatical and year's leave to complete the MFA program at the Northwest Institute of Literary Arts (NILA), without which, none of this would have ever happened.

Wayne Ude, Director of NILA, and all the other talented professors and fellow students there, especially my mentors Carmen Bernier Grand, who believed in me from the beginning and who, along with Bonny Becker, offered insightful criticism and suggestions.

Kristi Buerger, who took the time to carefully read the manuscript and offer her knowledgeable suggestions as a seasoned, former Bristol Bay setnetter.

Sue Aspelund, former Deputy Director of Commercial Fisheries for the Alaska Department of Fish and Game, and longtime setnetter in Bristol Bay, for her astute recommendations and suggestions.

Michelle McCann, my editor, for her support, enthusiasm, and careful critiques. She made all the difference!

Doug Pfeiffer and the talented staff at Graphic Arts Books for believing in *Bristol Bay Summer* and providing top-notch professional support.

Finally, this book would not have been possible without Dan Beishline, the Alaska Bush pilot who first introduced me and my two children to Bristol Bay more than thirty years ago (and who erected the tent that was later demolished by the Japanese typhoon).

Bristol Bay Summer Discussion Questions

1. From whose point of view is *Bristol Bay Summer* written?

2. In writing, we talk about an author's voice. How does your previous answer about point of view affect the voice of the story?

3. Each main character—Zoey, Thomas, Alice (Zoey's mom), Patrick, and Eliot—has a problem at the beginning of *Bristol Bay Summer.* Discuss what those problems are and if you think by the end of the book those characters have changed. For example, what is your opinion about Zoey's situation at the start of the story? Do you think her anger is justified? Or, do you think she should just "get over it"? What is she like at the end of the book?

4. Where do you think Lhasa's name came from? Any ideas why she was named that? Does it tell you something about Zoey's mom?

5. What do you suppose the "real Alaska" is as opposed to the "other" Alaska? Do you agree? Disagree?

6. A major theme of *Bristol Bay Summer* is family and what it means to Zoey. In the beginning of the book, Zoey wanted a normal family. What is a "normal" family? Over the course of the book, we see different families: Rose's, Thomas's, Patrick's, and of course Zoey's. What does Zoey eventually learn about the true meaning of family? What does family mean to you?

7. What do you think killed Midnight? If you were writing the book, would you have let Midnight die? Why?

8. What do you think Zoey wishes for when she blows out her birthday candles?

9. How does art help Zoey? Do you have some kind of similar outlet? How does it help you?

10. What is the point of the crises that happen in the book, for example when the engine quits in midair or the Japanese typhoon ruins their campsite? Was there any kind of foreshadowing in the story that warned you these things might happen?

11. What does Zoey find out when she calls her dad? Why is this important for Zoey's journey toward healing? What do you think of Zoey's dad? Does he make you mad or not? Why?

12. What do you think Zoey means at the end of the book when she tells Eliot "Sometimes you lose the thing you want the most, but sometimes it comes back to you in a different way. If you just give it a chance."

13. Do you think Patrick was acting irresponsibly by bringing Alice, Zoey, and Eliot to Bristol Bay with him? Think about the same question but substitute Alice's (Zoey's mom) name for Patrick.

14. Do you think Thomas will visit Zoey in Anchorage in the future? If so, how do you think that will go? Do you think Zoey will go back to Bristol Bay the next summer? Explain why.

15. See what you can find out about the proposed Pebble Mine in Bristol Bay. How might it affect the fishermen like Zoey and the Gambles?

*For a complete Study Guide, please go to the author's website: annieboochever.com.

CPSIA information can be obtained at www.ICGtesting.com
Printed in the USA
BVOW03s0822280415

397959BV00004B/4/P